Ju
Cowboy

Copyright © Olivia Jaymes

JUSTICE HEALED
Copyright © 2013 by Olivia Jaymes

E-Book ISBN: 978-0-9899833-2-7
Print ISBN: 978-0-9899833-3-4

Cover art by Sloan Winters

DEDICATION

To my wonderful husband and son. Thank you for all your love and support. I wouldn't be able to do this without you.

Chapter One

The smell of stale beer and sweat roiled Sheriff Tanner Marks's stomach bringing his hastily eaten cheeseburger up into his throat. He hated being in a bar on a Saturday night. Any bar. They held too many memories and none of them very good. Some of them downright lousy.

Funny how all bars looked and sounded the same. The soles of his shoes stuck to the sticky floor. The jukebox blared from the corner and the stench of alcohol, Old Spice, and pheromones were overpowering. Some couples were dancing on one side of the room while drunk, loud cowboys whooped it up in front of the wide-screen television on the other. A few Romeos were trying to hit on the better looking women.

A typical night in a small town watering hole.

"I hate this shit," Tanner said to his best deputy. Deputy Sam Taylor was a tough son of a bitch with a calm, cool demeanor. Tanner would trust him anywhere.

Sam chuckled and adjusted his cowboy hat. "Just a regular Saturday night in Springwood, Montana, boss."

"In the pool room, Tanner." Patty, the owner of this fine establishment, strode up to him and pointed to the back of the bar. "Get them out of here. They're going to bust up my place."

He strode straight for the back room, which boasted not one but two pool tables, and saw his son, Chris, exchanging fists with another cowboy from a nearby ranch.

"Shit. Not again." He headed straight for the fray but looked over his shoulder at his deputy. "Call for another deputy. Larry's just down the road, I think. We'll be taking them in."

Tanner was tired of making excuses for his son. If Chris was going to act like an idiot, he could spend the rest of Saturday night behind bars. Sam pulled out his cell while Tanner plunged himself into the fray, pushing them both back and ducking the wildly swinging blows. The two men appeared to have had too much to drink, and they would both spend the night in Tanner's drunk tank sleeping it off. Tanner was going to have to call Stacey about Chris. Again.

Tanner managed to separate the two, Sam holding the other cowboy, kicking and yelling, by the arms. Chris was seething with anger at being thwarted.

"Fuck you, Dad. Let me go." He lunged forward and unexpectedly knocked Tanner backwards.

He was steadying himself on his feet when a fist landed squarely on his jaw, spinning him around and sending him into a pile of metal chairs stacked against the wall.

He shook it off and grabbed Chris by the collar, holding him still. For once, his son seemed to get the message and didn't fight back. He stood there, a hateful expression on his face before turning his attention to the floor. Larry jogged into the bar with a grin and efficiently cuffed the troublemakers. Tanner rubbed his sore jaw and got to his feet. Sam slapped Tanner on the back.

"You okay, boss? You got quite a cut on your head."

Tanner reached up and winced as his fingers hit a spot above his right eye. He brought his hand down and his fingers were covered in blood.

"Shit. I'm getting too old for this, Sam." He was going to be black and blue tomorrow morning from the fall into the chairs.

"You probably need a couple of stitches, boss. I'll drive you to the doctor."

"I'm fine." Tanner waved it off, but Sam grasped his arm.

"You're bleeding pretty bad. Go look in the mirror."

"In a minute."

Chris was breathing heavy and pulling against the cuffs, which was only going to hurt him more. But this was Tanner's son in a nutshell. He had a

2

beautiful wife and baby at home and yet here he was drinking and fighting. Tanner scanned his son for any serious injuries but he appeared to have escaped any real harm. He'd have a fat lip and some bruised knuckles, but little else.

"Do you want me to call Stacey, son?" Tanner tried to keep his voice even and calm, despite the crushing disappointment and guilt twisting in his gut.

"You can't do anything for me, old man." Chris practically spat out the words, turning away.

"I can keep you from doing time for assaulting a cop. You need to start making better choices, Chris. You should be home with your wife and daughter."

"Like you were? How many Saturday nights did you get drunk, Dad? How many?" Tanner heard the hurt in his son's voice and would have done anything in the world to turn back the clock. But Tanner knew that wasn't an option.

"I don't know. I lost count. I do know I didn't get in fights and end up in jail. I didn't lose job after job so I couldn't take care of my family. I took care of you, son."

Chris shook his head, his mouth a flat line. "Paying the bills doesn't make you a father."

"Drinking yourself blind and punching another guy doesn't make you one either," Tanner countered. "Don't fuck this up like I did, Chris. You'll end up alone."

Chris turned away and let the deputy lead him out of the bar. Sam put his hand on Tanner's shoulder. "It's not your fault, you know."

Tanner exhaled slowly. "Actually, it is. It's what he saw growing up."

Sam shook his head. "He also saw you straighten up and get sober. A grown man makes his own decisions. Only Chris will decide when he's had enough. And you know when that will be."

Tanner did know. He was just trying to save Chris the same heartache. He would change when he hit absolute rock bottom. It was then a person had no choice but to change.

"You need to put something on that cut. There's the men's room."

Sam was right. Blood was dripping in Tanner's eye making it hard to see. A quick trip to the foul smelling men's room told him the ugly truth. He had a deep gash above his eye and he was going to have a lulu of a headache tomorrow. He tried to wipe off his face with a few paper towels, but only managed to smear the blood, making him look like something from a horror movie. He exited the bathroom with a wad of towels on his forehead and found Sam waiting for him.

"Okay, I need a couple of stitches."

Sam held up his hands. "I'll drive you to Doc Shay's. Larry will take the men to the station and let them sleep it off. I assume you're not pressing charges against your son for assaulting an officer of the law?"

Tanner shook his head and felt the beginnings of a small hammer pounding against his skull. He walked slowly out of the bar assuring concerned citizens as he passed that he was fine. He headed to the SUV but Sam grabbed the door handle, coming out of nowhere.

"I'm driving you. You're still shaky on your feet."

Tanner tossed Sam the keys with a scowl. "You're acting like my mother, but I'm in no fucking mood to argue. I'm not too old to take a punch, for fuck's sake."

Tanner slid in the passenger side while Sam started up the SUV. "You can still take a punch, boss, but those chairs you landed on weren't feathers and cotton balls. No one could walk away from something like that without getting their bell rung."

Tanner exhaled, closed his eyes, and leaned back against the headrest. Doc Shay would patch up his forehead and then Tanner could take a couple of aspirin and sleep. If that bar fight call had come in ten minutes later, Tanner

4

would have been off duty. It was the karma gods fucking with him again. They'd made sure he saw how Chris was ruining his life.

The town wasn't that big so it didn't take long to get to their destination. Within minutes Tanner felt the SUV come to a stop. Tanner opened his eyes and winced. They were sitting in front of the suburban home and office of Dr. Gregory Shay. Tanner liked the man, but he hated doctors in general. They always seemed to find a reason to shove a needle in his ass. He'd served his country in the hot, dry Middle East, but he hated needles more.

He swung out of the seat. "Let's get this fucking over with."

* * * *

"Now there's your husband." Dr. Madison Shay laughed and pointed to the television screen where Brad Pitt and George Clooney were looking hot and sexy in *Ocean's Eleven*. She and her friend Sherry Martin had been playing the "There's Your Husband" game since they were teens. Sometimes the males were sexy and handsome, sometimes not so much, but it never failed to make them smile and laugh.

At thirty years old, Madison should have been too old for the game but Sherry had been egging her on all night, first at the restaurant and now while watching the movie. So far, Madison's husbands included George Clooney and Carl Reiner.

"I'll take Matt Damon any day," Sherry declared. "He's very hot."

"You have Dan. He's handsome and sweet. He's a great guy." Madison popped open another can of Pepsi.

Sherry rolled her eyes. "At the rate we're going, I'll be the oldest living bride in America. I'm a wedding planner and I can't get my own man to propose. How messed up is that?"

"He'll propose. Didn't you say he was just trying to get his business up and running?" Dan owned a local real estate business.

"Before that he wanted to finish graduate school. What's the next excuse? He wants to pay for the wedding with our social security checks?"

"Trust me, you'll be married before I will. Guaranteed." Madison hadn't had a date in three years. By choice. She was hopeless when it came to men. She never knew what to say, do, or wear.

Sherry tapped her chin in thought. "About that. We need to find you a man."

Madison sighed. "We've been through this before. I don't understand men, and they don't understand me. It's like we're from different planets."

"You just need me to coach you." Sherry jumped up from the couch and started to pace excitedly. "I can tell you what to talk about, and help you pick out clothes." She looked down at Madison's faded and ripped blue jeans and SpongeBob T-shirt. "New clothes. We can go shopping. Buy you some dresses and high heels. You have great legs."

"I'd look like Big Bird if I wore high heels." At five foot-seven, Madison wasn't overly tall, but she was also slim which gave the illusion of more height.

"More like a supermodel," Sherry retorted. "You're not thirteen anymore. The glasses and braces are gone. You grew boobs. Use 'em."

"I am perfectly aware of the function of breasts. I went to medical school."

Sherry giggled. "I don't think we're thinking of the same function. Boobs are to make men drool."

Madison stretched out the neckline of her shirt and looked down at her chest. "Drool? Are you kidding?"

Sherry nodded. "Drool. You need to show some cleavage, girl."

"Low cut scrubs. A novel idea. How about some popcorn?" Madison headed into the kitchen with Sherry right behind her. Madison popped the popcorn bag into the microwave and pressed a few buttons. "Listen, I appreciate you wanting to help me. But I'm fine. I like being on my own and not having a man to worry about."

"I'm going to help you," Sherry announced. "Give me a month and you'll be in love."

Real fear entered Madison's heart. "Please, I beg of you. Don't."

The popping stopped and Sherry reached around Madison and pressed the cancel button, then pulled the steaming bag from the microwave. "You'll thank me later. You need a nice man." Sherry dumped the popcorn into a large bowl. "Let's see... there's Elmer Marsh who works construction. He has a good body."

Madison tossed a few kernels into her mouth. "Elmer? We went to high school with him. He barely graduated. He used to call me four-eyed Maddie."

"You want brains then? How about Teddy Perkins? He's an attorney." Sherry appeared to be warming up to this idea. Madison needed to put it in the deep freeze immediately.

"Teddy Perkins used to steal my lunch money and called me carrot top. Not in a nice way. He made my life a living hell until the day I left town. Now you want to fix me up with him."

Sherry sighed. "Were there any boys who weren't mean to you? There had to be someone."

Madison thought for a moment. "Jerry Jarvis. He wasn't mean to me. Actually, he never spoke to me once in twelve years of school."

Sherry slapped her forehead. "Jerry Jarvis always had one hand down his pants and the other knuckle deep in his nose."

Madison sprinkled some salt on the popcorn. "Whatever happened to him anyway?"

"He's the mayor. Can we get back to you?"

The loud peal of the bell for the back door interrupted Madison's plea to be left alone. If someone was ringing that bell, they wanted a doctor.

"Hold that thought. We have company."

Madison and Sherry hurried to the back of the house, which was through the kitchen, down a hall, and behind a set of thick double doors. The office was actually an addition built onto the existing house. Her mother had been a stickler for separating her father's work life from their home life. Friends entered through the front and patients entered through the back. The only problem was, in a small town, friends and patients were usually one in the same.

Madison pulled the back door open and found two large men in uniforms. She recognized Tanner Marks immediately. She'd had a case of hero worship for him years ago after he'd shooed away some bullies. He'd aged in the last twelve years. There was a touch of grey at his temples and a few more lines around his eyes, but his square jaw was just as strong and his shoulders just as wide. The other man was around the same age and just as tall, with dark hair and eyes. Between the two of them, they took up the entire doorway.

She stepped back into the waiting room so the men could enter. She eyed the blood soaked paper towel Tanner held above his right eye. "Come on in."

"Um, is Doc Gray here?" the stranger asked.

"Dad is in Seattle visiting his sister. Is this a medical emergency?"

A pause.

"Yes. The sheriff needs a few stitches over his eye."

"I'm a doctor. I can do it. " Another pause. "I assure you I am a board certified physician. You can bring him in here." She gestured toward the examination room.

Some Montana men could be real chauvinists. For a moment she thought they might turn around, but instead they entered the office and shed their heavy coats. It was colder than hell for the beginning of February, but it was toasty inside the house.

"Will you follow me?" Madison led them back into the examining room. She walked over to the sink and started to wash her hands.

"Hey, Sheriff. Deputy Sam. Can I get you some coffee or something?" Sherry offered.

Both men shook their heads. "None for me thanks," Tanner replied. "But I appreciate the offer."

Sherry grinned and gave Madison a sideways glance. "So polite. Being a gentleman seems to be a lost art these days. I'll wait in the other room if you don't mind."

If Tanner thought the gentleman remark was strange he didn't say anything. Instead, he pulled off his cowboy hat and tossed it into a chair. With the paper towels no longer covering his forehead she could see a deep gash over his eyebrow about three centimeters long. She dried her hands and waved toward a chair. She snapped on a pair of rubber gloves as he sat down. She gingerly probed the wound looking for any foreign material that would need to be removed before stitching it up. He sucked in a breath when she hit a particularly sensitive spot.

"Sorry. Can I ask how you did this?"

His jaw was starting to bruise so she had a pretty decent idea of what had happened but she wanted to be sure. If he needed to go to the next town over for an MRI, she wanted to get him there as soon as possible.

"I was breaking up a fight and caught a fist. Fell into a stack of metal chairs." His expression was sheepish. She pulled open a drawer and retrieved a flashlight, looking into his pupils, testing for a reaction. So far, so good.

She held a finger up in front of him. "Follow my finger with only your eyes." Luckily, he passed with flying colors.

"Can you tell me your full name?" she asked.

Tanner frowned. "Tanner Eugene Marks."

She heard the other cop snicker and Tanner shot him a dirty look.

"Good. What day is it?"

Tanner rolled his eyes. "Saturday. Do we really need to do this? I don't have a concussion, Doctor. I've had them before and I don't have one now. I just need a few stitches."

She'd dealt with every kind of patient in the world while working in the emergency room of a big city hospital. She smiled sweetly. "Where did you get your medical degree, Sheriff? I got mine at the University of Kansas."

A muscle worked in his jaw but he sighed and sat back in the chair. "I don't have one," he conceded.

"Then we'll move on. Any nausea or vomiting? Spotty vision? Headache?"

"No. No. Yes. Just a small one. Right above my eye."

She finished the examination as efficiently as possible then pulled out the supplies for his stitches.

"I'm going to numb the area so I can clean it and apply the sutures. Do you have any allergies to medication?"

Tanner shook his head. "No, ma'am."

She smiled at that. "You don't have to call me ma'am, or even doctor. My name is Madison."

He frowned as if he was thinking really hard. "Doc Shay has a daughter named Madison."

"Guilty as charged, Sheriff. I've been gone a long time, I guess."

His eyes widened in recognition and she winced inwardly. He was remembering her as the tall, gawky, geeky girl she'd been, complete with braces and glasses. She'd grown into her height so to speak and Lasik did wonders these days. Unfortunately, the geeky part was permanent. She couldn't get rid of it if she tried, and after all these years she stopped and embraced it. Her life was much easier without trying to be something she wasn't.

"Welcome back, Madison," Tanner said slowly. He seemed a little bemused.

"Thank you. Now let's get this done so you can go home and rest."

He barely flinched when she gave him a shot to numb the area and he sat perfectly still as she stitched up his forehead. He was going to have a scar there, but to quote her father when he stitched up young boys after a skateboard accident or a dirt bike spill, "Chicks dig scars."

She printed out the instructions for caring for his wound and he folded it up and shoved it in his pocket where she was sure it would remain. Unread. She picked up her prescription pad, her pen scrawling on the paper.

"I'll write you a prescription for the pain, Sheriff."

"No, thank you." His eyebrows were pulled down.

Her pen stopped. Was this some macho thing? He was being foolish. When that local wore off, he was going to have a whopper of a headache.

"You can take ibuprofen, but you'd sleep better with some pain medication."

"No." His voice was flat but firm. She ripped the prescription off and held it out to him.

"Just in case."

He shook his head. "No, thank you, Doc. I won't be taking it."

Silence seemed to stretch between them until the deputy, who had been quiet the entire time, cleared his throat. She jumped at the sound but simply turned and held out the prescription to him.

"Will you take it for him?"

The deputy shook his head. "He's the boss. If he says no, then it's no. What do we owe you?"

Madison placed the paper back on the desk. Stubborn men. She had an IQ of 140, but she knew little about the opposite sex. She'd learned plenty in medical school about the male anatomy, but the male mind remained a mystery.

"I'll send you a bill. Does my father have your insurance on file?"

Tanner nodded. "Thank you for seeing me so late. It saved us a drive into the next town."

"Any time." She led them back through the tiny waiting room and to the back door. "If you have any problems, please call me. Day or night. I'm used to interrupted sleep."

Tanner gave her a lopsided smile. "Me, too. Thanks again."

The deputy tipped his hat and they walked out into the night. She heard an engine fire up and drive away. She shut and locked the door behind her, heading into the kitchen where Sherry was munching on the bowl of popcorn with a Cheshire cat smile.

"What are you grinning about?"

"Is Sheriff Marks going to be okay?"

Madison shrugged. "He only needed a few stitches. He'll be fine."

"Good." Sherry waggled her eyebrows. "I'd hate for him to be out of commission. He's become central to my plan."

Madison felt that foreboding again. The kind she always felt when Sherry was planning something that was going to get them detention at school.

"Plan?"

"You know, I'm going to find you a man."

"I thought we agreed to forget about that." She might as well save her breath. When Sherry decided on a course of action, heaven help them all.

"I never agreed."

Madison sat down heavily in a chair. "What does Tanner Marks have to do with your plan, I ask with stone cold fear in my heart?"

Sherry grinned. "There's your husband."

Chapter Two

"Go home to Stacey and Annie, son."

Tanner opened the cell door and looked down at Chris, sitting on the mattress, his body language defiant. He was full of hate and rage and Tanner didn't know what to do about it. While he was drinking, Tanner had been a happy drunk, the life of the party. He'd never missed a day of work or let his alcoholism affect his day to day responsibilities. Chris was a sullen, angry drunk who blamed everyone else around him for his own decisions, wandering from job to job and borrowing money from his mother.

Did I fail him this much?

Chris stood and walked past Tanner without a word. He wasn't done with Chris quite yet. Tanner caught Chris's arm, but his son didn't turn around, only pulled his arm from Tanner's grasp. That was fine. He could hear what his father had to say from a foot away.

"This needs to stop. Annie's getting older and she's going to see what you do. Do you want that?" Tanner might as well have saved his breath. He already knew Chris's answer. "Come with me tomorrow night to my meeting. Just once. Please, Chris. Not for me or your mother, or even for Annie. Do it for yourself. You can't be happy like this."

Tanner had lost count of the times he'd begged Chris to attend an AA meeting. It appeared this time wouldn't be any more successful than the last. Chris walked away without a backwards glance.

Tanner stood there, his heart twisting in his chest, and watched his only son reject him yet again. With a sigh, he checked his watch. He needed to get on the road. He had a meeting at ten o'clock and it was an hour away.

A drive that turned into an hour and a half due to snow covered roads. By the time he walked into the roadhouse, all the other area lawmen were there and, it appeared, waiting on him.

"Shit, I'm sorry. The roads were bad. Hopefully they'll be plowed by the time we leave."

Tanner was part of a group of six lawmen who met once a month to discuss what was going on in crime and law enforcement. It had started as just an idea, but it was now a powerful weapon in keeping the peace. They were able to share ideas, crime trends, and even help each other out when things got tough. Only a few months ago, they'd come together to help Seth Reilly protect a woman in witness protection. That woman was now Seth's wife.

One look at Seth's face showed a happy, satisfied man. Tanner felt a twinge of envy. He'd give anything to be loved like that, but in all honesty, he wasn't sure he deserved it. He'd made so many mistakes in his life. Besides, he was content with what he had. The secret to happiness was to not want what you couldn't, or shouldn't have.

Reed Mitchell waved off the apology. "We were all late. I just got here about five minutes ago. The roads aren't any better up our way. I didn't even know it was supposed to snow last night."

Jared Monroe laughed and poured a cup of coffee, pushing it Tanner's way. "It's Montana in February. It's going to snow all the fucking time. That's why we all drive four-wheel drive SUVs."

Tanner added a little sugar and wrapped his cold hands around the cup while Seth Reilly passed around an envelope of pictures from his wedding in Las Vegas. Tanner and the other men had been at the ceremony last month. Seth and his lovely bride, Presley, had been married by an Elvis impersonator with dozens of friends and family in attendance. Even the Marshal who had placed Presley into Seth's protection had been there.

It had been a fun wedding but Tanner was a traditional guy. If he ever married again, he would want a traditional wedding. His first marriage had taken place with a justice of the peace and a fifty dollar gold band. The reception had been a barbecue in his in-laws' backyard.

14

Logan Wright pounded his fist on the table like a gavel. "Can we stop acting like teenage girls at a sleepover and get this meeting started?"

Griffin Sawyer chuckled. "All the marital bliss making you nervous, Logan? Think a preacher's going to magically appear and make you marry your latest lady?"

All Logan's women seemed to have two things in common. They were sexy and they were only out for a good time. Logan Wright had a reputation in half a dozen counties for being hot between the sheets and was a love 'em and leave 'em type. He attracted a certain kind of woman but few dared to think they could change him. To Logan's credit, he made sure he didn't spend time with women who had expectations.

Logan refilled his coffee cup. "Doubt the lady I was with last night had marriage on her mind."

Tanner sipped at his coffee and grimaced at the bitter liquid. He loved nothing more than a good cup of coffee and this sure as shit wasn't one. "Can we get started? We're already running late."

Reed nodded. "I'll start. Tanner, are you seeing a rise in violence in your area? My town is the closest to yours and it's been bad lately. I think we might be in for a full-on drug territory war."

Tanner nodded. "I am. I think it's time we called in the DEA and get their take on this. My hands are full with trying to stop kids from getting hooked on meth. But the trafficking on our roads is getting worse. Much worse. With budget cuts, my request to hire two more deputies was turned down."

Griffin scowled. "I had to lay off a deputy due to budgets cuts. Then they bitch about response time and crime rates. Shit, my men can only do so much."

Reed nodded. "I had to cut two deputies back to part-time. I wasn't exactly flush with manpower before, but now? Fuck. We just don't have the resources to do the anti-drug education in the grade schools and check on the probation violators."

"And now it looks like we have a drug war on our hands," Tanner said. "I had another John Doe turn up dead a few weeks ago. That makes four in the last six months."

Tanner didn't mention out loud that the deaths lined up from when Fenton Jacks bought a small ranch and settled in the area. Tanner had his suspicions regarding Fenton, but so far he'd only mentioned it to Logan and Seth. It didn't help Tanner's ex-wife, Abby, was planning to marry the guy in the spring.

"I've got some contacts in the DEA, an old Navy buddy. I'll give him a call," Reed offered.

"Sounds good," Tanner agreed. "Has anyone had a visit from our vigilante?"

Griffin raised his coffee cup with a grim smile. "I'm the lucky recipient this month."

Jared shook his head. "Sorry, it's not an exclusive club. My town as well."

Seth's eyebrows shot up. "Twice in one month? I thought we'd heard the last of him a few months back."

"Maybe he took the holidays off," Logan said. He wasn't as against the vigilante as the rest of them were. He turned to Griffin. "Who did he get in your town?"

"An accused child molester."

"Looks like he did the world a favor." Logan's expression was hard.

"He was accused. It wasn't proven. Shit, you are one tough bastard, Logan. Do you even care about the law?" Jared asked, his eyes narrowed. Jared was all about law and order.

Logan leaned forward so he was out of his chair, and pressed his hands to the table. "I care so much about the law that I want decent folks to be able to live their life without fear of their kids being assaulted or their property being

16

taken. I think young girls should be able to walk the streets at night unafraid and families should be able to leave their doors unlocked. I think people should be able to send cash in the fucking mail. That's how much I love the damn law."

Tanner put his hand on Logan's shoulder, pressing him back into the chair. "We all feel the same, Logan. We're all balancing keeping the peace with protecting people's rights."

He felt Logan relax so he turned to Jared. "Who did he get in your town?"

Jared gave Logan a hard look. "An alleged drug dealer. But I had my doubts about the man's guilt."

Reed reached for the coffee pot. "But you arrested him?"

"I brought him in for questioning. But after talking to the guy, it just didn't feel right. I didn't arrest him due to lack of evidence and was going to keep my eye on him. He turned up with a bullet in his brain two days later."

Tanner tapped the table with the coffee stir. "You know what bugs me about this? How does he know? Our towns are spread out in a three hundred mile or more radius. How does he fucking know? And what else has he done that we don't even know about?"

Griffin's lips twisted. "I think we need to face the fact we may have people in our own towns who are feeding him information."

"You're saying they know he's a vigilante?" Reed asked. "If so, that's a major weakness for him. The more people that know about a crime, the harder it is to keep the perpetrator a secret."

Griffin shook his head. "I don't think they know or we would have more evidence. I think they're being duped into giving him information."

The meeting droned on with each man giving his update. Tanner felt antsy today and wanted to get back to town. Normally, he loved hanging out with his cop buddies but now he simply wanted a meal and some decent coffee.

When the meeting ended, Logan followed Tanner to his SUV. "What does the other guy look like?"

Tanner chuckled, touching the bandage on his forehead. "Better than me. I broke up a fight in Patty's last night. Needed a couple of stitches."

Logan grimaced. "Ouch."

"It wasn't too bad." Tanner shrugged, remembering how gentle Madison Shay had been. Even the numbing shot hadn't hurt too badly. He'd been impressed with her calm, professional demeanor and amused at the SpongeBob T-shirt she'd been wearing.

Without a bra.

"Man, I hate doctors," Logan declared. "Of course, every time I see one they're trying to fix up something I've broken."

"That might have something to do with it. You okay?"

"Why wouldn't I be?" Logan leaned against the door of the truck.

"We were giving you a pretty hard time in there."

Logan grinned. He was a cocky son of a bitch, but one of the best friends Tanner had ever known. "I can take the heat. We seem to have a basic disagreement, that's all. If I have a chance to get the vigilante, don't worry, I'll bring him in. I'm not condoning what he's done. But he makes it hard to hate him when he picks the victims he does. That's all I'm saying." Logan's smile fell. "You seemed in your own world in there. Still thinking about Abby's new man?"

The thing about best friends was you couldn't fool them worth a damn. "Actually, I was thinking about Chris. It was his fight I broke up last night."

Logan shook his head in sympathy. "You need some tough love for him, man. It's not your fault."

"It is. They say alcoholism is hereditary. Besides, I spent half of his childhood drinking."

"And the other half making up for it. You never did the stupid-ass shit he's doing, either. If it's your fault he's an alcoholic, who is to blame for you? Your dad? Your mom? Who's the lousy asshole you can blame?"

Tanner's parents were church-going people who only drank on Saturday night. They might have imbibed a lot, but it was only one night of the week. "My parents don't have anything to do with this."

"And Chris's issues don't have a damn thing to do with you. As long as you let him blame you, he gets to do whatever the fuck he wants."

"Abby blames me."

"Abby and Chris are two peas in a pod. They both blame everybody else for their piss-poor decisions. It sounds like this Fenton guy is another sign of Abby's bad judgment."

Tanner sighed, tightening his collar around his neck. It was fucking cold out here. "According to her, her first bad decision was marrying me. Things went downhill from there. Luckily, we manage to be friendly most of the time now. She's a good person."

Tanner wasn't sure why he was defending Abby. She was more than capable of defending herself. Perhaps it was because Abby's personality and behavior didn't reflect well on Tanner's judgment. He'd married and had two children with her after all.

"As long as you don't need anything from Abby, she's great."

Tanner exhaled, his breath turning to steam. "I just want Abby to be happy. If Fenton Jacks can do that, well, more power to him."

"Have you checked him out?"

"Not really." Tanner had been wrestling with this. He wanted to dive into Fenton Jacks's past and see what he found. If not for Abby's sake, then for his two children. But if he found something, Abby was going to hit the roof that he checked on her fiancé. It was a case of damned if he did, and damned if he didn't. Abby mad was something Tanner had learned to avoid like the plague when she controlled how often he could see his own damn kids.

Now they were older and she didn't have the same power, but old habits died hard.

"You waiting for a sign or something?" Logan asked. "If you don't do it, I will, for fuck's sake."

Now there was an idea.

Tanner smiled. "That's true. If you decided to check up on him, I couldn't stop you."

Logan was grinning again. "Damn straight." He slapped Tanner on the back. "Looks like I have an assignment. Purely because I want to do it, not because you want it done." Logan turned on his heel and headed to his truck.

Tanner waved. "Let me know what you find."

Logan climbed up in the cab of his truck. "You'll be the first person I call. Drive careful, man."

Tanner hopped into his own SUV, firing up the engine and turning the heat on full blast. It had been a cold winter already and there was still more to go. He pulled out onto the road, glad to see the plows had been through while he'd been inside. He pointed the truck toward Springwood, his stomach rumbling with hunger. It looked like he would be making a stop somewhere for a late lunch.

* * * *

Madison shrugged off her heavy winter coat and slid into the booth. "Why are we here again? I thought we were going to head to the mall."

Sherry sat across from her and handed Madison a menu. "The roads are too snowy to drive into the city. We can get some lunch and chat."

Madison looked around the dimly lit sports bar. The walls were covered with over a dozen flat screen televisions, and most of the diners were men. Even the menu seemed to cater to the male appetite with several flavors of chicken wings and an entire page of artery clogging meals including chili cheese fries and a steak the size of a pot roast.

20

"I'm going to need to check our cholesterol after this meal. It's not good to eat too much red meat or cheese."

Sherry gave a long-suffering sigh. "You're eating unhealthy today. No lectures." Her finger wagged in Madison's face. "I mean it. I want to enjoy my meal of poison. Got it?"

"Got it. What's the worst thing on the menu? We should get two of those."

Sherry laughed. "One extra large order of chili cheese fries coming up. Then we'll move on to the entree. Oh, and don't forget dessert. They make a great chocolate cake here."

Madison could feel her arteries hardening but she had to admit the wafting aromas from the food were tempting. She rarely let herself eat whatever she wanted.

The waitress came to take their appetizer and drink order and before she knew it Sherry had ordered something fat-laden and two beers. The waitress bustled away and Madison frowned.

"I don't drink beer."

"You need to loosen up. A beer will help you."

"Why do I need to loosen up exactly?"

Sherry didn't answer. Instead her attention was caught by something behind Madison. Sherry waved and Madison twisted in her seat to see who had come in. It was Dan, Sherry's boyfriend and another man who looked vaguely familiar standing by the door. Sherry was beckoning to them.

"I did this for your own good," Sherry said, never taking her eyes from the men heading for their table. "I need to see how you interact with a man so I know what we need to work on."

Madison wanted to throttle Sherry. She leaned forward so only Sherry could hear her. "I can't believe you did this. I don't want a man in my life. I told you that last night."

"And I told you that I'm going to fix you up with Sheriff Tanner Marks. You'll make a great couple. I want you to be happy."

"So why this guy?"

"It's sort of like Animal Planet. I need to see you in a mating situation."

Madison pressed a hand to her forehead. "I'm going to kill you."

Sherry shrugged. "Probably. Now smile because here they are."

They certainly were. Dan slid in on Sherry's side and the other man slid next to Madison. She scooted over as far as she could but he was still right there next to her. He had a big grin on his face and she wanted to slam her head on the table repeatedly. This was going to be a disaster of monstrous proportions.

"Brent Hubbard." The man held his hand out. "Remember me?"

How could she forget? He'd called her "four-eyes" and "carrot top" in school. She shook his hand and tried to scoot a few more inches away, but she was already pressed against the wall.

"Nice to see you again, Brent." Lightning didn't strike her, which was a bonus as she was lying through her teeth. She should probably put aside her animosity toward those who had teased and bullied her in school, but Brent had been particularly loathsome, not letting up until she was in tears. Luckily, in junior high and high school his family had moved from Springwood. Apparently, Brent had moved back.

"Nice to see you. Wow, you sure look different than you did before. You could be a model now, and you were so funny-looking as a kid."

"Was I? I don't remember."

"I sure do. You had all those freckles with your bright red hair. And those glasses and braces. You're looking good now." He looked her up and down with appreciative eyes that made her cringe.

Madison took a big gulp of her beer, deciding she did need it after all.

Brent laughed. "I'm glad Dan invited me today. It's fun to see old friends from school."

She and Brent had never been friends but he seemed to have no memory of torturing her when they were children. Perhaps she'd overblown it in her own mind?

Nope. He'd been a real pill.

The waitress brought their chili cheese fries and took the men's beverage order. Brent and Dan were waxing poetic about college basketball while Sherry tried to turn the conversation to more personal topics. Madison was content to stay quiet which she knew frustrated Sherry. Despite the basketball talk, Madison had found out Brent owned the hardware store in town and was divorced.

"This is so great," Brent enthused. "You're a great listener. We should all go out together again some time." Madison gave Sherry a look that promised retribution. When it was time for Sherry's flu shot, Madison was going to use the biggest fucking needle she had.

"So, Dan," Madison interrupted. She needed to change the subject quickly. "How's the real estate business?"

Dan rested his arm on the back of the booth and around Sherry's shoulders. He looked like a man in love. It was only a matter of time before these two got married. "It's going well. The market's picking up so I can't complain. How's the doctor business?"

"I can't complain either. I start in Dad's practice tomorrow morning."

"You're a doctor?" Brent asked, clearly amazed. "You always were smart. Holy shit, a real doctor?"

"A real one," she replied.

Brent whistled. "A real doctor. I bet you're loaded. Doctors really rake it in."

How one man could be so socially inept Madison had no idea, but Brent was giving it all he had. She decided to ignore his remark about money.

"Dad wants to retire in a year or two. I'd always promised him I would take over the practice–I just didn't realize it would be so soon."

Dan nodded. "Your dad is a good man and respected in this town. It will be a loss when he retires but now that you're here to take his place I think the town's in good hands. Sherry said you were working in an emergency room in a big Chicago hospital."

"I was. It was exciting work but the hours sucked."

Sherry laughed. "The hours aren't much better here. Last night we had an unexpected visitor. Sheriff Marks needed a couple of stitches."

"That explains the bandage over his eye then." Dan nodded toward the other side of the sports bar.

Madison looked over and straight into the gaze of Tanner Marks. He was looking right at them and he didn't avert his eyes when she turned his way. He simply nodded and then finally turned his attention to one of the televisions showing basketball. She felt a little sorry for him. He was sitting all by himself at a table in the corner.

She turned back to her own table and picked up her menu. "What are you going to have, Sherry?"

Sherry was studying Madison, a smile playing around her mouth. "We're both going to have cheeseburgers and then chocolate cake."

Madison knew when she was beat. This entire afternoon had gotten away from her the minute they'd stepped inside this place. She might as well give in gracefully.

"That sounds good. Let's make those double cheeseburgers."

Sherry giggled. "That's a great plan."

Dan was shaking his head, but dropped a kiss on Sherry's temple. "I'm glad its Madison's plan. I've learned to fear your plans, baby."

Madison feared them as well. Sherry had only shown her the tip of the iceberg today and Madison knew enough to be afraid. Very afraid.

Chapter Three

Sherry never did anything by half-measures and the next week was evidence of that fact. Madison saw Tanner Marks everywhere. Yes, it was a small town, but this was ridiculous. She saw him on Monday night at the library when Sherry invited Madison for dinner and to browse for books. She saw him at the pizza place on Wednesday night when she was having dinner with Sherry and he was having dinner with his daughter. She saw him again on Friday at the drug store and had to duck into the cold remedy aisle. She didn't want him to think she was following him. He'd arrest her for stalking.

The last run-in hadn't been engineered by Sherry. At least Madison thought it hadn't, but these days she couldn't be sure. Sherry in her determined mode was a formidable opponent. She wouldn't be happy until Madison and Tanner were married with three kids and a dog.

It was a snowy and cold Saturday morning but Madison wouldn't have any fake meetings with Tanner. Sherry was safely working, organizing an out of town wedding. Madison was going to walk down to the coffee shop and get a latte and a bear claw. She'd finished her first week in her father's practice and it hadn't gone too badly. Most people were welcoming although there had been a few males who had balked at a female doctor.

As she walked down the street, she was surprised by how many people stopped and greeted her. She'd been gone so long it was a wonder she was remembered at all. It took her twice as long to get to her destination, and she was almost frozen as she headed to the counter to place her order. She stuffed her gloves in her coat pockets while she waited for the barista to make her vanilla latte. The coffee shop looked almost empty with only a few customers at the tables and one at the counter. She saw a nice table by the window overlooking the street and slung her coat over one of the chairs. She headed back to the counter where her coffee and bear claw waited. She took a taste of her coffee and turned on her heel, choking on the hot liquid and almost dropping her sweet roll.

Tanner Marks.

She coughed, her eyes watering at the pain of a burnt esophagus. He appeared to be waiting for his order as well. He wasn't in uniform today. Instead he was dressed as a civilian wearing jeans, cowboy boots, a flannel shirt and a heavy coat. Snowflakes were melting on the brim of his cowboy hat.

"You okay?" His brow was furrowed, his expression concerned.

"Fine. Hot coffee, that's all." She gave him a quick smile before ducking away to her table. She tried to relax but her heart was pounding. She hadn't expected to see him this morning and now here he was. It was as if the entire universe was plotting against her. What was it about this town that made her feel like the awkward girl she'd once been instead of a competent, professional physician?

She saw him look around for a table but every one was filled, which was strange as there had hardly been anyone in the place when she'd come in. It would be churlish not to ask him to share her table. Her father had brought her up better than that.

"I have a table. Would you like to share?"

He looked conflicted for a moment, and then smiled. "Sure, that's nice of you."

He settled into the chair opposite and immediately she fidgeted in her seat and her stomach twisted. She never knew what to talk about or what to say to a man. And Tanner was definitely a man. All muscle packed onto a six-foot frame, he looked every inch the alpha male. He was probably over forty but had a better physique than most men half his age. His face wasn't too bad either with his square jaw, tan skin, and dark blue eyes. He kept his brown hair short but she could see that it had a bit of a curl at the nape of his neck.

All in all, Tanner Marks was a handsome man. The type that made her stutter and stammer and sweat through her clothes.

He took off his hat and set it on the table.

"Snowy morning. We're supposed to get a few inches today."

He wanted to do small talk. She wasn't very good but she would give it a shot. "I heard something about that. How's the forehead?"

He touched the bandage and chuckled. "Fine. When can I get these stitches out?"

Shit, she'd forgotten to tell him that. In the ER, she rarely saw people after she'd stitched them back together. "It's been a week. I can take them out today if you like."

He frowned. "Is your office open today?"

"No, but it's no big deal. It will only take a few minutes."

Tanner dug into his bear claw with gusto. "You probably had other plans besides taking out my stitches."

She shrugged. "Coffee, a stop at the grocery store. Nothing earth shattering."

"No plans with Brent?"

She didn't know who he was talking about for a minute, then remembered he'd been at the sports bar last Sunday. "Brent is a friend of Dan's, not a friend of mine."

Tanner sipped his coffee. "He looked pretty happy to see you. Did he ask you out? I bet he did."

Brent had, but it was none of Tanner's business. "I don't take bets."

Tanner chuckled and sat back in the chair. "Then he did ask you out. Did you turn him down?"

She nodded. "He's not really my type." He was a creep who shouldn't be allowed to reproduce, actually.

Tanner laughed, a sound rich and deep, and a few heads whipped around to look at them. "Madison Shay, you are probably the most polite woman I've ever met. First, you offer to share your table with me, and then you simply say Brent Hubbard isn't your type. He's not any self-respecting woman's type. The guy is a total jerk."

Madison exhaled in relief. "How did you know? Have you arrested him or something? I didn't know if you were friends."

Tanner pulled a face. "We're not friends and no, I've never arrested him. But I've been around him more than enough. We both belong to the Moose Lodge. He cheats at cards and brags about women I doubt he's ever even dated. Not a nice combination."

"He gave me a creepy vibe." She shuddered. "He asked me if I had had work done. You know, since I used to be so ugly before."

She wanted to slap her hand over her mouth. What made her say that she had no idea. His face darkened and his smiled disappeared.

"Did he actually say that to you? What an asshole."

Madison shrugged. "He did but let's face it. He wasn't saying anything out loud that other people weren't thinking."

Tanner's lips were pressed together in a thin line. "You were not ugly. All kids go through an awkward stage. Both of mine did. I'm sure I did too."

She'd seen Tanner's picture up in the trophy case at school. He'd been the quarterback and captain the year the football team won the state championship. He'd been handsome and confident. He probably never got teased or called names.

"The problem was my awkward phase lasted about fifteen years."

"Well, it's gone now. You certainly got the last laugh."

"What do you mean?" She still felt like that kid most of the time.

Tanner leaned forward. "You're a doctor, and you sure aren't ugly now. You could be a model. Most of the people you went to high school with never left Springwood. They never went to college. Maybe they went into the military like I did. If they didn't? They work a blue collar job, getting dirty and sweaty every day for way less wages than they need to live. And when they can't do that anymore? They work double shifts at the Walmart. If they're lucky. Seems to me you've got nothing to feel awkward about."

"I—I never thought about it that way." She'd been too busy feeling inferior. "I have been very lucky."

Tanner nodded. "If anyone mentions the past to you, it's probably just their way of not feeling inferior."

"Do you think that's why Brent said those things?" Maybe she'd misjudged him. She wasn't going to go out with him, but perhaps he wasn't a total jerk after all.

Tanner grinned. "No. Brent's just an asshole."

Laughter bubbled up. Tanner had a dry but fun sense of humor. "You seem pretty sure about that."

"It's one of my gifts. I'm a good judge of character." He shoved the last piece of bear claw in his mouth.

"Have you judged me yet?" The words were out before she could stop them. She wanted to snatch them back but it was too late.

He tilted his head and looked at her. "You're a good person, Madison Shay. You have a good heart."

"You barely know me," she protested.

Tanner drank the last of his coffee and stood up. "You took time out of your Saturday night to stitch me up and offered to take time today as well. You offered me a seat at your table."

"That's no big deal. Anyone would have done that."

Tanner looked around the coffee shop, now almost empty. "But Madison, no one else did."

She opened her mouth to answer but she had no words. Tanner Marks was a nice man and he had a way of making her feel good about herself.

It had to stop immediately. If Sherry found out Madison had shared a table with Tanner, she'd never hear the end of it.

Tanner shoved his hat on his head. "I'll call your office on Monday to get my stitches out. I won't bother you on your day off. Thanks again for the company."

Just like that, he was out the door and ambling down the street leaving Madison to finish her breakfast. He'd given her some things to think about. She'd been so busy thinking about her past she hadn't really thought about what other people were doing while she was in Chicago. It changed the way she looked at everyone and everything. The only thing it didn't change was the past.

That still sucked.

* * * *

Tanner walked into the rundown house on the outskirts of town, the copper smell of blood hitting him at once. He grimaced at the grisly site before him. Another murder. This one messier than the last. The two previous had been by gunshot. This appeared to be from a large kitchen knife abandoned on the counter. There also must have been more than one perpetrator because it would have taken at least two guys to hold the victim down.

"Sorry I'm late, Sam. I was headed to Doc Shay's to get my stitches out. I had to turn around and head this way when I got your call."

"No problem, boss. Looks like these guys were sending a message." Sam had taken the call from a worried girlfriend who couldn't get in the locked front door. Tanner had already contacted Reed's guy in the DEA who was supposed to be on his way.

Tanner pushed up the brim of his cowboy hat. "I hope the message was received and understood. I don't want any more fucking murders in my town."

The county coroner was bent over the body with his camera. Tanner was lucky Dr. Stewart knew his stuff. He was semi-retired after a career in San Francisco. "The victim appears to have bled out, but I'll know more when I get him on my table."

Tanner's brows went up as he surveyed the. "I would imagine having your limbs removed one by one would cause some damage, Doc."

"I imagine it was pure torture, Sheriff." The coroner never looked up but continued to take pictures of the scene. "Torture on purpose. These people mean business. When are you going to catch them?"

"As soon as I can. I've called in the Feds to help."

The sound and vibrations of a helicopter shook the ramshackle structure. Tanner stepped out into the cold and watched as the chopper circled and then landed in a clearing. A man stepped out and headed straight for Tanner, his arm outstretched. Tanner shook his hand.

"Tanner Marks? I'm Jason Anderson, DEA. I believe we have a mutual friend."

Tanner was used to sizing up people immediately and he liked Jason Anderson. He had an open, easy way about him. Most Feds liked to come in, act superior, and take over. Reed had chosen well.

"Nice to meet you. I didn't expect you so fast." Tanner nodded to the bird.

Jason's expression grew serious. "This is a priority. I'm hoping we can share information and help each other out. Your little town is smack in the middle of a drug war. It's only going to get worse if we don't do something. Innocent people will get involved and die."

"That's why I called. Come on in."

Tanner led the way back into the house. Jason was obviously a seasoned agent. He didn't even flinch at the gruesome scene.

"I've seen this before. In Miami and also in Kansas City. Your town is on a drug route to Canada, and people are fighting over it. Maybe more than a few organizations want it. We need to shut them down."

Sam shook his head. "What's so special about this area?"

"It's remote, off the beaten path. Not too many cops or state troopers. Just the drug mules and the cattle." Jason turned to Tanner. "I've got another

31

guy in the copter, but I wanted to talk to you first. He's a forensics expert. Would you mind if he came in here and gathered evidence?"

"I wouldn't mind at all. Our resources don't run to something like that. We usually call in the state."

"I've got a call into them," Sam said. "I secured the scene and made sure no one else came in. They said they'd call me back with an ETA."

"Call them and let them know the Feds are here."

Sam grinned. "That ought to chap their asses. They hate that shit."

Jason finally smiled. "We're used to being reviled." He stuck his head out of the door and waved. "Trust me. They'll show up anyway so they can see what's going on."

"What can we do to help?" Tanner asked.

"Let us gather whatever we can find here. Run it through the lab. It may match other open cases. How about you and I get some coffee and I'll fill you in on what we already know and you can do the same? We can let these men do their jobs."

"Sounds good. We can take my truck. I'll drive you back here when your guy is done." Tanner turned to his deputy. "Sam, keep the place secure. I don't want the perp coming back to the scene of the crime."

"Got it. I'll keep the Fed safe, don't worry."

Tanner and Jason exited the house, passing the forensics agent who was heading in.

"I'll buy the coffee," Tanner said. "Let's go."

They loaded into his SUV and headed to town. He was glad he'd called in Reed's friend. This shit needed to end. Tanner took the safety of his town seriously. Nothing would happen to the people of Springwood on his watch as long as he had breath in his body.

Tanner was sure the drug cartels would be happy to relieve him of his responsibilities. They'd be glad to see him dead, just like the poor bastard in the kitchen.

Chapter Four

"I want you to stop this nonsense," Madison said, pulling a book from the shelf. It was another Monday night at the library with Sherry and surprise, surprise, Tanner was also there. He'd disappeared back in the stacks but she knew he was around. "This is getting ridiculous. It's like the whole town is conspiring against us."

Sherry grinned and Madison slapped her forehead. "Oh my Lord, you have the whole town working with you? I'm so stupid. Did they take up every table at the coffee shop on Saturday so Tanner would have to sit with me?"

Sherry laughed. "You have a suspicious mind. Why do you think that?"

"Because there was no one in there when I arrived and no one when I left. But when it came time for him to find a table, suddenly the place was packed. How are you doing this?"

"I'm amazing," Sherry declared. "It turns out the town wants Tanner to be happy. We all think he'd be happy with you."

"He's not interested in me."

Sherry tapped her chin. "Interesting. You said he's not interested in you, not that you weren't interested in him." Sherry waggled her eyebrows. "I think you like him."

Madison slammed the book back on the shelf, barely looking at the cover. "This is not third grade. You are not going to pass him a note asking him whether he likes me." A horrible thought occurred to Madison. "You aren't, are you?"

"I hadn't thought about that tactic but it's not a bad one. Direct and to the point."

Madison studied her shoes. It felt like the walls were closing in on her. "Please," she whispered. "Don't do this. Stop, Sherry. I just can't."

Sherry clutched her arm. "Hey, it's going to be okay." Madison looked Sherry in the eye.

"You don't know that. I'm a mess when it comes to the opposite sex. I don't know what to do, what to say. I'm fine alone."

"No, you're not." Sherry shook her head. "Eventually Dan is going to marry me. I'm going to have kids. I don't want you to be alone when that happens."

"We'll stay close. Besides, I have my dad."

"Everyone always says they'll stay close, but you know we'll spend less time with each other. We won't be able to help it." Sherry squeezed Madison's shoulder. "And I hate to say it, but your dad won't be around forever. You need someone to love you."

"I have my work," Madison argued. It sounded pathetic, but it was true. She loved being a doctor.

"You do." Sherry nodded. "What else?"

She didn't have anything else but Sherry and Dad.

"I could get a dog."

Sherry smiled. "Tanner already has one."

"You're not giving up then?"

"Never. One date. Would it kill you?"

It might. She didn't have any fond memories of past dates. They'd all been pretty awful.

"I'm not talking about this anymore. I'm taking my books to the checkout desk so you and I can go for dinner."

Madison headed for the front desk and the smiling librarian, Sally. She had been a few years behind Madison at school. "I'll take these, please."

She set her stack of books on the desk, and Sally bit her lip. "Well, the thing is, I can't check those out yet."

Madison frowned. "I'm not following. What do you mean yet?"

Sally took a deep breath. "I can't do it now. I need to wait."

"Oh, the computer is down? I can wait." Someone came up behind her and Madison stepped aside, gaping as Sally proceeded to check out the other woman's books. The woman headed for the door and Madison stepped back to the front of the desk. "Can you do mine now?"

Sally shook her head. "I can't."

Madison leaned forward. "What are we waiting for?"

"It should only be a few more minutes," Sally said. She looked really uncomfortable. Madison was about to abandon the books and head for the exit when Tanner walked out of the stacks area. Suddenly, everything was clear.

"Sherry?" she asked Sally.

Sally nodded. "You two would make a nice couple." She reached for Madison's books and very slowly and methodically began checking them out. Tanner saw her and tipped his hat.

"Sally. Madison. How are you ladies this evening?"

"Fine," they said in unison. Madison noticed the stitches were out of his forehead.

"When did you get your stitches out? You cancelled your appointment this morning."

Tanner leaned against the desk. "Your dad took them out this afternoon. I had an emergency call this morning. Sorry I had to cancel."

Sally handed Madison her books. "It's okay. We were slammed with patients anyway. There's a flu going around."

Madison didn't know what to say next. She'd never been good at small talk, but Sherry was suddenly at her elbow. "Sheriff, how nice to see you. We were just headed to get some dinner at the pizza place. Would you care to join us?"

Madison was going to tie Sherry to a chair and make her watch horror movies. Sherry was a total wuss when it came to scary things. Then Madison would make Sherry eat something healthy.

Tanner looked back and forth between them as if to gauge the sincerity of the offer. "That's kind of you. I was going to eat dinner alone, but company sounds good."

"That's great," Sherry enthused. "I'm starving. Let's go."

At least Sherry would be there. She always knew what to say and could be counted on to fill the silence. Madison wouldn't need to chat or be entertaining. Unless Tanner found bowel resections entertaining, he wasn't going to be charmed by her conversation.

She kept repeating to herself the whole way to the restaurant. It's only pizza. It's only pizza.

No one could make her go out on a date if she didn't want to. She was a grown woman and she made her own decisions. She wouldn't be railroaded into something she didn't want or need.

* * * *

Madison was wrong. She could be railroaded into something she didn't want to do. She was currently sitting across from Tanner in the restaurant and Sherry was long gone. She'd received an "important" phone call as soon as they sat down and had quickly left Madison alone with Tanner.

They'd ordered a large with sausage and extra cheese, and talked about the cold weather. Madison was officially out of topics. This was going to be one long excruciating meal at this rate. She played with the paper napkin on the table and tried to calm her fast beating heart. He smelled really good. Kind of woodsy and warm. It was male without being overpowering, and it made her palms sweat with fear.

"So what was the emergency this afternoon?" she asked, grabbing at any topic she could.

Tanner leaned back in the booth. "Murder. Some guy got hacked up in his kitchen." He scraped his hand over his face. "Shit. I'm sorry. Sometimes I forget how to talk in polite company. Please accept my apologies."

Tanner's cheeks were a dull red. She felt better knowing she wasn't the only one uncomfortable. "Relax. I'm a doctor. We can talk about all sorts of gross topics and I'll be able to eat dinner. I have a cast iron stomach."

"Still, I should be careful. Not too many people like to discuss death and dismemberment over their supper." Tanner shook his head, still looking discomfited.

"I think what you do is very interesting, actually. Do you know why he was murdered? Do we get a lot of murders in Springwood?"

"Not until recently," he answered, thanking the waitress when she brought their drinks. "Our humble town appears to be on a drug route to Canada and the cartels are fighting over it. Hence the recent rise in drug related crime and also in dead bodies. Today was the third."

"And they cut him up? Most of the gang activity I saw in Chicago involved guns. You wouldn't believe what a semi-automatic weapon can do to the human body."

"I would, actually. I was in the military."

She hadn't known that. "Did you see action?"

He nodded. "The first Gulf War. I left the Army in 1996."

"I'm not a big fan of war. Most doctors aren't."

"I'm not either. There weren't many casualties in that war but I did see my fair share. Not a pretty sight. You must have seen some ugly things in Chicago."

"I worked in an emergency room at a city hospital. On the weekends it was like a war zone. Endless streams of bodies. Kids too young to be carrying a gun, let alone know how to use it. Innocent people caught in the crossfire."

The conversation was easy and comfortable. She and Tanner had something in common. She told him stories from the ER and he told her stories about being in the Middle East. By the time they'd eaten their way through more than half of the pizza, she'd realized she was having fun.

Tanner was a nice man. Because he was, he deserved to know what Sherry and the town were trying to do. It was only fair to warn him.

"Tanner," she began, not sure how to say what needed to be said. "Sherry is...well, trying to be a good friend. She's trying..." Madison couldn't find the words.

He scratched his chin. "Sherry's a sweet girl. Dan should marry her."

"He should." Madison nodded, starting to lose her courage. She wasn't brave about men at the best of times. "Sherry doesn't like that I'm alone." Madison tried again.

Tanner sighed. "A young woman such as yourself shouldn't be alone. It can be hard to be on your own."

"Sherry doesn't think you should be alone either. Neither does the town."

Tanner narrowed his eyes. "The town has an opinion about my life? Why am I not surprised? They have an opinion about everything."

Madison shredded her napkin. "She thinks we shouldn't be alone. Together." She said the words quickly and braced herself for his laughter. It was surely a joke to him that anyone would think he was even slightly interested in her.

He frowned. "Together? As in you and me?"

She nodded. "Yes. Sherry and the town are conspiring to throw us together. Haven't you thought it was strange that we keep running into each other? That there were no tables at the coffee shop? That Sherry suddenly got an important phone call and left us here together? They're plotting against us, Tanner."

Her voice had gone up an octave and Tanner seemed to recognize her distress. He held his hand up. "Calm down. I have seen quite a bit of you, but are you sure? The entire town couldn't organize a trip to the bathroom."

"Sherry can. She can orchestrate the perfect day for a bride without a hitch. Now she's organizing you and me. Sally wouldn't check out my books tonight until you were around. I wasn't going to be allowed to leave the library without seeing you."

Whatever reaction she had expected, the one she got wasn't it. Tanner laughed. He was still chuckling when the waitress brought the check. "The town honestly believes a beautiful young woman like you would want to be with a broken down old lawman like me? Holy hell, I'm at least ten or fifteen years older than you, divorced with two kids, one of which hates my guts. You could do a hell of a lot better than me."

He needed to take this seriously. "You're not broken down and old. You're a nice man, which is why I told you. Forewarned is forearmed."

His blue eyes twinkled. "Forewarned? Are they going to force us to fall in love and get married? We're adults, Maddie. I think we can handle them."

She hadn't been called Maddie since she was a kid. "You think this is something to take lightly? We're here together, aren't we? They can engineer anything they want if we don't pay attention."

Tanner rubbed the back of his neck. "You have a point. Although having dinner with a pretty lady isn't something I would normally fight. It's you I feel sorry for."

Madison slapped the shredded napkin down on the table. "Stop. You're not old and I am not to be pitied because I'm having dinner with you. The fact is this was quite pleasant."

Well, crap, she hadn't meant to say that out loud.

"It was. I usually eat dinner alone."

"Me too. Something frozen and microwaved."

The corners of his mouth tipped up. "I know those dinners well. Sometimes I just eat standing up with the fridge door open."

Her eyes widened. "I've done that too."

He chuckled. "Now you know why they're trying to fix us up. We have a few things in common."

Madison wasn't so sure about that. She'd never told Sherry about her predilection for eating dinner over the kitchen sink.

"They should still mind their own business. But when Sherry decides something, well, it's almost impossible to change her mind."

The waitress came up and picked up the check along with Tanner's credit card. She hadn't been paying attention and now he was stuck with the bill. "You folks having a good evening? It's a nice night for a romantic stroll. Lots of stars." The woman smirked and headed to the cash register.

"See?" She rolled her eyes. "The whole town is in on it."

"Even if the whole town is in on it that doesn't mean we're going to be forced to date. We have free will."

Madison sighed. "You're right. I'm just being paranoid. They can't force us to do anything."

"Exactly. All we need to do is simply ignore them. They'll get tired of this and move on to something else before long. Small towns are full of gossip. Somebody is bound to do something that snags their attention."

"That's true." Madison smiled at Tanner. "You are a nice man. I thought you'd be appalled but you took the news really well." She reached for her wallet and extracted a twenty. "Here's my share of the pizza."

His eyebrows shot up. "Woman, if my father knew I let a lady pay half the check he'd have my hide. Dinner is on me."

Stubborn cowboys.

She thought about arguing but she could see from the set of his jaw she wasn't going to win. She relented, stuffing the bill back in her purse. "Thank you then. That's very kind."

The waitress dropped off the receipt. Tanner signed it and then stood, shrugging on his jacket. She pulled hers on and felt his warm hands at the collar, helping her.

"Let me walk you to your car."

She couldn't think of a blessed reason for him not to, so he walked with her down the sidewalk to where she'd parked her car. He waited, standing there, while she started her engine and drove away. She forced herself not to give into the urge to look into her rearview mirror.

Chapter Five

If it weren't for his daughter Emily, Tanner wouldn't have even come to the Valentine's dance tonight. She wanted him to meet her new boyfriend, Tyler Givens. She'd met him in an art class she was taking in Billings, and he was supposedly "awesome" or some such word. Now he was here and Emily hadn't shown up yet. So he had staked out some real estate by the food buffet and made small talk with the townsfolk who wandered by.

The Ladies Auxiliary had really gone all out this year for the annual fundraiser. The Civic Center, which was really just a converted warehouse for town council meetings and the occasional non-denominational wedding and reception, looked like Cupid had exploded. Hearts and snowflakes, clearly all handmade from red, white, and pink construction paper, hung from the ceiling while the tables were covered with red paper tablecloths and white paper lace doilies.

There was also a spot for photos with a splashy red and gold background that would have made Venus blush. They were charging ten bucks a pop but you couldn't pay Tanner to stand in front of that mural that was obviously designed by a horny teenage boy. Shit, even the angels had silicone boobs and lascivious expressions.

All in all, it was a banner year and the turnout was going to make the children's wing of the nearby hospital very happy. There was a crush of bodies on the dance floor and a steady stream of newcomers through the door. There wasn't much to do in a small town so when something went on it usually ended up packed with people.

"Tanner, I didn't expect to see you here tonight. Are you on duty?"

Tanner winced at the familiar sound of his ex-wife's voice. Since the kids were now grown, he tried to stay out of her orbit as much as possible. It wasn't easy in a town the size of Springwood but a determined man could make things happen. Abby was a good woman and mother, but she had a way of grating on Tanner's nerves. He was pretty sure it was on purpose.

He turned to find Abby and her new fiancé, Fenton Jacks. Abby was a tiny woman with short dark hair and a nice figure, even after two children. Fenton was a few inches under six feet with a soft middle. He wasn't a bad looking man. Tanner had even heard women say Fenton was handsome. But he had a perpetual smirk on his face that made Tanner want to smack it off.

Fenton had bought a small ranch about eight months ago. As far as Tanner could see, the man was a city slicker who didn't know one end of a cow from the other. Fenton's enthusiasm for small town life seemed suspect since he liked to brag about living all over the world. He also seemed flush with cash. Something else that made Tanner suspicious. Small ranchers were rarely rich.

Tanner nodded. "Abby. Fenton." Tanner looked down at his jeans, western cut shirt with silver bolo tie, and his dress cowboy boots. "No, I'm not on duty. Emily wanted me to meet Tyler tonight."

"Fine young man," Fenton boomed. Heads swiveled toward them. "We had him over to dinner the other night."

Of course you did, you smug bastard.

Fenton and Abby always made sure to let Tanner know how much Emily and Chris, especially Chris, liked Fenton. Tanner made a mental note to call Logan in the morning and see if he'd turned up anything with his investigation. Tiny pinpricks stabbed the back of Tanner's neck. This guy simply was not legit. It didn't mean he was doing something illegal, but he wasn't on the up and up either.

Abby placed her hand on Fenton's arm. "We liked Tyler. He seems like a good boy."

"I'm sure he is." Tanner looked over their shoulders for an avenue of escape. It was all cordial at the moment, but it could turn on a dime.

"I saw Chris today," Abby said.

Apparently the cordial part of the evening was complete. Tanner's shoulders stiffened but he kept his expression bland.

"How is he? I haven't seen him in a few days."

Since I let him out of jail for drinking and fighting two weeks ago.

Abby's lips pressed together. "He's lost his job at the Hogan ranch. This is the third in the last year."

Tanner's hopes plummeted. Logan and Sam were right. What Chris needed was some tough love. Fast. "I hope you didn't give him any money, Abby. You're only enabling him to keep drinking and losing jobs."

"He has a wife and a baby, Tanner. I had to do something," Abby insisted.

"No." Tanner shook his head. "Chris needs to do something. He needs a trip to rehab."

"You never needed rehab." Abby waved away the suggestion. "You stopped drinking and Chris can, too. He just needs someone to help him."

Tanner didn't like his ex-wife talking about his drinking problem in front of her future husband. He also wasn't thrilled with how she characterized his struggle. Apparently he'd made his twenty-year love affair with the bottle look like a day at the fucking park. He remembered it very differently. The withdrawal alone had been physically excruciating.

"Getting sober can only be done when he really wants it. If he doesn't, it's doomed to fail."

"He wants to," Abby insisted. "He promised me he's going to stop drinking. Stacey told him that if he didn't stop drinking she was going to leave him."

Personally, Tanner thought that was a good idea. Chris wasn't seeing all the things he could lose with his self-destructive behavior.

"I hope he means it this time, Abby. He's said those things before."

"He means it this time." Fenton puffed out his chest. "Besides, he has me to watch over him now. He's going to come work on my ranch. Things are going to be fine."

44

It was all Tanner could do not to knock that smug smile off of Fenton's face. He was implying that Tanner hadn't been up to the job of parenting, but Fenton had everything under fucking control. Tanner gritted his teeth and seethed inside, but tried to appear outwardly calm.

"Don't cut him any slack, Fenton. Don't baby him. He needs to quit drinking and learn some responsibility."

It appeared that Fenton wanted to say more but divine intervention was kind. The Eisleys interrupted with a question for Abby about the quilt she was making for their soon-to-be-born granddaughter and the four of them ambled off to find the bar. Tanner exhaled slowly, trying to let go of his anger. He shouldn't let Fenton and Abby wind him up that way. He knew better.

He refilled his cup of punch and found his attention pulled to the dance. Madison Shay had just walked in with her friend, Sherry, and Sherry's boyfriend, Dan. Madison didn't appear to have an escort and she looked slightly uncomfortable standing there, her smile strained.

But she looked beautiful tonight. Tanner remembered her as a gangly kid with long legs and freckles. This woman was a far cry from the child. She wore a white knit dress with a high neck and long sleeves, belted at the waist. It showed off the subtle curves of her slender body, and the red suede boots accented her long legs. She'd left her hair loose and it hung down almost to her waist in fiery curls and waves.

Holy crap, it was hot in here. Tanner ran his finger under his collar. A blast of cold air was just what he needed instead of standing here salivating over a lovely lady. He'd been too long between women. Tomorrow he might want to think about calling that widow he'd been seeing in the town over. She was always happy to hear from him. He headed for the entrance and a breath of fresh air but then realized he would have to pass right by her to step outside.

Sherry's eyes lit up and she made a beeline straight for him, tugging him over to where Dan and Madison were waiting. "Sheriff, it's so good to see you tonight. I had no idea you would be here."

The way Sherry was eyeing him gave credence to Madison's story about being fixed up with each other. He simply couldn't figure out why Sherry had chosen him. Madison was way out of Tanner's league.

"My daughter convinced me. She wanted me to meet her new boyfriend."

"That's so sweet. I haven't seen Emily in a long time," Sherry said.

"She spends most of her time in Billings but she comes here to visit once every couple of weeks. She's going to art school."

Dan chuckled. "Good for her. I can't even draw a stick figure. I'd love to have a talent."

Sherry linked her arm in his. "You do have talent, babe. The kind they don't teach in school."

Tanner laughed and Madison turned pink at the innuendo. It intrigued Tanner to see a woman as beautiful and sexy as Madison act so innocent. It made her seem fresh and unspoiled compared to the women he'd dated lately. He tended to gravitate toward females who were also divorced and didn't want a man around full time. The care and feeding of the male animal wasn't a part of their future plans.

A Trace Adkins song came on, and Sherry clasped Dan's arm and squealed with delight. "I love this song. Let's all go out and dance." She turned to Madison with a huge smile. "You remember how to line dance, don't you?"

"Kind of," Madison replied, clearly not as enthused as her friend. Sherry patted Madison's shoulder. "Just follow us. It'll all come back to you." She started tugging Madison and Dan toward the dance floor. "Sheriff, you're coming too, right?"

Tanner was about to make his excuses and head outside when he saw Abby and Fenton by the front door. He didn't want to run into them again tonight. A quick glance toward the food buffet and he could see Marilyn Cedars scanning the crowd hopefully. She'd been widowed about a year ago and was looking for a new daddy for her five uncontrollable children. Tanner

46

had his own issues without taking on five more. Make that six, if you counted Marilyn herself who chain-smoked and chewed her gum like the MGM lion. Discretion was the better part of valor or some shit like that. He dutifully followed Madison, Sherry, and Dan to the dance floor. As long as the steps weren't fancy, he could fake it.

Thirty minutes later he'd danced to several songs alongside Madison. She'd stepped on his boots a few times in the beginning but she moved with a natural grace he couldn't help but admire. She also had a self-deprecating sense of humor that made him smile. Damn if she wasn't the most attractive woman he'd met in a very long time. A sultry, slow song started, the lights going dim. Tanner looked down at Madison's pretty face and threw caution to the wind.

Fuck it.

He was ready to admit that he liked her and was attracted to her. She was too damn young or he was too old, but he enjoyed her company. They had things in common and she was pleasant to be around. He held out his hand.

"Dance?"

Her eyes widened and she looked ready to bolt for the exit. He was ready to slap himself upside the head thinking a woman like her would want to dance with a guy like him when she gave him a tremulous smile and placed her hand in his.

Instant electricity.

A zing went up his arm that jolted his entire body. He enfolded her into his arms and they began to gently sway to the music. He could smell the flowery scent of her shampoo and feel her heart beating against him. He closed his eyes and let his cheek rest on her forehead while the warmth of her body seeped into his skin. A simple dance had never been this good or this right. Her body fit his as if the good Lord had made her just for him.

Right there and then he decided. He was going to pursue Dr. Madison Shay. Heaven help her, he was a man on a mission with the first woman he'd truly liked in years.

Hopefully he wouldn't screw it up.

* * * *

Madison didn't want it to be this good, but Tanner's hard body so close to hers felt like heaven. He was solid and strong, and she let herself lean against him as they moved to the soft ballad. It was all over too soon and the song ended note by note and the lights came up, harsh and blinding to her eyes. She quickly pulled away as if she'd been burned. In a way she had. He was the bright light and she was a moth, helpless to the attraction she felt for him. She'd thought she'd been above all of the nonsense until their slow dance. Her body was on fire just being close to him.

But she'd seen what happened to moths and she wasn't planning to let that happen to her. She stared at the floor and mumbled a thank you before turning on her heel and heading straight for the foyer and then out the front door. The cold air hit her like an icy wall, freezing her in her tracks. Her breath came in frosted pants and she wrapped her arms around herself to ward off the bitter February weather.

She should have headed for the ladies room, but as usual, her mind hadn't worked correctly in the presence of a man and now she was probably going to get hypothermia. She quickly calculated her probable blood alcohol level after a glass and a half of wine and used that to predict how long she had before she would freeze to death. Not long. She needed to figure out how she was going to sneak back in, get her coat, and find a ride home. Walking home in this weather wasn't an option, and Sherry and Dan were having too much fun to abandon the party and drive her anywhere.

She rubbed her arms and almost jumped as something heavy was laid across her shoulders and a warm male scent surrounded her. She whirled around and Tanner was standing there, his brows knitted together.

"You'll freeze out here." He tugged the front of the coat together and his fingers brushed the sensitive flesh of her neck, sending sparks through her body. She swallowed the lump that had formed in her throat. He must think she was a total idiot.

"You don't have a coat." Her voice came out as a mere whisper.

Tanner shrugged. "The cold doesn't bother me. Besides, I'm not wearing a dress."

She licked her dry lips, not sure what to say. She never knew what to say to a man, especially a man as attractive as Tanner.

"Thank you." This time her voice sounded normal, but he still had that puzzled expression on his face.

"Maddie, have I offended you? I'm sorry if I have. Did I get too familiar on the dance floor? You hightailed it out of there pretty fast."

He thought he'd done something wrong. Madison shook her head. "You didn't do anything. It's me. I'm all wrong."

His frown deepened. "How are you wrong? I don't understand."

Madison took a deep breath. "The dance was nice. I just don't know how to talk to a man or anything."

"You do a pretty good job talking to me."

She realized with a start he was right. He was easy to talk to. It still didn't mean she wasn't a failure though. She struggled to find the right words. "I like being with you. It's just that when it comes to romantic situations, I've never had much luck."

He regarded her steadily and she felt the heat creep under her skin. She'd said it was romantic and he probably wasn't thinking that way at all. What a mess. Madison wanted to throttle Sherry about now. She knew well Madison's awkwardness with the male species.

"I haven't either, Maddie. I'm divorced so I failed at marriage. I've dated but haven't met one woman who captured any real interest. Until now."

Her heart beat a tattoo in her chest. "You mean me?" She barely pushed the words out.

This time he smiled. "Yes, you. You seem surprised. I was thinking you wouldn't be interested in me because I'm so much older."

"You're not that much older than me. I'm thirty."

"I'm forty-four. I'll be forty-five in a few weeks. I have two grown kids. Is that a deal breaker?"

"No." Madison shook her head. "What would be a deal breaker for you?"

He stroked his chin. "Addicted to drugs, alcohol, or shopping. I don't like cigarettes much but could tolerate them. Law abiding is a must, of course. Other than that, I'm pretty flexible."

He wasn't asking all that much. "What if I told you I'd never had any luck with men? At all."

"If you've dated a lot it doesn't bother me, if that's what you mean." Tanner shrugged.

"No. I mean I haven't had any luck. I've had twenty-six dates in my life with eight different men. You do the math." She waited for him to calculate the answer. "If you don't like to do mental arithmetic, that's an average of three point two five dates per man. Actually, I went out with one man seven times, so that moves the average even lower. Obviously there's something wrong with me."

He tipped his head to the side. "Are you sure? Maybe there was something wrong with them?"

"All of them?" Madison rolled her eyes. "What are the odds?"

Tanner held up his hand. "We don't need to calculate it. Maybe I should say this differently. What were the men like?"

"They were men I went to college and medical school with."

"There you go." Tanner nodded. "Maybe they weren't the right men for you. Perhaps you should try a different type. An older man who would appreciate you. Who isn't trying to build his career. I'm settled into mine."

She felt a warmth in her chest. "Would you appreciate me?"

"Madison Shay, I would do my level best. How about we try this?"

"Dating?" And sex, although she was too chicken shit to say it.

"Dating. I like you, Maddie." His voice was soft like a caress on her skin. It made her shiver and quake but not because of the temperature.

"I like you, too."

He gave her a lopsided grin. "Then how about another dance? Let's enjoy the evening. May I drive you home when the party is done?"

She nodded and let him lead her into the warm building. She froze as he lifted the coat from her shoulders. "Damn."

His eyebrows shot up. "What's wrong? Having second thoughts already?"

"Sherry is going to be completely insufferable now. I'll never hear the end of it that she was right."

His rich laughter echoed in the empty lobby. "If that's the biggest problem this relationship has we're in good shape. Would it help if I told her I had to beg you to go out with me?"

"She'd never in a million years believe that, Tanner."

He hung up the coat and draped an arm across her shoulders. "Maddie, you are good for my ego."

They walked back into the main room. She felt safe and warm in his company. He was good for her ego too. She liked Tanner Marks and she was absolutely scared stiff to admit it.

Chapter Six

"I want to hear every dirty detail," Sherry declared. Madison and Sherry were sitting in the kitchen and Madison's dad was whistling a lilting tune while talking on Skype with his sister. "I want to know how it went. Tanner brought you home last night after the party. Did he kiss you?"

"Shhh! I don't want my dad to hear you." Madison warmed up their coffees and pulled two pieces of toast from the toaster, dropping one on each of their plates. She sat back down and sighed. "No, he did not kiss me. Are you happy now?"

Sherry tapped her chin. "Hmm, he was probably just being a gentleman. Do you think he wanted to kiss you?"

"How would I know?" Madison rolled her eyes. "I know zilch about men and less about kissing. Let's face it. I'm the romantic equivalent of the Bermuda Triangle. Men date me then disappear, never to be heard from again."

Sherry's lips twitched. "I never thought of it that way. But don't worry. We can fix it. You just need Sherry's School of Romance. I'll be your coach."

"I sucked in athletics. I was picked last for everything."

"Luckily for you there are no other people on the team. This is one on one coaching. Now did he ask you out? When are you seeing him again?"

Madison nodded. "We're having dinner tonight. He's picking me up at seven."

Sherry immediately went into her drill sergeant mode. "We have so much to do," she said. "We should make a list."

"What do we need to do?" Madison lifted a forkful of scrambled eggs to her mouth. "It's just dinner."

Sherry cast an appraising eye over Madison's clothes. "For one, we need to go shopping. Your wardrobe leaves something to be desired, my friend."

Madison looked down at her gray sweatpants and blue sweater. They'd seen better days but she was only having breakfast with Sherry, not tea with the Queen of England. "There's nothing wrong with my clothes."

Sherry wrinkled her nose. "Let's forget that you've had those sweatpants since high school. Put aside the fact your sweater is faded from a thousand washings. If they were brand spanking new, I'd still want to replace them. They hang off of you like a tent. You need something that enhances your figure, not swamps it. What were you planning to wear tonight anyway?"

Madison shifted in her chair. "I hadn't thought about it yet. Maybe some jeans and a sweater."

"Task number one. New clothes. We'll drive into the city after breakfast. Task two? Let's talk about talk."

"Talk?" Madison's fork paused in mid-air. "Now I don't speak correctly?"

"You speak fine. We just need to tweak things a bit. First, let the man talk. Find out his interests. If they aren't your interests, well, just pretend they are or that you're fascinated by what he's saying." She smiled. "And whatever you do, do not, I repeat, do not have sex with him tonight. Men like Tanner Marks like to strive for things. Compete. Win. You need to be a prize he wants to work for."

Madison clapped her hand to her forehead. "It shouldn't be this difficult. I'm shocked the human race hasn't died out if this is what it takes to get a man interested in a woman. Do they all have such weak egos?"

Sherry laughed. "Luckily, no. And it's only in the beginning, when you first get to know them. They need some encouragement, that's all."

Madison frowned. "Sex on the first date is bad? I thought men really liked sex. The few times I've had sex they seemed to like it."

"Sex on the first date is bad. You don't want him to think you do that with every guy."

Madison gave up on her eggs. "Can't I just tell him I don't? I told him I'd only been out on twenty-six dates."

Sherry groaned. "He won't believe you. And now would be a good time to mention that you should try and keep an air of mystery around you. He doesn't need to know every little thing about your life."

Madison felt her indignation rise. "He won't believe me? That seems harsh. I don't assume he's a liar."

"Well, you should," Sherry countered. "Women lie to men about their sexual experience, so he'll be suspicious of a thirty year old that's not far from a virgin. And yes, my friend, men lie. Some lie like dirty dogs to get in your pants. They'll say or do anything that will get you to go to bed with them. Remember Todd Baker? He took me out my senior year and got in my pants, then showed up with Tracy Gildbrand at the game the next day. Asshole."

"Tanner wouldn't lie to me." Madison was sure of this.

"He probably wouldn't, but you need to know that many men do. Reality is a heartless bitch."

"Says the woman who creates fantasy weddings for other people. Do you give this pep talk to your brides?"

"A version of it. I tell them even if the wedding is a disaster, they're still just as married."

Madison's eyebrows rose. "Maybe you're the heartless bitch."

Sherry shrugged. "I'm simply managing their expectations. Perfection is not a reasonable expectation."

Madison sipped her coffee and leaned over in her chair to make sure her father was still in the living room. "I hope you're right. I like Tanner and I don't want to scare him off."

"Oh, that reminds me. Don't talk about gross, bloody stuff, *Star Wars*, *Star Trek*, *Dr. Who*, global warming, or grisly death of any kind. Got it?"

"That's pretty much all I know. Science and geeky stuff. Besides, we've already talked about gruesome things." Sherry shook her head and frowned. Madison sighed and capitulated. Perhaps she should be taking notes on her hand so she could remind herself in the middle of the date. "What should I talk about?"

"Him. Ask him about his interests. Movies, books, sports, his childhood. Men love talking about themselves. Do that and he'll think you're wonderful."

"Okay." Madison pushed her plate away. "I can do that."

"You can do what, sweetheart?" Madison's dad entered the kitchen and headed straight for the coffee pot.

"Oh, just go shopping with Sherry today. What do you have planned? How's Aunt Carole?"

Her father smiled. Madison's mother had died when she was thirteen and Greg Shay had done everything he could to be both parents for his daughter. Madison never doubted his devotion and love. It had been an easy decision when he'd asked her to come home to help him with his practice and eventually take over.

"Your aunt is doing well. She's says it's cold and rainy in Seattle, but then it rains all the time there."

"Is she going to come visit this spring?" Aunt Carole usually spent a week in Montana for Easter.

A strange expression flitted over her father's face but was gone in an instant. "Not this year. She has some things going on at work." Her father added cream and sugar to his coffee and absently stirred the hot liquid. "In fact, she was asking if I could come back and spend some more time with her. She needs some advice and has asked me to help."

Madison sucked in a breath. "Is Aunt Carole sick?"

"No, no." Her father waved the concern away. "I shouldn't have been so vague. Forgive me. She's having some renovations done and she's asked me to help oversee them. You know how anxiety-ridden your aunt gets about these things."

Aunt Carole was the president of a bank and one of the most capable women Madison had ever known, but certainly home improvement projects could be stressful. Carole had divorced her husband about five years ago and did often turn to her brother for advice.

"I'm sure I can handle things, Dad," Madison assured him. "How long will you be gone?"

"I'm not gone yet." Her dad's eyes twinkled. "I won't leave for a week or two. Not sure how long I'll be away. I'm so glad you're helping with things. It's nice having you here."

"It's good to be back." Madison was surprised, but she truly felt that way. Being in Springwood was a good thing, and she was determined to put her rocky childhood behind her.

Her dad opened the freezer and looked inside, pushing around the contents. "What do you want for dinner? We have steaks and there's chicken in here, too."

The moment had arrived. "I won't be home for dinner actually, Dad. I have dinner plans."

Her dad turned with a smile. "You and Sherry going out somewhere? The barbecue place has a brisket on Sunday nights."

"Um, no. I'm having dinner with Tanner Marks." Madison braced herself for a reaction. Her father never thought the men she dated were good enough. He'd been disdainful of them all. At least the ones he'd met.

Greg Shay's jaw went slack but he quickly recovered. "Tanner Marks is a fine man and a good sheriff." Her father paused. "He has had some issues in his past, but they do seem to be in the past."

"What issues?" Madison frowned. "I wasn't aware of anything."

Madison's father sighed. "He had a drinking problem years ago. He liked to hang out at the local watering hole, have a few too many, and close it down several nights a week."

"I had no idea." It didn't sound like Tanner in the least. Her head swiveled to Sherry. "Did you know?"

Sherry nodded. "I thought everyone knew, honestly. Is it a big deal?"

Madison shook her head. "No, it just surprised me that's all. Dad, you said he had a drinking problem. Does that mean he doesn't now?" Tanner had always seemed completely in control when she'd been around him.

"From what I've heard he hasn't touched the stuff for about ten years. Sober as a judge. He was a wild one back in the day, though. I heard he was the life of the party. People have conjectured that's why he and Abby divorced. His son, Chris, appears to have inherited the propensity to drink. He's constantly in the drunk tank or getting in a fight."

"Tanner's been sheriff for thirteen years," Madison said in amazement. "The town elected him Sheriff knowing he liked to drink? I guess this little town isn't as closed-minded as I thought."

Greg Shay chuckled. "Remember this is Montana. A hard drinking, hard partying man isn't considered a problem as long as he takes care of business. And Tanner Marks has taken good care of this town. Sheriff Tunney used to keep some rotgut whiskey in his desk and drink during the day. No one thought a thing about it."

Madison rubbed her chin. "Alcohol addiction is complex. It's not just genetic factors, but environment and personality." She looked at her dad. "How did I not know this? Was it a well-kept secret?"

"Why would you know?" He shrugged. "You were too young to hang out in bars. No one thought much about it so they didn't gossip about him. He wasn't a man to fall over his own feet even drunk so even if you saw him it wouldn't have been obvious."

"Does this bother you?" Sherry queried. "It was all so long ago I didn't think it was a big deal. You could always call him and cancel."

Madison shook her head. "It doesn't bother me in the least. Can you imagine the strength of character he must have to overcome his body's desire for alcohol? I'm not even going to go into how serotonin and dopamine can play into addiction."

Her father nodded. "You make a good point." He leaned down and kissed her cheek. "Have a good time tonight."

"Thank you, Dad." Madison smiled.

"Thank you for growing up into such a fine young woman. Now if you ladies will excuse me, I'm heading over to Harvey's today. I'm helping him work on that bookcase he's building." Her father hurried out of the kitchen and Sherry grabbed Madison's hand.

"I knew you wouldn't care. That's what makes you two so perfect for one another. Your ability to see past the superficial stuff."

"It actually helps me relax." Madison sat back in her chair with a smile.

"How on earth does this help you relax? You won't have to pair your wine with the entree?"

Madison laughed. "It means he's not perfect. It means he has flaws. I can deal with a man who has the occasional dent in his armor. It makes him more human."

Sherry sighed. "I guess I see what you mean. I like that Dan isn't perfect. I like some of his flaws. Like how he snores after he eats pasta and how he's the worst speller in the world."

"I'll just ask him about it," Madison said, lifting their plates from the table and heading to the sink.

"No," Sherry gasped. "You can't do that." She looked scandalized.

"That's a no-no, too?" Madison rinsed the dishes and dried her hands. "Fine. There are way too many rules in dating."

"You'll remember all them. Don't worry."

"I've got lots of things to worry about but I don't think that's one of them. Let's get on the road and I'll let you browbeat me into buying clothes I would never choose myself."

"Deal." Sherry bounced out of her chair. "I know just what you need. We're going to start with your underwear."

Madison groaned. It was going to be a long day. And she liked her underwear just fine.

* * * *

Tanner was shoving a load of towels into the washer when he heard a rap on his front door. Scout, his four year-old German Shepherd lifted his head from where he was lying on the kitchen floor and whined. He wanted to bark and run around but was too well-trained to do it. Tanner walked to the front window, stopping to scratch Scout behind the ears.

"Good boy," he crooned.

One look outside made his gut clench. It was Stacey, Chris's wife. She appeared to be on her own. He opened the door, Scout immediately behind him and ready to rip off a limb if the visitor was unwanted.

"Hey, Stacey. Come on in. How about a cup of coffee?"

Tanner acted as if it was a social call but he knew better. Stacey's features were pinched and she looked like she hadn't had a good night's sleep in a while. Scout recognized her and danced around her legs while she pet him. Stacey picked up one of Scout's toys and tossed it into the living room. Scout went scampering after it with a happy bark.

Stacey entered but seemed to hover in the foyer. He put his arm around her shoulders and led her into the kitchen. She sat down at the table, staring at her purse. He waited while she gathered her thoughts. He liked Stacey and she deserved better than what she had with his son. Tanner had hoped she would be a calming influence on Chris but the opposite effect seemed to have taken place. He was wilder than ever since he married Stacey nine months ago.

"I've left Chris." Her simple statement broke his heart but didn't surprise him. He'd wondered how long she could hang in there. Tanner sat down at the table across from her. Her eyes were bright with tears and her lips trembled. Scout brought his toy into the kitchen, dropping it at Stacey's feet. As if he knew she was upset, he rested his head on her thigh in comfort.

"I'm sorry to hear that, but I had a feeling it might be coming. Where are you staying? What about Annie?" he asked gently.

At the mention of her daughter, she smiled weakly. "She's with my parents. That's where we're going to stay for awhile until I can figure out what I'm going to do." Her face crumpled. "I talked to my mom and dad. I'm going to file for a divorce and ask for full custody of Annie. Don't worry. I'll make sure you get to see her, Tanner. I just can't have her around Chris anymore. I can't trust him."

Alarm shot through him. "Has he hurt you and Annie?"

She shook her head but the tears were starting to fall. "No, but he's so angry, Tanner. He yells and scares the baby. He scares me. I can't take it anymore. He says that everything will be better now that he's working for Fenton, but I need to see it before I can believe it."

Chris had done a number on trust with his loved ones. Tanner knew from experience it would take a long time to build it back up. Working for Fenton wasn't a magic cure-all for what ailed Chris.

He patted her hand. "You did the right thing. Until Chris sees the consequences of his behavior, he won't change."

She lifted her tear-stained face to him, her eyes beseeching. "Will you talk to him again? Try and convince him to go to the AA meeting with you? I want Annie to have her father, but not this way."

She scrubbed her eyes with the back of her hand and anguish filled Tanner's soul. He wasn't sure she would understand that Chris had to want to do this himself.

"I'll talk to him," Tanner found himself saying. "I don't think it will make any difference, but I will. Chris doesn't have any respect for me."

"You're wrong." Stacey shook her head. "He does. He knows you quit drinking cold turkey. But he doesn't have the confidence to think he can do that himself."

Tanner didn't agree with Stacey's assessment but that wasn't the important thing at the moment.

"Do you need anything? Does Annie need anything?" Chris's regular bouts of unemployment had wrecked their finances. Stacey, Chris, and Annie were basically living hand to mouth.

"My parents are taking good care of us. We're okay." She stood, clutching her purse as if it was a lifeline. Scout sprang to life, watching her intently.

Tanner stood as well, placing a reassuring hand on her shoulder. "Whatever you need, day or night, you call me. Promise?"

Stacey sniffled and ruffled Scout's fur. "Promise. Thank you, Tanner. I know we can always count on you."

He walked her to the door. "Does Abby know yet?"

Stacey stepped out onto the porch. "I assume Chris will tell her and Fenton. You know Abby and I don't have the greatest relationship."

Abby had never thought any woman would be good enough for her baby boy, hence her chilly demeanor when dealing with Stacey.

"You're probably right. I'll talk to you after I've talked to Chris. Still the same cell number?"

She nodded and headed down the driveway to her old car. Tanner had wanted to buy them more reliable transportation when Annie was born but Stacey had been too proud to allow it. He watched her drive away, impervious to the bitter cold and lost in thought about his herculean task. He'd promised to talk to his son.

And he would do it. He'd promised Stacey. He didn't think it would make a damn bit of difference but he'd try. One more time.

Tanner glanced at his watch and scowled. Finding his son was the issue. What dive watering-hole would be open at eleven o'clock in the morning on a Sunday?

None.

That meant Chris was sleeping it off somewhere. Tanner headed back into the house to grab his coat and keys. He had some drunken, hung-over butt to kick.

"Scout, watch the house for me. I'll be gone for awhile."

The dog barked as if he understood every word, parking himself on the living room rug. He was sprawled as if he didn't have a care in the world. Tanner chuckled as Scout's eyes closed. The dog would be snoring within minutes. Tanner would love to be as carefree, if only for a day. But he wasn't a dog, he was a father. A father who needed to have a talk with his son. It wouldn't be the last.

Chapter Seven

Madison almost fell into the chair. Her feet hurt, her head hurt, and her credit card was screaming after the workout she'd given it. She grunted with relief and flexed her feet, stretching her toes inside her warm Ugg boots. They had literally shopped until Madison couldn't take it anymore, so Sherry had dragged them both to one of the mall restaurants for a bite to eat. Madison could only hope the shopping portion of the day was complete.

"You need to exercise your shopping muscles more." Sherry laughed, helping Madison stack the purchases in the two empty chairs at their table. "You're out of shape."

"I think my credit card actually caught fire at the last store. I'm sure I'm going to hear from my bank when they see a long list of charges at the mall."

"When they call you can tell them your friend helped you be stylish and sophisticated."

Madison couldn't argue. Although the delicate and lacy underthings Sherry had insisted on Madison buying wouldn't be seen by many, if anyone, the other garments made her feel amazing. When she'd put them on and gazed in the mirror, it was hard to believe it was herself gazing back. The old saying about clothes making the man were true, or in this case the woman.

"I really do need to thank you. I never would have thought to even try on most of what you picked out. They didn't look good on the hanger."

Sherry leaned over the table. "The secret of shopping. Sometimes great clothes look terrible on the hanger. They need a great figure to fill them out. You have one. I swear everything you tried on looked like it was made for you. I almost hate you." Sherry grinned. "And lunch is on me since you took my advice without too much fuss. I expected to have to do much more persuading."

The waitress came to the table and took their drink order. Sherry ordered a Coke and Madison ordered an iced tea.

"I want to look nice. When I wear those clothes, I have more confidence."

Sherry slapped the table. "Exactly. That's what I've been trying to tell you."

"I need all the confidence I can get when I'm with Tanner, or any man for that matter."

"Fake it 'til you make it, my friend."

Madison opened her mouth to reply she wasn't sure how to fake anything, but a squeal interrupted her. She turned to find two women standing at their table with huge smiles. They both had a few bags so clearly they had been shopping. One was hugely pregnant and probably needed to sit down and rest.

"Sherry, I thought that was you," the pregnant woman said. "I told Lisa it was you, but she said it wasn't." The woman turned to Lisa. "I told you it was Sherry. And look, it's Madison, too. Gosh, we haven't seen you in years. How are you?"

With a jolt, and not a pleasant one, Madison realized the two women were Lisa Millstone and Carrie Eller. They'd been in the popular crowd at school and had made Madison's school years difficult.

Try awful and horrific.

Madison shrunk back into the chair on instinct as if waiting for them to make a remark about her red hair or her glasses, but then she remembered she didn't wear glasses anymore and the freckles had faded some.

"I'm fine, thank you." Madison forced the words between gritted teeth. "How are you?"

Carrie patted her large stomach. "Huge and ready to have this baby." Her smile grew wide. "Hey, are you taking new patients? When I have this little girl here, it would be great to bring her to a female doctor." Carrie bit her lip. "Not that your dad isn't great. He is. But it would be nice for a girl to see a woman doctor, you know what I mean?"

Madison shifted in her seat. Carrie seemed perfectly sincere and appeared to have grown out of her former catty demeanor. "I am. Just call the office when you're ready."

Carrie beamed. "I will."

Lisa eyed the huge mound of packages Sherry and Madison had amassed. "I see we've been shopping seriously. I do hope this is for a date with the sheriff. We're all rooting for you two."

Heat flooded Madison's face. "Oh God, does everyone know? It's so embarrassing."

Lisa laughed. "What for? You two look good together. I saw you both in the coffee shop the other day."

Madison pointed to Sherry. "When are you going to admit that you had something to do with that?"

"Guilty." Sherry raised her right hand as if in court. "Lisa and Carrie have been excellent partners in crime."

The waitress slid their drinks in front of them and drifted away without a word.

"It was fun," Carrie enthused. "As an old married woman with two kids and one on the way, I don't have much romance in my life."

"Three kids?" Madison asked. "That's great. Who did you marry?"

Carrie grimaced. "My first husband was Steve Trotter, but it didn't last." Madison stiffened in shock but tried not let it show in her face. Carrie and Steve had been one of the golden couples in high school. "He was a big, fat, lying cheater. I divorced him and met Larry. Do you remember Larry Poplar?"

Madison did. He'd been a nice guy but never in Carrie's league. "I do remember him. Congratulations."

Lisa sighed. "You had it right, Madison. Getting good grades and going to college before settling down. You're a doctor. That's amazing. I wish I'd done something like that. Not a doctor, of course. I'm not that smart. But something, you know. I have a crappy job as a receptionist at a law firm. My boss is a jerk. Always yelling and screaming about a case."

Madison was definitely in the twilight zone. These women were saying they admired her? "I'm sure you are smart, Lisa. You can do anything you want."

Carrie laughed and shook her head. "No, you can do anything you want. Us mere mortals have to take what we can get."

"There's nothing special about me," Madison protested, but inside she felt changed. When she'd come back to Springwood, somehow the town and the people had been frozen in time. She'd pictured everything and everyone as they were. Madison hadn't stayed the same, so why hadn't she given that much credit to the people around her? Life was hard on everyone. It was so basic, yet for all her IQ points she'd completely missed it. She reached for the bags on the chairs. "Would you like to join us? We haven't ordered yet."

Sherry gave Madison an approving smile. "That's a great idea. We can move all this stuff."

Lisa looked unsure. "We don't want to intrude—"

"You aren't intruding. I'd like to catch up with you both," Madison said. She really meant it. It was time to put a stake into the heart of her insecure past and move the hell on. This was the first step.

"We'd love to." Carrie grinned. She and Lisa sat on the now cleared chairs. "This baby has a craving for cheese. Anybody want to split an order of mozzarella sticks?"

They all nodded and Madison felt lighter as if a weight had been lifted. Things could be different if only she let it happen.

* * * *

Tanner's cell rang just as he was pulling into Chris's driveway. Logan had promised him to look into Fenton's background and hopefully that was what this call was about. He answered the phone but left the engine idling and the heater blasting.

"Hey, Logan. What's up?"

He heard Logan chuckle. "I'm calling about Fenton Jacks, of course. Plus another interesting development. Which do you want first?"

"Fuck you, Logan. You know what I want first. Talk to me."

Tanner loved Logan like a brother, but he could be a real pain in the ass. He loved to joke around long after Tanner had lost his sense of humor.

"Funny thing about Fenton Jacks. He doesn't exist. Not really."

"Really?" Tanner's gut had been right, as usual. Now that his suspicions were confirmed, he wondered why he'd ever questioned them. "Tell me more, my friend."

"Now I'm your friend?" Logan laughed. "What if I'd given you the news that Fenton Jacks was a fine, upstanding citizen and loved by all?"

"Stop stalling," Tanner growled.

"Man, you're easy to rile. Okay, so here's the scoop. Fenton Jacks doesn't exist. At least he didn't until he showed up in Springwood. The man has no past to speak of. It looks like he walked into town with a million dollar bankroll and some fake identification papers."

"At almost the very moment a drug war broke out."

"Funny coincidence, huh? I thought about that. Has he ever said anything about where he lived before he moved there? Family names? Anything that I can run down?"

Tanner snorted. "After what you've told me, I don't feel the least guilty investigating this guy. He wants to be my kids' stepfather? Screw that. I'm going to call the DEA agent I've been working with. Give him this guy's picture and info. Maybe they can run some facial recognition on him."

"Good idea. What can I do?"

Tanner admired Logan's workhorse attitude. He was a stalwart friend and nothing was ever too big a favor. "Fenton talked about a sister once. Natalie

Harmon from Kansas City, Missouri. I don't suppose you could run that down while I pursue him? He has a picture of her at his house so I assume she's a real person."

"Got it. I'm all over it, Tan. I'll call you if I get something. Now for the other thing. Seth called me."

Tanner was immediately on guard. "Is everything okay? Is Presley all right?"

"They're great. This doesn't have anything to do with Presley." Seth's wife, Presley, had been in the Witness Protection Program due to attempts on her life by her boss. It had turned out to be something completely different, but Tanner knew Seth was still very protective of his wife. "Seth got a call from Marshal Evan Davis. He needs our help."

Davis had come across as a pretty capable guy when Tanner had met him at Seth and Presley's wedding. "With what?"

Logan chuckled. "He won't say yet. You know those Fed guys. It's all super-secret double-naught spy shit. He wants to talk to us about it. Can you be available for a conference call on Monday morning at ten?"

"Sure. I admit I'm intrigued."

"Me, too. Maybe he's got another woman for Witness Protection. Hell, he only needs five more and we'll all be married. If that's the case, count me out."

An image of Madison floated into Tanner's mind. He'd given in to the strong feelings he had for her and asked her out on a date. Already he was anticipating her company. He liked being with her. She was easy to be around and she understood his job, or seemed to. Abby had forever harangued him about the military and then law enforcement. She'd hated the pay, the hours, and the danger. She'd never understood his need to help and protect. Madison appeared to share that with him.

"Let's hope it doesn't come to that. Listen, I need to go. Stacey asked me to talk to Chris." Tanner sighed. "She's left him and taken Annie. I'm in his driveway now."

Logan whistled. "Holy shit, why didn't you say so? Do you think it will do any good?"

"No." It broke Tanner's heart to admit it, but Logan would know the truth if Tanner tried to lie. "Until Chris wants to get better he won't. He's working for Fenton now, for fuck's sake. It's gone from bad to worse."

"It probably ain't going to get any better very soon so buckle up for the ride, Tan. Are you going to say something to him or Abby about Fenton?"

"I don't have enough details yet. But the minute I do, I will. In the meantime, I just want to try and keep Chris sober."

"Good luck. You're going to need it."

Logan signed off and Tanner hung up, tucking his cell back into his pocket. He turned off the truck and walked up to the front door of the small, run-down house Chris and Stacey rented. It looked sad with its peeling paint and rickety shutters, reminding Tanner of the first house he and Abby had lived in after he got out of the Army.

The inside was more cheerfully decorated with bright, happy colors. Stacey had done everything she could to make the house a real home. Tanner had to admit he missed a woman's touch in his own house. More and more often these days it felt cold and lifeless.

Tanner rapped on the door and waited, listening for a sign of life. Chris's truck sat in the driveway so he should be home. Tanner banged on the door again but there was still no answer. He tried the door and it swung open easily. Whenever Chris had come in from a night of partying, he hadn't locked the door.

Tanner wasn't sure how long Stacey had been gone but the house was a mess. Litter was tossed everywhere along with a pizza box and a few empty beer bottles. He shook his head in disgust and headed back to the bedroom.

Chris was in a lump on the bed, the sheets tangled around his waist. Even in sleep, his son's face was drawn into a scowl instead of peaceful repose.

Hardening his heart, Tanner grabbed the end of the sheet and gave it a hard tug, rolling Chris's body off the bed and onto the floor with a thud. He groaned and raised his head, blinking against the light as Tanner pulled back the drapes and let the sun shine directly into the room.

"Get up, son. We're going to have a talk."

Chris ran his fingers through his dark hair, but it was already standing on end. "Fuck you, Dad. Get out of my house."

"I paid this month's rent so I think I'll stay," Tanner replied, hating every word that was coming out of his mouth. No one had warned him tough love was tougher on the parent than the child.

Chris finally looked up, his eyes narrowed and his lips curled in a sneer. "It's just like you to hold that over my head. I told you I'll pay you back. Does it make you feel powerful to lend me money? Next time I'll ask Mom."

"Abby paid your rent last month. And no, I don't feel powerful. I feel helpless watching my only son piss his life away." Tanner leaned against the dresser and crossed his arms over his chest. "Stacey came to see me this morning."

That got Chris's attention. He wrapped the sheet around him and sat on the edge of the bed, his head hanging. "Is she okay? Is Annie alright?"

"She's fine. Stacey is at her parents' house. You want to tell me what you plan to do about this situation?"

His son looked up, rebellion written in the rigid lines of his frame. "She doesn't understand. She's always on my case. That job was a piece of shit. They treated me like crap and paid me worse. Things will be better now that I'm working for Fenton."

Tanner had to fight to hold his tongue about Fenton Jacks. He didn't know enough about the man yet. But he would. Instead, he concentrated on the task at hand. "Stacey understands you fine, son. You drink and lose job after job. It's not complicated. It is pathetic. You need to straighten up."

"For Stacey? For Annie?" Chris jeered. "When do the violins start?"

"No, for yourself. That's the only way this will work. You have to get sober for you."

"Fenton says there's nothing wrong with a guy sowing his wild oats."

His son quoting Jacks made Tanner want to bury his fist in the wall. "He's right. To an extent. But when a man takes on the responsibilities of a wife and child those days are gone. Tell me one thing, Chris. Are you happy? Are you enjoying being the biggest drunk in Springwood?"

There was silence and then Chris looked up, his eyes blazing. "Yes. When I'm with my buddies, everything's great. When I'm with you or Stacey, all I get is lectures. I'm tired of not being good enough for you. Mom and Fenton think I'm just fine the way I am."

Tanner exhaled slowly, frustration warring with sadness. "You are fine, son. You are also a drunk. The two are not mutually exclusive. You need to get help. Come with me tomorrow night to my meeting. Just once. Try it. Wouldn't you like to wake up just one morning without a rotten taste in your mouth and a pounding headache?"

Chris stared at the carpet. "I'll think about it, okay? If I come to the meeting, will it get you off my back?"

It was the best he could hope for. Chris had never even entertained the idea before. "Just come to one meeting. Library at seven. I'll come by and pick you up."

Chris shook his head. "No, I'll just meet you."

Tanner put his hand on Chris's shoulder. "Maybe we can get a bite to eat afterward. You know, talk."

Chris looked up, but the corners of his mouth were turned down. "Let's not get ahead of ourselves. Just the meeting."

Swallowing his disappointment, Tanner agreed. "Fine. I'll meet you a few minutes before seven in front of the library." He headed to leave, but turned back. "And Chris? Try and stay sober until then. Don't show up drunk."

Chris didn't answer and Tanner hadn't really expected one. He locked the front door as he left and climbed into his truck with a heavy heart.

The chances of Chris showing up tomorrow night were slim.

Chapter Eight

Madison and Tanner made small talk as he drove to the restaurant. He'd asked her about her day and she told him about shopping with Sherry and seeing some girls from school. Madison did not mention buying new underthings. When she asked him about his day, he vaguely answered something about taking his dog for a walk.

Dressed in khaki colored slacks and a navy sweater with a white collar peeking out, he looked and smelled really good. His jaw appeared to be freshly shaved and the tang of his aftershave tantalized her nostrils. Instead of tousled by the wind, his dark brown hair had been combed into submission. All in all, he was gorgeous. Her palms were sweaty and she rubbed them on her brand-new emerald green corduroy trousers. If she didn't calm down, she was going to stroke out before dessert.

"I hope you like Italian food. I don't come here much but this place is really good." Tanner pulled into a parking spot outside of a beige stucco building. "I think it's new since you left town."

He was around to her side of the vehicle before she could climb out of the car, offering her a hand, which she gratefully accepted. The parking lot didn't look like it had been plowed well. In the dim light, she could make out patches of ice here and there as they carefully made their way to the entrance.

"I haven't been here before but I do like Italian." Tanner held the door open for her and she stepped into the warm restaurant decorated in muted earth tones. The tempting aroma of tomatoes and garlic made her stomach growl and her mouth water. "It smells so good in here."

Tanner chuckled. "It does, doesn't it? I'm glad you brought your appetite. I hate to see a woman pick at her food."

"No worries. I'm hungry."

The hostess led them to a corner table near the back of the restaurant. They shed their coats and settled into their chairs. A waiter magically appeared from nowhere.

"I'm Albert and I'll be your waiter tonight. May I get you something to drink? Would you like to see the wine list?"

Madison enjoyed the occasional glass of wine with a good meal but she remembered the conversation from earlier today. Tanner was waiting for her response.

"Not for me, thank you. Iced tea?"

"I'll have the same," Tanner answered. The waiter hurried away and Tanner placed his large, warm hand over hers on the table. "It's okay. You could have ordered wine if you wanted it."

Did he read minds as a hobby? She hurried to try and smooth it over.

"I don't really drink much. As a doctor, I'm on call a lot."

He smiled. "It's okay, Madison. I don't have any secrets. I'm sure you know I don't consume alcohol. I have a drinking problem."

The way he phrased it alarmed her. "Have? I'd heard you haven't had a drink in ten years." She winced at what she had revealed. She'd been gossiping about him, but he didn't seem fazed.

"It's been about nine and a half, actually. I say have because once an alcoholic, always an alcoholic. There isn't a cure. I can never drink again. Ever."

The waiter slipped their glasses in front of them. "Are you ready to order?"

Madison hadn't even opened her menu.

"Can you give us a few minutes?" Tanner asked, his gaze never leaving Madison. She could have sworn she heard the waiter sigh, but he disappeared as quickly as he'd come.

"I didn't know," she said. "I guess I was too wrapped up in my own problems to recognize anyone else's. Dad told me today."

74

"Hell." Tanner grimaced. "I'm sure he was thrilled about an older, alcoholic man taking out his baby girl. Did he object?"

"No, but he doesn't get to do that. I'm a grown woman and I make my own decisions."

Tanner sipped his iced tea. "You didn't think about canceling? Not even for a moment?"

"Not even for a moment. I'm a doctor, remember? I've been educated in addiction."

"So have I. The hard way." Tanner laughed and she relaxed. He was obviously comfortable with the topic and with himself. She admired the easy way he carried his burden. He wasn't screaming about being a victim or how life was unfair. He'd faced his problem head on and dealt with it.

She flipped open the menu. "What do you recommend here?"

"I usually get the chicken parmesan but if you want something lighter they make an excellent grilled salmon."

"I think I'll splurge tonight."

His gaze ran up and down her body making her shiver with awareness. "You're a beautiful woman, Maddie, with a perfect figure. You should eat anything you like."

Heat rushed to her cheeks. "Thank you, but I'm also a doctor. Too much of anything isn't good for you. Moderation is the key." She took a deep breath. "Hearing that you have a flaw helped."

"I've got several. Don't we all?"

Madison shrugged. "I certainly do. I guess I don't think of you that way. I think of you as a sort of...well, hero."

Tanner jerked back in his chair. "A hero? I'm no hero, Maddie."

"You are." Maddie nodded. "When I was thirteen there were some girls teasing me during the town carnival. You told them to stop or you'd call their parents. Those girls never bothered me again."

Tanner shook his head, his brow furrowed. "I wish I remembered that day, honey. But I don't."

It seemed unreal that a day that had lived in her memory for almost seventeen years was completely forgotten by him. Maybe she'd dreamed it or blew it out of proportion after all this time.

No, it had happened. She was sure of it.

"I was grateful all the same."

"What were they teasing you about?" he asked.

"The usual. My hair, my freckles, my glasses, my braces, my brains, and don't forget my clothes. That was the list most of the time."

He seemed at a loss for words. "That was a long time ago. I'm sorry I don't—"

She held up her hand. "It's okay. You don't need to apologize. Just because it was important to me, doesn't mean it was important to you. You were just being nice, that's all."

"I wish I remembered," he said, grabbing her hand and giving it a squeeze. "I wish I really was the hero you thought I was. I'm just a man, Maddie. Flesh and blood."

He certainly was. Very attractive and very male flesh and blood. The lustful thoughts made her shift in her seat and what wasn't already pink with embarrassment turned bright red. He quirked an eyebrow.

"Something I said?"

The waiter sidled up to the table before she could answer. They ordered and the waiter dissolved away, leaving her with the open question waiting for an answer.

"I—I'm not very comfortable on dates. I told you I never know what to say or do."

"How about you tell me about medical school? That might put you at ease."

"I'm supposed to let you talk about yourself." Madison chewed her bottom lip.

"You are?" Tanner frowned. "Why?"

Madison sighed. "Sherry gave me dating advice. I'm supposed to let you talk about yourself. She said men love to talk about themselves. I'm also not to talk about gross, bloody things, *Star Trek*, *Star Wars*, *Dr. Who*, or have sex with you." She buried her face in her hands. "Oh God, I shouldn't have said that."

She peeked through her fingers and he was grinning. He reached across the table and tugged her hands away. "You can talk about all the blood and guts you want. I can handle it. I love *Star Wars*, by the way. I've never seen *Dr. Who* but I'd like to hear about it." His expression gentled. "As for sex, well, I'm very attracted to you, Maddie. You've probably figured that out. But I don't want to rush you. When the time is right, we'll know."

Her heart accelerated at his tender tone. She was relieved and disappointed all at once. He excited her and she couldn't remember the last time she'd been this sexually attracted to a man. But he was right. She wasn't ready to make love with him tonight.

"You're a nice man."

Tanner groaned. "Don't say that. Next thing you'll be telling me that I'm a great guy but you just don't feel *that* way about me."

She fiddled with her napkin. "I doubt that will happen."

He smiled. "It won't happen for me either. Now tell me about medical school, pretty Maddie. I promise I won't say a word to Sherry about it."

She shook her head. "I'm still too nervous. How about you tell me something about yourself instead? How about you tell me about you?"

An hour, two chicken parmesan meals, and a shared tiramisu later and she'd learned quite a bit about Tanner. "You didn't like the military?"

The waiter placed two cups of coffee in front of them. Tanner added a dollop of cream and a sugar. "I don't like people telling me what to do. The military was a means to an end."

"Law enforcement."

Tanner snorted. "That was far from my mind. I just wanted a steady paycheck. I hadn't done great in school so my options were limited."

"You got to see the world." She sipped her coffee. "That must have been nice."

"It was." He nodded. "I was stationed in Germany for awhile. I liked it there, but Abby was homesick. She never enjoyed being an Army wife. Or a sheriff's wife either, for that matter."

"Did you leave the Army for Abby?"

"Sort of. She was tired of it, and my dad had talked to Sheriff Tunney about giving me a chance as a deputy. I thought things would change if I came home."

"Did they?"

He frowned. "Yes, but not for the better. I'd promised Abby I would stop drinking. I told her everything would be better when we came back to Springwood. I lied."

"Is that why you divorced?" It was a nosy question and none of her business but it had slipped out before she could censure herself.

"That's a good question." He stroked his chin. "We never were deliriously happy, even in the early days. We married too young and we wanted different things. But Abby actually left me after I got sober. I hadn't had a drink in about six months when she came and said she couldn't take it anymore."

That didn't make much sense. "What couldn't she take anymore? You'd stopped drinking."

"I think she couldn't take being a sheriff's wife anymore. She'd always pictured her life differently." It looked as if he were struggling for the right

78

words. "Easier, more glamorous. I don't know if that's the right way to put it. She hated having to clip coupons and watch every dime when I was in the Army. She wanted something better for herself. I don't blame her. It wasn't easy with two kids and a husband who was at the bar all the time."

"It wasn't any of my business asking you about that." Madison ran her finger around the rim of her coffee cup.

He captured her hand and his eyes were a soft blue. "If we're going to give this a real shot between us I don't want you to think I'm hiding my past. You can ask me anything."

She'd relaxed as the evening had unwound and she felt the same way. "You can ask me anything as well."

He slowly smiled. "Are you sure, Dr. Shay? I want to know everything about you."

"There's not much to know." Madison shrugged. Her life was an open book. A boring one.

"Tell me about growing up? Were you always the smartest kid in school?"

She was working to put her childhood behind her. "I was. And boy, no one ever let me forget it."

Tanner laughed. "Tell me more." He signaled the waiter for more coffee.

"Don't blame me if you fall asleep while hearing this. It's not that interesting."

"Let me be the judge. Why don't you start with how you and Sherry became friends?"

That brought a smile to Madison's face. "That's actually a pretty entertaining story. We were in fourth grade and Sherry was the new kid in school."

They were both laughing by the time he helped her on with her coat and led her to his vehicle. Now all she had to do was worry about the goodnight kiss.

* * * *

Madison looked nervous. Extremely nervous. She was biting her lip, bouncing one leg over the other, and avoiding eye contact. Tanner had to hide his grin as he opened the SUV door and helped her out. He knew why she was so tense.

It was time to get his goodnight kiss.

If he were honest, he'd been thinking about it all night. The way her full lips had moved as she told him about her childhood and then college. Her perfume had wafted around him, leaving him hard and aching. There would be no relief tonight. He'd go home to no one but Scout and take a cold shower before falling into bed. If he were lucky, he wouldn't wake up with dog breath in his face.

He held her hand as they walked to the door. She fumbled with her purse and pulled out her key ring before looking up at him. Her mouth was shiny with some kind of gloss and he couldn't wait to kiss it off, licking it with his tongue. Her eyes were wide and she had a deer in the headlights expression.

"Um, would you like to come in for some coffee?"

It was sweet to invite him in, but if he accepted he'd want to take things further than a kiss. He was pretty sure her father was home and Tanner hadn't been caught necking with a girl on the couch since high school. Besides, they'd had three cups of coffee at the restaurant. He wouldn't sleep all night as it was.

He shook his head. "I don't want to wake up your dad. How about a movie on Wednesday night? There are a couple of good ones showing at the mall in the city."

"That's sounds good. I haven't seen a movie in a long time."

The air was thick with tension and Tanner didn't know how to make it better. There seemed only one solution. He ran his hand from her shoulders down her arms and then pulled her close to his own body. Bending his head, he captured her soft lips with his. At first he thought he'd misread her signals,

80

but then her mouth parted under his and his tongue delved into the warm cavern.

She tasted of chocolate and coffee and something unique and indescribable. He angled his head so he could deepen the kiss and her arms crept around his neck, pulling him down. His groin tightened painfully and only the layers of winter wear kept him from pressing her curves as close as he could get her.

At some point, they'd moved and she was leaning back against the house, her fingers tangled in his hair. He lifted his head and looked down at her drowsy, well-kissed expression. Her lids were half-closed, her cheeks flushed, whether from the cold air or the heat of their kiss, he wasn't sure.

"That was a hell of a kiss, honey." His voice was hoarse and he didn't bother to hide his reaction to her innocent seduction. She licked her lips and he had to stifle a groan.

"It certainly was. I'm not sure I've ever been kissed quite like that."

He brushed her cheek with his fingers, knowing exactly what she was talking about. Something major had happened here on this front porch and it was more than just the meeting of their mouths. In fact, the entire evening had been leading up to this. He'd been lonely for so long, had gotten used to the feeling. In one night, Madison Shay had knocked him off his comfortable path and made him remember what it was like to feel.

"I haven't either." He pressed a quick kiss to her lips. If he didn't leave now, he would start thinking of all the reasons he should stay. "I'll call you, okay? About Wednesday?"

She nodded and he stepped back, instantly missing the feel of her body. He lifted the keys from her fingers and unlocked the door. "I'll wait until you're inside and I hear the lock."

She didn't say anything for a moment. "Thank you for dinner."

He pushed a stray hair back from her face, her skin like satin under his fingers. He felt her tremble under his touch. He was in big fucking trouble with this woman, and surprisingly he didn't mind. He was scared as hell.

"Thank you for coming. Go on inside. It's cold out here."

Tanner stood there while she entered the house, the door closing behind her. He exhaled slowly as he listened for the fall of the deadbolt, then turned to head back to the SUV. He swung into the driver's seat and quickly checked his phone. He'd had it on silent during the date and grimaced when he saw six messages from Seth.

He punched a few buttons until he had Seth on the line. "Seth Reilly."

"Sorry, I just got your message. What's up?" Tanner asked.

"Shit, man. I was worried about you. I've got a murder in Harper. Jared and Logan are here, too."

"Jared and Logan? Why are they there?"

Seth sighed. "Because we're not sure if it's drug related or the vigilante. Can you come here and look at the crime scene? See if it matches your drug murders? Logan and Jared are here as they've seen the most action from the vigilante."

Tanner started up the engine. "I'm on my way. Give me directions."

Seth rattled off the location and Tanner turned on the siren and lights. So much for a hot romantic evening. This night was going to end in a stone-cold murder.

* * * *

Tanner pulled up to the old barn as close as he could get to the yellow tape surrounding the scene. There were various law enforcement vehicles scattered around and one helicopter. Looked like Jared had called in his DEA friend, Jason Anderson. Tanner showed his badge to the deputy on watch and ducked under the tape, striding to where Seth, Jason, Jared, and Logan stood.

Even from this distance, with nothing but lights brought in by the cops, Tanner could make out the bloody scene. He turned on his flashlight and shined it down on the body.

"Have you decided anything or were you waiting for me?" he asked.

Logan slapped him on the back. "It's just not a party unless you're here, man."

Tanner walked around the body looking for similarities and differences to his own crime scenes. "I could have passed on this party tonight. I had a date."

He knew he'd be setting off a shit storm by telling them, but Logan was always on his case about finding a woman. Shit, Logan didn't want to be tied down but he sure as fuck liked to see other guys with one woman. Maybe it simply cleared the field for him.

Seth chuckled. "A date, huh? Wait until I tell Presley. She'll want to double date."

Tanner shook his head. "No way. Presley is walking, talking trouble. I don't need any more stress in my life." He grinned at his friend. "No offense. I'm not sure I could handle all the excitement."

Seth laughed. "None taken. I handle it just fine. Wouldn't have it any other way, honestly."

Jared groaned. "Can we stop with the woman chatter? Tanner, what are you thinking?"

Tanner looked up at Jason who had yet to speak. "Sorry to see you again under these circumstances. But in this case, I think the DEA isn't involved. This looks like the vigilante to me, not like the drug related murders I've been seeing. There's no torture here, just a clean kill. What made you think it was drug related?"

"The deceased was a known drug mule," Jason replied. "Same cartel that's been trying to take over the drug route through this area."

Tanner snapped off his flashlight. "I've never seen this guy. How did the vigilante find out about him, I wonder?"

Jared crossed his arms over his chest. "I arrested him about six months ago for possession with intent to deliver."

Seth shook his head. "And I arrested him last week for using his girlfriend as a punching bag."

"Charming guy," Jared observed. "The vigilante does have a way of choosing his victims."

Jason's pocket buzzed and he pulled out his cell, looked at the screen, and then sighed. "Shit. I need to get out of here. We've got a big bust going down at the border." He tucked his phone away. "I'll leave the crime scene guys here as a favor from your friendly federal government. Unfortunately, I can't help much with a vigilante murderer. I could call in a profiler if you like."

Jared looked around. "I don't know about you guys but I think we should take him up on his offer. A profiler couldn't hurt."

The men nodded in agreement. "Then I'll talk to my friend at the FBI. He'll tell me the name of the best. I'll call you." Jason turned on his heel and was gone. The coroner nudged the men aside so he could begin gathering evidence.

"Are you still happy about the vigilante, Logan?" Seth asked.

Logan scowled. "I've never been happy about it. I just haven't obsessed about it like you all have. But yes, I think it has gone too far. I'm tired of getting dragged out of a warm bed to come to a murder scene."

Jared waggled his eyebrows. "Just how warm was the bed you left? Scorching?"

"Warm enough." Logan snorted. "Give Seth the hard time. He's the happily married man just back from his honeymoon."

Seth had a grin a mile wide. "No comment. Tanner's the one with a date tonight."

84

Three sets of eyes swung his way and Tanner just shook his head. "A gentleman never talks. Madison is a lady. A real lady."

Jared laughed. "He's got it bad. Next thing you know there will be a wedding. Damn, I hope this love shit isn't catching."

Tanner shoved at Jared shoulder. "Shut the hell up. It was just a date."

But Tanner knew it had been much more. He wasn't ready to call it love, but he was ready to admit to the deep connection he felt when he was with Madison. The only question in his mind was if he was worthy of it. He'd messed up so many things, he sure as fuck didn't want to mess this up with her. She was too special.

Chapter Nine

Reed Mitchell was standing on the steps of the library Monday night when Tanner finished his AA meeting. To Tanner's complete and utter surprise, Chris had actually shown up. He'd refused to sit next to Tanner but he could see the shock on Chris's face as he took in the identities of the other attendees. Tanner was sure Chris hadn't known that most, if any, of those people were battling alcoholism.

Chris had sat in the back, slumped down in the chair, with his hat pulled down as if it would keep him anonymous. He needn't have worried. No one in that room would ever speak about anyone else. Tanner had tried to talk to Chris when the meeting ended but he'd bolted from the room and out of the library so quickly he'd practically left marks in the tile.

Tanner was just happy Chris had shown up. It was progress.

Reed pushed up the brim of his hat and grinned. "Catching up on your reading? I've been standing out here for fifteen minutes freezing my nuts off."

Tanner slapped Reed on the back. "Call me the original bookworm. How did you find me and what are you doing here?"

"I asked Logan. He wanted to talk to you but he's on duty tonight. I've been deputized in his stead."

"Isn't that a demotion for you?" Tanner joked. "Come on. There's a pizza place on the next block. My treat."

Reed shoved his hands in his pockets. "If they have heat, I'm in."

It was a quick walk to the restaurant and they settled into a table before ordering two coffees and a large with everything but anchovies. "So what did Logan want to talk to me about that was so important he sent you? It's not another murder, is it?"

"No, it was the conference call you missed with Marshal Evan Davis this morning."

"Shit, I wanted to be there but I had two deputies call in sick with the flu. I was out on a call. What was it about?"

A smile played around Reed's mouth. Reed was a good man, a smart cop, but something of a mystery. Women loved him, men wanted to be him, and Reed didn't appear to give a damn either way. He was dedicated to his job and little else. While Logan played at being a ladies' man, Reed didn't play at anything at all. Tanner doubted Reed had ever pursued a woman in his entire life, yet he was never short of female companionship on the rare occasions he took time from his work.

Tanner would trust Reed with his life. There weren't many people he could say that about. In fact, the list was comprised of the five lawmen in the group plus his deputy, Sam.

"The Marshal wants our help."

Tanner wrapped his hands around the steaming coffee cup. "Okay, with what?"

Reed's lip curved up slightly. "He wouldn't say. Said he couldn't."

Tanner laughed. "So he wants our help with something but he can't tell us. Do we have to be blindfolded the entire time as well?"

"Luckily he didn't mention it. He asked us to help him guard something that was being transferred from the border of Canada down to Colorado. Right through our jurisdictions."

Tanner stroked his chin. "He's a U.S. Marshal. I'm guessing it's a prisoner transfer."

Reed nodded. "That's what the rest of think. As for Colorado..."

"Florence." Tanner finished the sentence for Reed. "Holy shit, it must be one bad dude if they're taking him to Florence. That place has the worst of the worst." Tanner frowned. "Why aren't they flying him? Wouldn't that be easier?"

"Jared asked that question but Davis simply said that no one would expect the cargo to be driven instead of flown."

"Then he's expecting trouble. When do we get details? We can't plan until we know what we're dealing with."

The waitress placed the piping hot pie in the middle of the table. Tanner's stomach growled. He'd missed lunch since he'd been shorthanded.

"Davis promised to let us know a week ahead. He can't tell us any sooner than that. Damn, this is good pizza. I've got to come visit Springwood more often."

Tanner chuckled. "We do have good pizza. The owner had a restaurant in Chicago at one time."

Thinking of Chicago made Tanner think about Madison. He'd been busy all day but it hadn't stopped him from replaying their kiss a dozen times or more. Maybe he could call her tonight. Just to say hello and see how her day was.

"So when do I need to mark this on my calendar?" Tanner asked.

"That's the thing. Davis doesn't know. Apparently they only give him about five days notice. They don't give any warning to the guy being transferred. From what I've heard, they just show up in his cell and move him."

"And that's where we come in."

"Exactly," Reed replied, signaling to the waitress for a coffee refill. "We arm ourselves and make sure this guy gets to Florence. Piece of cake."

It didn't sound all that difficult. The prisoner would be in cuffs and shackles, probably riding in an armored vehicle. It was a babysitting job at best.

"Let everyone know I'm in. It sounds like a nice break from domestic disputes, cattle rustling, and Saturday night drunken fights."

"Don't forget drug cartel murders." Reed helped himself to another slice.

Tanner grimaced. "That's not the usual around here. I can't wait until Jason Anderson can help us turn this tide around."

"Did you give him the picture of your wife's new man?"

"Fuck. Logan tell you about that?" Tanner didn't give a shit that Reed knew, but it was fun to bust his balls a little bit.

Reed grinned. "He did. I guess Logan can't keep a secret."

Actually, Logan was as tight-lipped as they came. He'd kept Tanner's secret regarding his Monday night meetings for years.

"I did. Anderson said they would run it through facial recognition."

"Fuck technology. What does your gut tell you?" Reed was an instinctual cop, rarely wrong.

Tanner leaned forward and set his coffee cup on the table. "I think Fenton Jacks is somehow messed up in this drug war. It's too much of a coincidence him showing up when he did."

"Then I don't envy you. At some point, you're going to have to tell your ex Jacks is a criminal. It ain't going to be pretty."

It was going to be hell on earth. Somehow, Abby would blame Tanner.

"I could send her a text." Tanner tried to keep a straight face.

"Hell, why not a message in a bottle? It'll get there eventually." Reed laughed.

Tanner sobered. "I don't want my kids mixed up in this. Shit, I don't want Abby in it either. If Jacks hurts them in any way, I'll take him out myself."

"The rest of us will be right there with you." Reed's eyes had narrowed and his expression grown cold.

If Jacks so much as harmed a hair on their heads, Tanner would make the man wish he'd never been born. Family was everything to Tanner, and no one was going to mess with his.

* * * *

Madison was having dinner on Thursday with Sherry, Lisa, and Carrie and no one was more surprised than Madison herself. She found she actually liked spending time with Lisa and Carrie. Whatever they'd been as kids, they were different now. Carrie had even pulled Madison aside and apologized for being a "total bitch." Apparently, she'd been as insecure as Madison but it had manifested itself differently.

Carrie checked her watch. "I only have a sitter for an hour and a half. Hubby has the night shift. Spill it. Inquiring minds are dying to know."

"We had fun. Monday and Wednesday. We went to see that new car chase movie. It was okay," Madison answered primly. She wasn't one to talk about her relationships much. If she'd ever had any worth talking about that is.

Lisa waggled her eyebrows. "Two dates in three days. Very good. When do you see him again?"

"Friday. He's fixing me dinner at his house and then we're going to watch some movies."

Sherry nodded. "Then you're going to have sex with him?"

Madison felt her cheeks get hot. "That's kind of a personal question. All we've done is kiss so far."

"How was it?" Lisa grinned. "I bet it was hot. The sheriff looks like he knows his way around a pair of lips."

That was the understatement of the year. Tanner was the best kisser ever. Madison didn't have a ton of kissing experience but she'd be willing to bet her medical license Tanner was in a league all his own.

"It was hot," she admitted. "But I'm not sure I'm ready to sleep with him."

Carrie tapped her lips with her finger. "Well, it's the third date."

Sherry and Lisa nodded as if Carrie had said something very wise. Madison looked from one to the other. "So? It's the third date? Is that supposed to mean something?"

"That's the *get naked* date. Everyone knows that," Sherry answered.

Madison sat up in her chair. "I didn't know that. Maybe Tanner doesn't know it." She smacked her forehead. "How did I not know this?"

Of course she knew why. She'd had very few third dates. The vast majority of the men she dated never made it past date number two.

90

"Calm down." Sherry patted her shoulder. "You're going to get yourself all worked up. It's only sex. You've had sex before. You're not a virgin."

"I might as well be," Madison retorted. "I haven't had much luck when it comes to sex."

The women laughed and Carrie leaned across the table. "I think you will with the sheriff. I'm guessing he's had some experience. Damn, he's good looking. If I wasn't a happily married woman, I'd be all over it."

"Me too," Lisa joined in. "I usually like my men younger, but for him I'd make an exception."

"If everyone thinks he's great, how come he wasn't dating anyone?"

Sherry looked around the dining room and then leaned forward. "He dates women out of town. I heard he was seeing a widow over in Harper for awhile."

Madison didn't like the twist of jealousy inside her. She'd always felt the emotion wasn't a positive one. "Do you think he's still seeing her?"

Carrie's eyes went wide and she slapped her glass down on the table. "No way. Tanner Marks does not dabble with women."

"We never said it was exclusive or anything," Madison said, her mind running over every word he'd spoken, looking for trouble. "I mean, I couldn't get angry with him for it."

Lisa's brows drew together. "I would. If a man asks you out three times in one week he better not be laying the pipe anywhere else."

Madison almost spit out her tea. "Laying the pipe? Oh God." She couldn't stop the fit of giggles at the very elegantly dressed Lisa's choice of words.

Lisa waved her hand in the air. "You know what I mean. Laying the pipe. Slamming the sheets. Tapping the keg. Whatever you want to call it."

They were all laughing, the sound turning several heads in the restaurant. Madison wiped the tears from her eyes. "I don't want to call it any one of those things." She sighed. "I want it to be making love."

"You're a romantic." Carrie smiled. "But sometimes it's okay if it's just hot and raunchy."

"I'm not a romantic," Madison protested. "I'm practical, down to earth. I'm a doctor."

"A doctor who's fixing to get laid proper for the first time in her life." Sherry grinned. "You lucky girl. Be sure to wear your new underwear."

Madison groaned. Just when she was relaxed and comfortable around Tanner, a spanner was thrown in the works. How could she be calm, cool, and collected tomorrow night when all she would be thinking about was sex?

* * * *

"Come on in." Tanner took a step back so Madison could enter his house. Her gaze quickly scanned the interior decorated in shades of brown and blue. It was clearly a male dominated home. There were no comfy pillows on the sofa or a crocheted throw on the back of a chair. There was a large German Shepherd with a wagging tail who was crowding around their legs trying to sniff her. Tanner caught the animal by the collar and tugged him back.

"Easy, Scout. Let the lady get in the door and get her coat off." He smiled apologetically. "We don't have too many visitors so he gets excited when people come over."

She held out her hand so Scout could get her scent. Apparently he approved. His tail wagged even faster and he pulled at Tanner's grip.

"Sit." Tanner's commanding and deep tone had an immediate effect on Scout. His bottom went down to the floor in a second. Madison had to fight the urge to sit down herself. His voice was that compelling.

"He's sweet. Scout? There's a character in my favorite book—"

Tanner laughed. "Mine, too. I didn't do very well in school but I did like *To Kill a Mockingbird*."

"How many dogs have you named Scout?"

Tanner chuckled and helped her off with her coat. "I swear this is the first. Although I did have a black Lab named Atticus and a cat named Finch."

"Is he a police dog?"

Tanner laced his fingers in hers and led her into the kitchen. "Retired, although every now and then he helps out. He's got hip problems that keep him from active duty on a daily basis. Now he's just part of the family."

Madison knelt down and rubbed the silky fur. "He smells good. Did he just have a bath?"

"If a lady is coming to dinner, then every member of the family has to clean up. It wasn't a pretty sight, let me tell you. He was royally pissed at me this afternoon for bathing him. He pouted in front of the fireplace until I gave him a treat."

Laughter bubbled up. "I think I know who's in charge around here."

Tanner winked. "He let's me think I am. Can I get you something to drink?"

She looked into his glass. "Is that tea? That sounds good."

He poured her a glass and she sat at the table. "Did you have a good day? You said you had a full day of patients scheduled."

They'd gone out on Wednesday night and seen the latest blockbuster movie. He'd been so tired he'd fallen asleep and then spent the rest of the evening apologizing for it. He told her about the drug route war and the vigilante, in addition to a bout of flu that was keeping his deputies from work. She'd known all about that flu bug as it had filled her waiting room all week.

"I did. I'm exhausted. I hope this flu bug has wound its way to the end. I had my first patient at seven this morning."

Tanner was pulling items from the refrigerator. "It's good we're having a low-key evening in tonight. I was planning to broil a couple of steaks. How do you like yours?"

Just how low-key was he planning to keep it? She'd worn her best underwear but she wasn't sure she was ready to sleep with him tonight.

Although her body was definitely not against the idea. Just the sight of his wide shoulders and handsome face made her warm. Her brain, on the other hand, was the one dragging its feet. She really liked Tanner. A lot. If they made love and then he dumped her, it would hurt. She'd never been hurt by a man before and she wasn't all that keen for it to happen now.

"Um, medium." She finally remembered to answer. "Can I help?"

He shook his head, pulling the broiler pan out of the oven. "Everything is under control. I've got baked potatoes to go with the steaks, salad for a starter, and ice cream for dessert."

She smiled. "What kind of ice cream?"

"Chocolate fudge. My daughter told me all women love chocolate."

"It sounds delicious. I think I like having a handsome man make dinner for me." She wanted to sound relaxed and normal. He leaned down, his palms resting on the table.

"Handsome, huh? For that you get a kiss."

His lips were firm and warm, and the kiss was over way too soon. She was breathless as he turned back to the kitchen counter.

"So, how's the drug thing going?" She sounded like an idiot. Awesome.

"No more dead bodies which is always a plus." Tanner slid the broiler pan in the oven. "We're working with the DEA so I'm hoping to get news very soon."

"We?"

Tanner started setting the table. "There are some guys I meet with once a month. Other lawmen like myself of smaller towns. We share information and work together if we need to. Most of them are affected by this."

"And the vigilante?" Madison helped him with the flatware.

"And the vigilante. They're good men. I'd trust them with my life." He smiled. "I'd trust them with your life."

Her stomach fluttered and at first she thought she had ringing in her ears. Tanner was looking at her expectantly. "That's you, right?"

Her phone. Shit. "Yes." She grabbed her purse from the floor and rummaged for her cell.

Sherry. *This better be damn important.*

"Hey, Sherry. What's up?"

Madison listened with growing alarm.

"Tonight? You want to fly out tonight?" Her voice sounded squeaky but she couldn't help it. "Hold on. I'll ask him." She looked up at Tanner. "I don't suppose you know of any place in Vegas where Sherry and Dan can get married? Apparently Dan has agreed to it and Sherry isn't taking any chances that he'll back out. She wants to fly out tonight. Like now."

Tanner grinned. "As a matter of fact I do. Can I talk to her?"

Madison handed him the phone and listened to his end of the conversation. When he hung up, he turned the stove off. "Looks like we need to pack a bag and head for the Billings airport. We'll stop by your place on the way. We can pick up some takeout and eat in the car."

She was having a hard time taking all this in. "Billings? Bag? I think I've missed something."

"Your best friend is getting married, Maddie. You're her maid of honor and I just promised Sherry I'd get you to the church on time, so to speak."

"Now?" she croaked. "This minute?"

"Not a moment to spare." Tanner sported a wide smile. "They want to get married as soon as possible. I'll make the reservations while you pack a bag. It will only take me a couple of minutes to get my things together, but I know women don't like to be rushed."

She was going to Sin City with Tanner Marks. With a name like that, sinning with this gorgeous man was probably a given. She didn't know whether to shout for joy or run in fear. Deciding to make up her mind later, she stood and squared her shoulders.

"It sounds like a great trip. Let's go."

Chapter Ten

It had all been a whirlwind.

Tanner had taken Scout to Deputy Sam's house, and Madison had informed her father of the impending nuptials in Vegas. He'd been amused but happy for the couple. She and Tanner had hit the road for the Billings airport, meeting Sherry and Dan there along with Dan's brother Jim and his wife Karen.

The plane ride had been uneventful, and now they were checked into the Mirage Hotel on the Vegas strip, heading to their rooms.

Scratch that. Room. Singular.

Apparently while Tanner made airplane reservations, Sherry had been making wedding chapel reservations. That left Dan to book the hotel rooms. He'd booked three, which just showed that men couldn't be trusted to make travel arrangements.

They were walking down a long corridor and Madison's heart was beating so fast she might as well have been walking to her own doom. She was that damn nervous. The fabric under her arms was damp and she'd licked her lip gloss off six times since the plane had landed.

"This is it." Tanner stopped and set down the suitcases. She slipped the card into the slot, the light flashing green before she pushed open the door. He had insisted on carrying the luggage and she stood back to let him pass.

The room was large with a king sized bed on one side and a large flat screen television on the other. The wood was dark and the bed linens luxurious. She tugged the curtains aside and the lights of Las Vegas twinkled in the night sky.

"We have quite a view." Her voice managed to sound natural. Pretty much.

Tanner came up behind her and wrapped his arms around her middle, nuzzling her neck.

"I won't complain. I think the best view is right here in this room." He dropped a kiss on her shoulder and walked over to the hotel directory. "Are you hungry? We can go downstairs to one of the restaurants or order room service."

Trying to slow her racing heart, she shrugged as casually as she could manage. "I wouldn't mind getting something to eat and exploring the hotel. I seem to have gotten my second wind sometime around one in the morning."

It was three in the morning now and she should be exhausted, but the thought of slipping between the sheets with Tanner was keeping her wide awake.

"It might have been the multiple cups of coffee you drank on the way to the airport and during the flight." Tanner was smiling as he flipped open his suitcase. "Suits me to walk around. Like you, I should be tired but I find I'm not sleepy. Just let me change shirts and we can head out."

Nothing had prepared her for seeing Tanner's bare chest. She was a grown ass woman. A doctor, for heaven's sake. But her body went into overdrive as he stripped off his shirt revealing a muscular torso Michelangelo would have been proud to sculpt. Her gaze trailed down from his impressive pectorals taking in each individual ridge of his abdomen. Holy crap on a cracker.

By the time her gaze wandered back up to his face, his eyebrows had shot up but his expression was amused.

"Honey, if you don't stop looking at me like that we're not going to get out of this hotel room all weekend."

She lifted her chin, tired of denying what she truly felt. "Maybe I don't want to leave this room. Maybe I want to do something else."

He came close and his clean, male scent surrounded her. "Maybe right this moment isn't the time." His hands massaged her shoulders. "You're tense. And nervous. Honey, there's nothing to be worried about. I want you more than I want my next breath. If you want to make love, well then, we'll make love. But let's go relax. Have a bite to eat and just enjoy being with each other. This room—and that big bed—will be here in an hour or two."

She took a deep breath and felt the knot in her muscles loosen. "I don't have a ton of experience."

"Do you think I give a damn about that? It will be good because it's you and me. Trust me, Maddie."

His voice was like a silken caress, soft and soothing. She smiled for the first time in hours. "I do trust you, Tanner. For the first time in a long time, I trust someone."

"Then let's go have some fun. We need to loosen you up a little bit. This is Vegas, baby."

She giggled and let her hands slide around his lean middle. "Show me Vegas, cowboy."

He was right. The bed could wait. But she knew it wouldn't wait long. She was going to make love to Tanner. It was only a matter of time.

Tanner tugged on a fresh shirt and they were out the door. The hotel was breathtaking and after a quick meal in one of the restaurants they explored every inch of it. It was five in the morning by the time they returned to their room. There was nothing she enjoyed more than spending time with Tanner. She hoped he felt the same.

Suddenly shy, she grabbed her small suitcase. "I need a quick shower."

He nodded and switched on the television while she ducked into the bathroom, setting a new record for showering. She shaved her legs and armpits and brushed her teeth. She debated whether to leave her hair in a braid or let it loose, finally deciding that lying down on a braid would be uncomfortable. Wearing a short blue nightshirt with penguins on it, she padded into the main room. She didn't have any sexy nighties and of the things she slept in, the shirt was the newest and fit the best. At least she had a pair of her new panties on underneath.

"I, um, saved you some hot water if you wanted to shower."

Tanner was lying on the bed, leaning against the headboard with his jean clad legs crossed, his shirt unbuttoned, and his feet bare. He tossed the remote on the mattress and grinned.

"Damn, you look good." He hopped up from the bed and strode to where she was standing, burying his nose in her neck and making her heart gallop. "Smell good, too. Give me five minutes."

He darted into the bathroom and she took several deep breaths to calm down before slipping between the sheets. She leaned back against the headboard and started to give herself a pep talk.

She'd had sex before. It hadn't been anything to write home about, but she'd done it. She was stressing about a perfectly normal biological function. People all over the world were probably having sex at this very moment and they weren't having a cow. She was thirty damn years old and she wanted this. She wanted Tanner.

She simply didn't want to disappoint him.

"You're frowning." Tanner was standing at the end of the bed wearing nothing but a hotel towel wrapped around his waist, his dark hair wet. A few trickles of water were sliding down his shoulders and along his muscled arms. Suddenly she was finding it very hard to breathe, especially since her stomach was performing a Cirque de Soleil performance in her abdomen.

"Was I? I'm just tired, I guess."

His expression softened. "We've both been up twenty-four hours straight. What time are you supposed to meet Sherry to pick out dresses?"

"Noon for lunch, and then we shop afterward. I think she wanted all of us, including you guys, at lunch as well. What will you guys do while we shop?"

Tanner laughed. "Bachelor party? Seems like he needs a send-off into matrimony."

"Sherry will kill you. She thinks Dan's had plenty of years to be a bachelor. I can't say I disagree, honestly."

Tanner came and sat on the bed next to her. "By the time I was his age, I'd been married for almost twelve years with two kids. I'd seen combat. So you may be right. Maybe we'll take him to the blackjack tables."

Her fingers itched to feel his skin under her palms. She gave into temptation and leaned forward, letting her hands glide up his arms, over his biceps, and onto his solid shoulders. "She'd approve of that."

"Aw, honey." Tanner cupped her chin. "If you're tired, we can wait. We don't have to do this now."

One glance down at the towel told her a different story. An impressive tent dented the terry cloth material and her entire body started humming. He was as aroused as she was. She shook her head. "I'm not tired. I mean, I'm not too tired. Make love to me, Tanner. Please."

"Yes, ma'am." He pushed her back onto the bed, his hard body hovering above hers. "And just for the record, you never have to say please."

* * * *

Madison's body against his felt like heaven. Tanner's cock was painfully hard and he had to recite baseball stats in his head to cool down. He needed to take this slow and easy. She was obviously nervous and he couldn't say he was completely calm. He wanted this to be good for both of them. The relationship was amazing and the sex needed to match.

His tongue traced her full lower lip before he captured her mouth in a deep kiss. She tasted sweet and spicy, a flavor he could easily become addicted to. He explored the warm cavern of her mouth, never hurrying. Her hands were clutching his shoulders and he slid his palm under her nightshirt so he could trace the curves underneath.

Madison moaned in response and he broke the kiss reluctantly, wanting to feel skin on skin. "Let's get rid of this, honey. It's in the way."

100

His hands pushed up the hem and she obediently lifted her arms so he could pull it over her head, and toss it aside. She was wearing nothing but a lacy pair of pink panties and his cock jumped under the towel that was now twisted between them. He threw the towel across the room, heedless to where it landed. He couldn't tear his gaze away from the beautiful, womanly form before him.

"Jesus, Mary, and Joseph, you are gorgeous." His voice sounded like gravel, his throat tight from the rush of emotion he felt being with Madison like this. It had never been this important, this right.

She blushed from the tips of her toes to the top of her head, every inch turning a rosy pink. He swept her into his arms for another kiss, enchanted by her sexy shyness. He almost jumped off the bed when her soft hand encircled his cock. He cursed as his balls pulled tight, and she snatched her hand back as if she'd been shocked.

Her eyes were wide and he placed her hand back on him. "I was just surprised, honey. I'm so excited I could blow like a teenage boy on his first date."

To his surprise, she smiled. "It makes me feel better to know I'm not the only one."

"You are definitely not the only one. Damn, that feels good." Her soft hands were stroking him teasingly, and then she reached down and cupped his balls, wrenching a groan from his throat.

She slid off the bed and onto her knees on the floor. Her gaze locked on his cock. "You're beautiful." Her fingers traced a pulsing vein. "The skin feels soft and smooth but underneath is hard like steel."

He sucked in a breath. She was testing every bit of control he had. "I'm sure it's not the first you've seen." She was a doctor, after all.

"It's the first I've wanted to do this with." She dipped her head and swiped at his cock with her tongue. It was as if her saliva was electrified. He felt the vibration down his cock, through his balls, and straight to his spine. Reflexively, his fingers tangled in her silky long hair.

"Holy shit. Are you trying to kill me?"

She looked up at him and it might have been the same look Eve gave Adam in the Garden of Eden. Just like that, Madison had gone from a nervous, unsure woman to a seductress. She ran her tongue around the mushroom head of his cock and he hissed as heat swept through his body. She engulfed as much of his dick into her mouth as she could, her tongue teasing the sensitive underside. His fingers tightened on the back of her head.

Each stroke of her lips and tongue sent him closer to the edge and heaven. It was only with supreme will that he was able to pull slightly away. "Honey, you need to stop. I can't hold back anymore."

His words had the opposite effect. If anything, she sucked and licked harder and this time there was no stopping the tide. His balls pulled up close to his body and the pressure in his lower back was unbearable. He came hot and hard, his seed shooting out and into her waiting mouth. He watched in fascination as she swallowed every drop. When he was done, his body was wrung out, and he collapsed back on the bed.

Madison crawled up his body and snuggled with him while he caught his breath. He wrapped an arm around her waist and pulled her close, smelling the floral scent of her shampoo and skin.

"I should spank you for that, young lady."

He felt rather than heard her giggle and his heart did a flip in his chest. "I didn't know you were kinky, Sheriff. What else don't I know? Do you want to tie me up, too?"

He quickly rolled on top of her, trapping her underneath him. His hands held her wrists by her head. She was completely at his mercy and appeared to like it. Her eyes were glowing, her nipples were hard points digging into his chest, and her lips were parted in excitement.

"I might like doing that. I could take my time and make you come over and over." He nibbled on her collarbone. "I can see your father never disciplined you. You're out of control."

She laughed. "Maybe it's Vegas making me naughty."

"Nope." Tanner shook his head. "I think you're always like this, but you've managed to hide it well. I can see I've got my hands full with you. Literally."

She shook her head, her fiery hair like a halo around her face. "I'm not. I just decided to be brave. I wanted you to feel like I feel."

"I do." He kissed her then, not soft and slow like before. This kiss was deeper, hotter, and more carnal than the others. Her tongue tangled with his and it was a meeting of equals. She was his match and he was going to enjoy the continual battle for control. "You should have pulled off when I told you to though. Are you mad?"

Tanner had his share of sexual experience, and it told him women didn't like to swallow. She didn't seem upset or angry, but he didn't want her to think he was a thoughtless, selfish bastard.

Her wrists flexed under his hands. "No, why?"

It was his turn to blush. "I think you got more than you bargained for when you were on your knees."

She shrugged. "I'd never done that before so I was curious. It was fine, Tanner."

"Never done that before?" Her expression was perfectly serious. "For someone who's never done that, you did a damn fine job."

"I'm a doctor." Madison smiled. "I know where all the nerve endings and sensitive spots are. At least where they're supposed to be." She paused and licked her lips. "You tasted salty, and a little like coffee."

"You don't have to swallow, honey. Ever again, I promise."

"I'm not upset. I liked watching your face when you had an orgasm. The muscles on your neck and jaw tightened, and your eyes closed."

His beautiful, analytical Maddie. With any other woman in the world, the conversation would have been strange. With her it felt totally natural. It was time to get her mind off of his response and get back to hers. He leaned down and captured a nipple with his lips, drawing it up and worrying it with his teeth before soothing it with his tongue.

One look at Madison's face told the story. Her lids had drifted shut and she was no longer pushing against his hands, her body relaxed. She'd surrendered to his control and dominance.

"Time for you to come, Maddie. I want it all. Don't hold anything back."

* * * *

From the moment he'd been so affected by her touch, she'd felt empowered. It had only grown, even as she had fallen to her knees. She'd always viewed a woman servicing a man as something weak. Now she knew differently. She'd been on her knees but he'd been in her power. It was heady stuff and something she wanted to experience again and again.

At the moment she was his willing supplicant. His lips and tongue were doing naughty and delightful things to her nipples and she arched her back, wanting and needing more. Her entire body felt as if it was on fire, flames licking at her skin. She wanted to watch his expression as he explored her but her lids simply became too heavy to lift.

His lips kissed a wet trail down her abdomen and his tongue traced circles on her inner thigh. Her legs fell open of their own accord. He was in the driver's seat and she was happy to hand him the keys. She was hungry for the kind of ecstasy she'd heard and read about but had never experienced for herself. Tanner was a man who could deliver her into heaven with a simple touch or kiss. Making love with him was out of this world pleasurable.

His teeth caught the elastic waistband of her panties and he tugged them down her legs, one side then the other, until she felt them fall from her toes. She was exposed to his gaze and she forced her eyes to open. The irises of his eyes were dark and his expression hungry, almost feral. He pushed her thighs further apart, insinuating himself so her legs were thrown over his shoulders.

She knew what he was going to do. He was going to put his mouth on her cunt and she felt her honey gather in anticipation. Always before this had been embarrassing and unpleasant. This was how it was supposed to be. She was his tonight, and it was clear he planned to enjoy every inch of her.

He pressed a thick finger inside of her and she moaned as the walls of her vagina stretched. It had been so long since the last time she'd had sex, but she rested comfortably knowing she was designed to accommodate him.

"You're so tight and wet for me, Maddie. Do you want my cock in your pussy?"

She felt another wave of heat at his simple and direct question. "Yes. I do."

He pressed a second finger inside her and began to move them in and out, sending tingles to her toes. "Say what you want, honey. Tell me what you need."

"I need you, Tanner."

"Say it, honey. I ache to hear it. Do you want me to say it first? I can't wait to be balls deep in your hot little cunt. It's going to feel better than anything ever has."

She'd never taken part in any sort of dirty talk but she didn't want him to think she wasn't aroused. "I want your cock inside of me. I need it."

Pressing a kiss on the sensitive skin where hip met thigh, he blew on her clit, her body tightening in response. Her clit was swollen and begging for his attention, and she slid her legs further apart to urge him on.

"Your pussy is so pink and ready for me, all shiny with your cream. I need a taste."

She screamed as his tongue lapped at her clit. Overwhelmed at the colliding sensations, her legs shook and her body trembled. His fingers were rubbing her G-spot and his mouth was torturing her slowly, shredding any semblance of control she'd imagined. The room spun and she grabbed onto the sheets, her fingers clawing for purchase when the first wave of her orgasm ripped through her.

"Tanner," she whispered, her voice soft in the quiet room.

She could barely speak and then only his name. Her voice sounded as if she was someone else, someone who knew pleasure well. The fire inside her was out of control and she let it burn until it finally subsided, leaving her weak and wrung out.

His mouth was pressing kisses on her oversensitized flesh. It bordered on pleasure-pain but she didn't fight it, didn't protest. He'd brought her too far to turn back now.

"Easy, Maddie. I need a condom and then we're going for a ride."

He was gone for only a moment, and then was back ripping open the foil packet with his teeth before rolling it on. She held out her arms, eager for him to be inside of her. He came down and the solid weight of his body pressed her into the mattress. His cock nudged her slit and then pressed forward. Her tight muscles resisted at first, then loosened as he slid inside. By the time he was in to the hilt she was panting.

Wrapping her legs around his hips and her arms around his shoulders, he pulled out slowly. The ridges of his cock ran over her G-spot and she mewled with frustration until he thrust inside her again. His groin rubbed her already sensitive clit, sending frissons of pleasure to every part of her body and tightening the coil in her belly.

His strokes sped up and soon their breathing was ragged and her nails were raking the flesh of his back. She whimpered in his ear, urging him faster and harder. She needed everything he could give her. She teetered on the precipice, her world narrowed to only the two of them in this bed. He reached between them and touched her clit.

It was all she needed to send her over. Her climax lit up fireworks behind her lids and the coil in her abdomen sprung free, making her flush with

106

pleasure. Deep inside she knew this was what a man and a woman were made for. This was what they were designed to do.

She simply hadn't known it would change her forever.

He froze, thrusting deep one last time. His head was thrown back and his expression was tortured. He let out a long breath and shuddered as his hot seed emptied into the condom. She could feel him swell inside her. She kissed him everywhere she could reach until he was still, his forehead pressed to hers. He kissed her nose, their bodies covered in a fine sheen of sweat.

"Honey, that was something else. Are you sure you don't do this all the time? You're dynamite."

She giggled and stroked his back. "I'm sure. You're not too bad yourself, you know. Very adequate."

He lifted up on his hands. "Adequate, huh? You really are begging for that spanking, Maddie." He pulled from her body and she winced slightly, unused to their activity. "Let me take care of the condom."

He levered up from the bed and disappeared into the bathroom. She heard water running and a flushing sound before he came back out with a washcloth in his hands. "Let's get you rinsed off, honey." The cloth was warm and soon she was lying drowsy and sated in his arms. "Sleep. We have a big day ahead of us."

He tucked her into the nook of his arm and shoulder. She never wanted this feeling of comfort and safety to end. She felt a shiver of fear run up her spine as she examined the feelings that had welled up tonight.

Love.

There, she'd said it and the world hadn't exploded. She could hear Tanner's soft snoring next to her, completely unaware of how she felt. She'd never loved anyone before.

That wasn't true. She loved her father and she loved Sherry, but she'd never loved a man before. And she was pretty sure she was falling in love with Sheriff Tanner Marks. She was halfway to a heartache if he didn't love her back. She didn't know how to make a man fall for her. It had never been something she'd cared to know.

She waited until Tanner's breathing fell into an even pattern before she slipped out of bed. She rummaged in her purse until she found her phone and pulled up her Google search. She typed in her question and wondered if there would be any results at all. Normally, she'd ask Sherry a question about men but this wasn't the time or place.

How to make a man fall in love with you.

There were over six hundred million search results. Well, crap. It was either really easy so everyone knew how, or really hard and everyone thought they knew but didn't. She glanced over at Tanner sleeping peacefully in bed, his face almost boyish in repose, and her heart lurched. She'd just spend a few minutes looking at the search results.

It couldn't hurt, right?

Chapter Eleven

"Everything is under control." Fenton's hand tightened on the phone. He didn't like explaining himself to people, even if that person happened to be his boss, Lionel Warner. "We're ready when the time comes."

"What about the sheriff? Aren't you fucking his ex-wife? Do you think that's wise? You're painting a target on your back."

Fenton flicked a glance to the closed office door. Abby was in the kitchen conferring with his housekeeper about dinner. "What about the sheriff? He doesn't know a thing. Why would he? He's the Andy Griffith of a backwater, piss ant town, for fuck's sake. He's not Rambo."

"I did a little checking on your Andy Griffith. Something you should have done. He was a fucking Army Ranger in Desert Storm. He won a Distinguished Service Cross. I don't think they just hand those out to anyone. Don't underestimate him."

"He's a drunk," Fenton countered, tired of arguing. "At least he was. Doesn't matter. I've got the ex-wife and the son in my pocket. They think I'm a hero, not him."

Chris was already in debt to Fenton. Soon he would have Chris doing jobs for the cartel. No way would Sheriff Marks turn his baby boy over to the law. Outing Fenton would out Chris. The kid was Fenton's insurance policy.

"What about the wife? You're not really going to marry her are you? She'll fucking flip when she finds out you're not a humble rancher."

The plan had never included marrying Abby Marks, but it wasn't out of the question. She was pleasant and non-demanding as long as she had a large spending account. She wasn't the smartest tool in the shed, which was also a bonus. Fucking her was good and if she didn't squawk about his business dealings, she might make a decent cartel wife.

"Who knows what will happen? Once the job is done, I won't need to be here any longer, right?"

Fenton hated Montana. It was too cold and there was nothing to fucking do except screw Abby and a few other women he had on the side in Bozeman and Billings.

"You're there for more than the job. We need to take over that fucking route. That's your real job. This other is just a one time thing."

Holding on to his patience, Fenton blew out a breath. You didn't act annoyed or impatient with Lionel Warner. If you did, your loved ones might never see you again. Fenton should know. He'd helped people understand the consequences of crossing Warner many times.

"We're making progress. We should have complete control within sixty days."

Warner cleared his throat. "Thirty days, Jacks. Stop fucking around and get it done. I want that route free and clear, understood?"

Fenton swallowed hard. "Understood. When will I hear from you again?"

"When I have something to say to you." Warner hung up leaving Fenton staring at his phone.

He dropped it on the desk and swung around in his office chair so he was facing the window. What some people might call Montana beauty he called desolate wasteland. The house was a dump and the town was a yawn. Once he completed these two jobs he would take a trip to New York. Now there was a town where something was always happening. He might even take Abby with him.

First he simply needed to make sure everything went like clockwork on this upcoming job. No problems. No snafus.

No loose ends. In and out. Surgically clean.

* * * *

"Are you nervous?" Madison asked. "You look completely serene."

The ceremony was only a few minutes away and Sherry looked beautiful in her white satin dress. It was a long, simple style, sleeveless with a scoop

110

neckline and a plunging back. Her hair was piled on top of her head and her nails sparkled pink and silver.

Madison, Karen, and Sherry had spent a few hours that afternoon shopping and having their hair done. The results were miraculous. Madison had never felt so glamorous. Sherry had insisted Madison wear a silky black dress that only came to mid-thigh. Strapless, it pushed up what cleavage she had and hugged every curve. She'd topped off the outfit with black high heels and a black velvet choker with a ruby-colored rhinestone in the center. Madison had protested that it wasn't a wedding outfit, but Sherry had overruled any other choice, proclaiming her "hot and sexy."

"I am serene. I'm marrying the man of my dreams. Finally. I know I'm doing the right thing."

Karen laughed and shook her head. "Just wait. The thing you love about him most right now? Well, that's the thing that's going to drive you up a wall in a few years. You'll still love him more than anything, but you'll be able to push each other's buttons like nobody's business."

Tanner had done a great job of pushing all the good buttons Madison had. In fact, he'd joined her for a second round in the shower this morning, climbing in while she'd been washing her hair. Getting clean had never been so much fun.

Sherry was staring at Madison as if she'd never seen her before. Madison rubbed her nose. "Do I have something on my face?" Sherry shook her head. "What then?"

She grabbed Madison's elbow and pulled her off to the corner where no one could hear. "You're different. I've been so wrapped up in the wedding today I didn't notice. But you're different." Her eyes lit up. "You slept with Tanner? You go! How was it?" Sherry's voice was a whisper but Madison still felt the heat creep into her cheeks. Luckily the others appeared engrossed in their own conversations.

"We should be concentrating on your wedding, not my sex life. We can talk about this later."

"We can talk about this now. Don't bother denying it. The guilty truth is written all over your glowing face and from the look of it, it must have been good. You look like you got caught with your hand in the cookie jar."

Blessedly the doors to the chapel opened and the woman who had helped Sherry and Dan fill out all their paperwork beckoned to them.

"It's time, everyone. Follow me."

The six of them followed the smiling hostess into the chapel, all of them taking their places. Tanner and Karen sat and watched as Jim and Madison flanked the blissful couple as they recited their vows. Tears welled up in Madison's eyes as she heard the catch of emotion in Dan's voice as he promised to love and honor Sherry all the rest of his days. Sherry was beaming as she promised the same, their hands entwined.

Quickly it was Madison's big moment when she would hand over the ring for Dan. As Sherry took the ring from Madison's fingers, she caught Tanner watching her, his eyes warm. Before she knew it, Elvis was singing "Love Me Tender" and Dan and Sherry were dancing right there at the alter, their expressions so full of love it made Madison's heart ache with longing. As the music faded away, they headed back down the aisle to make way for the next couple.

Dan had a big grin on his face. "We have a surprise for everyone as thanks for sharing this occasion with us. I talked to the concierge at the hotel and he was able to get us tickets tonight to the *Criss Angel: Mindfreak* show after dinner."

Karen shrieked in delight and jumped up and down. "Are you serious? I love Criss Angel."

Jim put a calming hand on her shoulder. "We can all see that, sweetheart. Simmer down."

Jim's stoic personality didn't seem to bother his wife. She grinned and gave Jim's shoulder a nudge. "You knew all the time, didn't you?"

"I might have simply made a suggestion, that's all."

"I love you." Karen gazed at her husband with adoration.

Madison looked up at Tanner, so handsome in his dark blue suit. "Did you know, too?"

Tanner chuckled. "Let's just say we were busy while you ladies beautified. There are more surprises, you know. Dan wanted to make this really special for Sherry since she wasn't getting a big church wedding."

"More surprises? I didn't realize you were devious, Tanner Marks."

"Just trying to help out."

Dan slapped Tanner on the back. "He certainly did help out. He turned on the charm and got us reservations at STACK tonight." Dan checked his watch. "In fact, we need to head out or we'll miss dinner. We're catching the late show afterward."

They filed out, heading for the rented limousine. Madison tugged on Tanner's sleeve to slow him down, separating them from the other two couples. "Charmed? Should I be jealous?"

Tanner smiled. "Would you be? Don't worry, Maddie. I'm a one woman man, and you're that woman."

That was what she wanted to be.

* * * *

Madison and Tanner were finally alone. If you considered alone to be the two of them and several hundred people in a casino. Sherry and Dan were headed to their room to enjoy their wedding night and Jim and Karen were going to soak in the jetted spa. Tanner was going to teach Madison to play blackjack. She'd rather go up to the room and make love but the reading she'd done on Google was very clear. She needed to enjoy the things Tanner liked to do. If he wanted to play blackjack, then she would smile the entire time.

113

The article had also suggested she ask for his help with something which was how they'd started talking about blackjack. When she'd said it would be great to get a few pointers from him, she simply hadn't thought it would be right now.

"Go ahead and have a seat." Tanner motioned to a chair at the gaming table, shaped like a semi-circle.

"Um, I thought I would just watch you." Madison tried to back up a few steps but Tanner was right behind her, urging her forward. She was only doing this to make him fall in love with her, not because she had a deep-seated need to give her money to this establishment.

"The best way to learn is by doing. I'll be right here with you." He handed her the stack of red and blue chips. "Place one there so they know you want to play."

Well, crap.

Sighing, she sank into the chair. Each person at the table was dealt two cards face up and the dealer dealt himself one card face up and one face down.

"You have a two and an eight. That's called a hard hand because you don't have an ace. Tap your cards so he knows you want another one."

Tanner's hands were on her shoulders and she had to force herself to concentrate on the cards and not the warmth from his body or his yummy smell. She tapped her cards and the dealer dealt her a five.

"Tap again."

She tapped again and was dealt a three.

"Wave your hand over your cards to show you are holding." She waved her hand and waited for the other players at the table to bet. One of them went over twenty-one and got up from the table in disgust, stomping away.

"Now the dealer will play his hand. If he has sixteen or less, he has to take a card."

114

The dealer had a ten showing. He turned over another card, an eight, and then flipped over the card that had been face side down. A five. He had a total of twenty-three.

"You won."

She twisted around so she could see Tanner's face. "That's it? I won?"

"Although the game is called Twenty-One, the goal is really just to get higher than the dealer without going over. You did it."

Where her one chip had been, there were now two. Her analytical mind quickly calculated her odds of winning if simply beating the dealer was her only goal. "I can see how people could get addicted to this. I'll let it ride."

If he thought her saying "let it ride" was funny, he didn't act like it. Instead she allowed him to coach her until she had doubled her money. She could have figured out the odds for each play herself now that she understood, but the article had said it was important to make a man feel needed, to feel like he was helping her with something. She gathered her chips up into a plastic cup and pushed away from the table. The middle-aged man next to her looked up in surprise.

"You're not quitting are you? You're on a roll, little lady. You should keep playing."

She shook her head. "The odds aren't in my favor to continue winning at this pace. I should quit while I'm ahead."

Tanner chuckled in her ear. "I agree. Let's get something to drink, okay?"

With his hand under her elbow, he led her to the cashier where she exchanged her chips for cash, shocked at how much she had won.

"Are you hungry? We can get an appetizer at the bar." He was looking around and she captured his jaw with her hand.

"Can we go up to the room instead?"

He frowned. "Of course, Maddie. You must be exhausted. You probably want to get some rest."

She shook her head, going against the advice in the column. She couldn't play hard to get games. It simply wasn't who she was. If he didn't fall in love with her because of it, well, so be it.

"I want to make love with you. Is that okay?"

His eyes instantly darkened. "Honey, that is absolutely okay. I was trying to be thoughtful and not push you, but I've been thinking about it all damn day."

The article had talked about giving a man a job to do for you. It made them feel important.

"Will you take me upstairs and make me scream?"

Tanner hurried her toward the elevator. "It will be my pleasure."

It would be pleasure for both of them. She would make sure of it.

Chapter Twelve

Tanner couldn't get Maddie's clothes off fast enough. He'd practically dragged her to the room, his cock already hard and pressing against the zipper of his pants. There was something about this woman that turned him into a horny teenage boy. Maybe it was the innocence swirled with sensuality. Perhaps it was her innate intelligence mixed with a wide-eyed naiveté when it came to anything outside of her career. Whatever it was, it did it for him like nothing ever before.

Within seconds their clothes were in a heap on the floor and he was pushing her thighs apart, kissing a line straight to her cunt. It was already pink and shiny, and he couldn't wait to delve into her depths and bring on that scream she'd asked for so sweetly. His fingers played with her nipples, hard and pointed while his tongue swiped at her clit.

She was rolling around, partly laughing and partly moaning. He pressed her into the mattress firmly to hold her still. "Easy, honey. We don't want anyone injured."

She giggled and looked down between her legs at him. "I didn't know."

"Didn't know what, Maddie?" She looked so incredibly sexy lying there, her long red hair playing peek-a-boo with her breasts.

"That it could be fun. That I would laugh." Her eyes widened. "Oh shit, is it okay to laugh? I'm not laughing at you. It's just, it tickles there." She pointed to her inner thigh. His heart tightened in his chest. He was falling for this woman. Hard. There would be no soft landing if she didn't feel the same. He liked her. Hell, he respected her. When she looked at him with her eyes shining, just the way they were now, he felt... Shit, he didn't know what he felt. It was as if everything was okay and always would be as long as she was there.

Aww fuck, I've got it bad.

"It's okay to laugh. Sex is supposed to be fun. It doesn't always have to be serious," he assured her and was rewarded with a smile. His stomach was twisted into knots and his heart was pounding. This wasn't a casual thing and hadn't he known it wouldn't be all along? Isn't that why he'd hesitated in the beginning? He could picture them making a life together. That was something he'd never allowed himself to imagine. He'd fucked up so many things. Was it too much to ask to be given a second chance?

Am I worthy of it?

He didn't ponder the answer. He wasn't a man given to long bouts of introspection. He was a man who lived by his actions. That was the true measure of any man. Words meant nothing. Deeds were what counted.

He pushed her legs farther apart and let his tongue wander through the folds of her pussy. Her legs started to tremble and he'd already learned that meant she was close. He pressed a finger inside her. Tight and wet. He couldn't wait to be buried deep, driving them both to the stars and back. Her hands were clutching the sheets, her chest rising and falling rapidly with each movement of his tongue.

When her head was thrashing back and forth, he gave her mercy. His mouth closed over her clit and lightly sucked. She froze and then he heard the scream he'd promised her. She said his name over and over until she lay on the bed replete from her climax. He went back to kissing and nibbling the sensitive skin of her inner thigh. Soon she was giggling and pushing at his head.

"No fair. Now you know I'm ticklish."

He levered up and grinned. "I can't wait to find all your ticklish spots."

She sighed and came up on her elbows. "I have quite a few. People are supposed to grow out of being ticklish, but I never did." She bit her lip and looked up at him from under her lashes. "Thanks for the scream, by the way."

His lovely Maddie. He'd never been thanked for an orgasm before, but he could get used to it.

"Thanks for screaming. You're good for my ego."

She nodded, suddenly serious. "I've heard the male ego is a fragile thing. Do I need to praise or encourage you more?"

He tried to keep a straight face. "Maybe you could do some cheering? I liked that when I was in high school."

She was too smart for him and shoved at his shoulder with a groan. "I was actually trying to be nice. And I wasn't a cheerleader. Not even close. If you want one of those, you shouldn't be dating me. I saw your picture in the trophy case in high school. You were the big man on campus."

He'd been a stupid teenage boy. "It was a long time ago."

Her brows were drawn down in puzzlement. "You almost sound like it was a bad thing."

"It was okay." Tanner shrugged. It had been years ago and not something he thought about much, if at all.

Madison shook her head. "I didn't mean to bring the mood down. All because I said I wasn't a cheerleader."

He pulled her on top of him so his cock was snug against her pussy. "You'd make a cute cheerleader." He dipped his head and captured a nipple with his teeth making her back arch and her fingers tighten on his shoulders. "Go ahead, honey. Say what you want. You can do it."

She pulled him closer, her lips mere millimeters from his.

"Give me a cock, cowboy."

Hell, yes.

He leaned far over the side of the bed to snag a condom from his pants pocket. He was going to need to start buying these by the case. Fucking Madison was the most exciting and pleasurable thing he'd ever done by a country mile. He couldn't get enough of her, his appetite endless.

Quickly rolling on the protection, he lifted her hips so she was hovering above him and she was straddling his thighs. She was holding onto his shoulders and biting her lip.

"You okay, honey?"

She nodded. "I've never been much good at being on top."

She kept looking down at his cock and rearranging her legs.

"You'll be fine," he assured her. "You're in charge. Just do what feels good. I'll love it. I promise."

His voice was becoming hoarse because she'd already started to lower herself onto his dick. So fucking tight and hot. Her cunt squeezed and hugged every inch of him until he was into the hilt, their bodies resting together. He tilted her chin up so she was looking into his eyes and their gazes locked.

She started moving, slowly and experimentally. His fingers flexed on her hips as she drew up, then slammed down hard. Hissing his approval, he used every ounce of strength to stay still. He'd given her the control this time. As hard as it was, she needed this to gain confidence.

She swiveled her hips and his eyes rolled back in his head. Sweat broke out across his skin as she tortured him stroke by stroke, thrust by thrust. He forced himself to keep his eyes open. Her eyes had turned a dark emerald shade, the pupils large and unfocused. Feeling her tremble, he knew she was close.

Tanner rolled her nipples between his fingers giving her a bite of pain, but he wasn't prepared for the reaction. Her nails dug into his shoulders and a moan escaped her full lips. She started panting and grinding herself down on him, her back arched, inviting more.

He gave it to her.

She was riding him frantically now, whimpering his name as her forehead fell on his chest. He reached around her and smacked her bottom. Not hard, but enough to leave a pink handprint.

"Yes," she hissed. Her pussy clamped down on his cock and he could feel the flutters of her climax ripple down his shaft. He spanked her again, and again felt the vibrations, but this time they sent him over the edge with her.

His balls pulled up and it felt like his body was being turned inside out from the middle. He cursed as her teeth bit into his bicep, the pain mingling with the pleasure and sending him further into orbit. They finally collapsed together, her on top of him as he stroked her back and ran his fingers through her silky hair.

Making love with Madison was no usual thing. It was an experience he'd never get over and knew wouldn't be repeated with any other woman. She was a once in a lifetime.

They lay there for quite a while but eventually he had to move and deal with the condom. He gently lifted her and put her next to him.

"I'll be right back, honey."

He quickly took care of things then padded back into the bedroom, cuddling up next to her. She turned in his arms, pressing a kiss to his chest.

"You spanked me." Her voice was muffled but he didn't hear any anger. If anything, she sounded amused.

"I told you I would." He chuckled and then pulled her up so they were eye to eye. "Are you mad? I won't do it again if you didn't like it. I was honestly just trying a few things to see if it excited you."

She tilted her head as if she was cogitating on the matter. "I like it," she pronounced. "You can do it again. Just don't tell anyone. I'm not sure a modern woman, a doctor, should enjoy being spanked by her lover."

"First of all, I wouldn't tell a soul. That's our business, and no one else's. Second, this isn't about being a modern woman or an old-fashioned one. It's not unusual for people in general to enjoy mild pain with their pleasure. It intensifies the sensations."

She nodded, apparently satisfied. "I'll look it up later. Do you like being spanked?"

This woman was going to be the death of him. He was starting to sympathize with Seth Reilly. The man had to be completely exhausted all the time.

"No." Tanner shook his head. "No. I like being dominant."

Watching her closely, he wanted to be sure she believed him. He was an ornery cuss in and out of the bedroom, but no one was going to spank him. Ever. His own daddy had given up when Tanner was six and started fighting back.

She lay back down, her head pillowed on his shoulder. "Good. I can't imagine spanking you."

"Let's keep it that way, Maddie. Close your eyes and we'll get some sleep. We've had a big day."

"I see you do like to be dominant. You're bossy, but in this case I agree with you. 'Night, Tanner."

"'Night, Maddie. Sweet dreams."

Tanner fell asleep to the soft rhythm of Madison's breathing, quieting his mind to all the questions left unanswered that were running free in his brain. There would be time enough to answer them.

Tomorrow. With Madison.

Everything should be with Madison, he decided moments before sleep took him. She made everything better.

* * * *

Madison soaped her long hair, letting the hot water run down her body. She was pleasantly sore in a few spots, but her body was humming after a night of lovemaking with Tanner. He'd woken her after a few hours of sleep and they'd sated themselves after rolling around in the sheets, their bodies tangled together. It was every sexy fantasy she'd ever had brought to life.

She checked her bottom in the mirror this morning and there hadn't been a sign of the baby spanks she'd received from Tanner. If anything, she wanted more. She needed to be fucked hard and fast by him while he spanked her bottom. It was hot and a little raunchy but she was a grown woman. She wouldn't be ashamed or embarrassed. Tanner had taught her that much. He didn't judge her and she wouldn't judge herself.

She was rinsing her hair when the shower curtain opened, the rings scraping loudly on the metal bar.

"Norman Bates, I presume?" She didn't bother to open her eyes. Instead, she tipped her head back so the shampoo slid out of her hair. It took ten minutes to wash, but it was the one thing she didn't want to give up.

Two large hands began massaging her scalp and running through the strands. "Sorry, just me. I don't have a weapon."

His hard cock nudged her belly and she giggled. "Are you sure? Feels like you might be armed and dangerous with that thing."

His hands glided down to her bottom pulling her against him and his lips pressed to hers, his tongue dipping inside. She groaned and wrapped her arms around his neck. He took his time exploring her mouth. His hands squeezed her ass cheeks before sliding up to cup her breasts. He played with them with his fingers and tongue until they were taut and hard.

She kissed her way down his chest, over the ridges of his stomach, until she was on her knees. His cocked bobbed in front of her and she didn't tease or make him wait. She swallowed him down in one gulp, the head of his cock bumping the back of her throat. His fingers went reflexively to the back of her head and his hips canted as he pressed for even deeper entry.

She relaxed her jaw and took him further, fighting her gag reflex. She loved how he felt heavy on her tongue and the way he filled every nook and cranny of her mouth. He let her lick and suck for a few minutes before pulling her to her feet.

"I want to fuck you." His voice was like gravel and broken glass. He positioned her with her back on the tile lifting her hips so her legs could wrap around his waist. She felt him hot and hard at her slit and suddenly a last shred of sanity reared up and cried out in her mind. She pushed at his shoulder. If they'd gone one more minute, it would have been too late.

"Tanner. Condom. We need a condom."

He let go a string of profanity that made her blush, but let his forehead rest against hers.

"Sorry, honey. I got carried away. I put one on the vanity. Give me thirty seconds."

He didn't need all thirty. Within twenty-five he'd lifted her back up and impaled himself in one hard thrust. She clung to his strong shoulders, her head buried in his chest as he pounded her into the decorative tile. Every stroke ran across her G-spot and stimulated her clit until she couldn't take it anymore. He fucked her like a metronome, hot, fast, and steady. She could feel her body starting to fly apart, twisting in the maelstrom of sensations.

Between the spray of the water, his hands, his mouth, and his pounding dick, she was lost to the pleasure. The sounds of their lovemaking echoed off the walls and only served to inflame them further. When her body shattered, she cried out at the intensity. The pleasure twisted her inside and out. She barely registered Tanner's own growl of completion, but she felt his hot seed fill the condom.

He kissed her tenderly as they caught their breath. He lowered her legs until her feet touched the floor of the tub, but held her until she could stand on her own. She was blown away by the power of what they created together. They were exponentially more as a couple than she'd ever imagined.

She looked up into his eyes. "I think I'm going to want to do that. A lot."

Tanner's smile widened. "Maddie, I'm your man."

That was what she was hoping for.

Chapter Thirteen

"Tanner Marks." Tanner gave Madison an apologetic smile as he answered his phone. "Give me a minute, Maddie."

She nodded, engrossed in a book, and he walked to the far side of the airport waiting area. Their plane was on time and should start to board in a few minutes. It was just him and Madison this time. Jim, Karen, Dan, and Sherry were taking a flight about an hour from now with another airline. It was all they'd been able to book at the last minute.

"It's Agent Jason Anderson. Am I interrupting? I could call back later." Tanner could hear clinking dishes in the background. It sounded like Jason was calling from a restaurant or maybe his own kitchen.

"No, it's fine. I'm at the airport waiting for a flight back to Montana."

"Vacation?" Jason sounded surprised. "Shit, I'm interrupting your time off."

"No, it's not like that. My girlfriend's best friend got married in Vegas last night. Madison was the maid of honor. It's okay. Talk to me. What have you found out?"

Jason wouldn't be calling him on a Sunday morning if something wasn't up. Tanner knew deep down that Fenton was dirty. He hoped Jason would be able to tell him just how bad it was.

Jason sighed. "It's not good news. Your friend was right. Fenton Jacks doesn't exist. Thomas Lydell does, and he's one bad motherfucker. Deep into the Warner drug cartel. He's climbed the ladder the old-fashioned way. He killed everyone in his way."

There was a silence on the other end giving Tanner a chance to wrap his mind around what he was being told. He'd known Fenton was a criminal but to hear he was a murderer was still a shock. His fucking kids spent time with this asshole. Shit, Abby might be Tanner's ex-wife but it didn't mean he wanted any harm to come to her.

"He's in Springwood to take over the route?" Tanner was proud of how calm he sounded despite his churning gut. He was already working out how he would get Fenton away from his family. Fuck that, he wanted Fenton out of his town. Period.

"He is. You've done us a favor, Tanner. We can zero in on him now and watch his every move."

"You're not going to arrest him?" Tanner's voice got a little loud and several heads turned his way, including Madison's. Her brows were knitted but he gave her a reassuring wave.

"He's managed to weasel out of every charge until now. We need to catch him in the act. I know you're concerned about your wife--"

"Ex-wife," Tanner interrupted curtly. "I'm concerned about my kids, too. I don't want them around him or any of his friends. I can't believe you don't have enough to pick this guy up right now."

Frustrated, Tanner paced the small area by the windows overlooking the tarmac. His fucking taxes at work. They knew this guy was a killer but they were going to let him wander around until he killed someone else.

"We'll have someone on him every minute of every day. I'm asking you to keep this to yourself, Tanner. And yes, I know that it sucks. We take him out now, the head of the snake will only grow back meaner and more deadly. They want that drug route and they'll do whatever it takes to get it. We need to bust not just him but the entire organization. We'll have a better chance of getting intel on the big boys. Lydell isn't going to roll over on his boss but the men lower down just might. They have less to lose."

"Only their life," retorted Tanner. He didn't like that Jason Anderson was making sense. He wanted to fly back to Springwood and run this guy out of town on a rail. Straight to the nearest state prison or federal lock up.

"If they're selling or running drugs, their life isn't worth much anyway. One step out of line and the big guys will take them out without a second thought. They're disposable and easily replaced."

126

Tanner's grip tightened on the phone and he wished his fingers were wrapped around Fenton's neck. "You're asking me to stand by while a killer hangs around my family, my town."

"I know." Jason's voice was low. "Please just give me some time to watch him. If we arrest him, we have to make the charges stick this time. This is our best chance. You're our best chance, Tanner. Listen, I trust your judgment. If there are people you need to tell, well shit, I won't be happy about it, but I understand. If you feel like your family or town is in imminent danger, then you need to do what you need to do. All I'm asking for is that you give me some space to do this investigation, and that if you do tell someone, it's someone you trust. Can you do that for me?"

Fuck. Fuck. Fuck. Fuck.

"If one thing..." Tanner snarled. "If one thing happens to my family I'll hold you personally responsible. I swear to God, Jason, there won't be a rock big enough to hide under. Do I make myself clear?"

Tanner jumped when he felt a hand on his back. Whirling around, he looked directly into the troubled gaze of Madison. He took a deep breath, trying to calm the hell down.

"You're clear. I promise we'll have a couple of people on him twenty-four seven."

Tanner held the phone away from his ear. "Are you okay?" asked Madison. "You look upset."

"I am upset, but I'll be fine." He opened his mouth to explain but the airline came over the loudspeaker announcing the flight. "We need to board." He put the phone back to his ear. "Jason, I need to go. I'll call you."

He pressed the End button not wanting to continue the discussion. He was pissed off and frustrated. He shoved the phone in his pocket and hoisted his carry on further up his shoulder. Jason had given him leeway to talk about Jacks, but Tanner wanted the asshole arrested right now.

Madison put her hand on his arm. "You were scaring me a little bit there for a minute. You looked so angry. What's wrong?"

He realized he couldn't tell her the truth, at least at this moment, and he didn't like that one little bit. Tanner wasn't a fan of keeping secrets, especially with someone he was supposed to be in a relationship with.

"Let's just call it bad news. Are you ready to board?"

She nodded, but her expression was shrewd. She knew he wasn't telling her something. He put his hand under her elbow and led her to where they were lining up to board.

"I had fun this weekend. Thank you for going." She gave him a big smile that made his heart lurch in his chest.

"Did you think I'd let you go to Vegas without me? No way. I had a good time. A very good time." In fact, he couldn't remember having a better time in his life before this. He enjoyed Madison's company, both in and out of bed. "I'd like you to meet my kids."

He'd just blurted it out and now they were making their way through the aircraft to their seats. Madison didn't answer and he was beginning to think he'd blown it. They settled down, buckled their seat belts, and she put her hand on his. "I'd like to meet your kids very much."

He relaxed under her touch. "I'll call Emily and Chris." He shifted in his seat, suddenly uncomfortable. Her opinion of him was now very important. "I have a granddaughter. Does that bug you?"

"No." She shook her head. "I knew that before we got involved."

"I'm older than you. I'll be forty-five on Friday."

Her face lit up. "A birthday. We'll have to do something special."

He lifted her fingers and kissed the knuckles. "Focus, honey. I just told you I'm going to be forty-five. That's not dog years."

She giggled. "I heard you. I just don't care. Your age is just a number. Are you upset that I'm thirty?"

"Men are never upset about a beautiful young woman."

"Well, I'm not upset about a handsome older man. Relax, Tanner. It's all good. Don't look for problems where there aren't any."

Maybe he was looking for issues. Things with Madison were great and that scared him. He'd rarely had anything in his life go smoothly.

"I just want you to be happy, that's all."

"I am happy." She closed her eyes as the engines started to rev underneath them. "Now hold my hand while we take off. I get nervous."

He clasped her hand, rubbing her wrist with his thumb. He'd set up dinner for them with Emily and Chris. His son might not even show up, but Emily certainly would. He could see Madison and Emily getting along well.

And while Emily was here, Tanner could talk to her about staying in the city for awhile. At least until Fenton was flushed out. That left Abby and Chris, and Tanner had no ideas how to convince them to stay away from Fenton when the truth couldn't be told.

He glanced at his watch, determination welling up inside him. He'd do everything and anything to keep his family and town safe. Now he just needed to figure out how to accomplish it.

* * * *

Madison shoved the clothes into the washer and poured in the detergent. It was kind of sad to be home after the weekend in Las Vegas, but she was looking forward to getting back to work tomorrow. Mondays were always a busy day.

"I made some hot chocolate. Come and have a cup." Her father stood at the doorway of the laundry room holding two large, steaming mugs and a big smile. "I want to hear about the wedding and your trip. It's been years since I was in Vegas."

She laughed and took one of the mugs from his hand and followed him into the kitchen. Settling into one of the chairs at the table, she asked, "When were you in Vegas? Did Mom go?"

Her father settled across from her, his hands wrapped around the mug. "Your mother and I did go for vacation a few years after we were married. You hadn't come along yet. We had a marvelous time. We saw a few shows and gambled a little. Not much. Your mother was very cautious. But still, we enjoyed ourselves."

"We saw Criss Angel after the wedding. It was a good show." Madison sipped the hot liquid and it almost burned her tongue, making her wince. She blew on the surface to cool it down. "The wedding was great. I thought it might be cheesy, but it really wasn't. I got choked up when they took their vows."

"Good weddings are like that." Her father nodded his head. "Dan and Sherry make a nice couple. I'll have to send them a wedding gift."

Her father's voice trailed off and his expression was troubled. He was staring out the kitchen window as if his mind was captured elsewhere, lines grooved into his forehead.

"Dad, is everything okay?"

Her dad set the mug on the table. "I need to tell you something and I'm not sure how you're going to react."

Alarm pierced her heart. "You are sick aren't you? I asked you this once but you said no." She sat up straight in the chair ready to call the Mayo Clinic, but he waved away her concern.

"I'm not sick." He sighed and reached across the table to pat her hand. "Madison, I've met someone."

"Met someone?" Her mind whirled the words around. Her father appeared to be miserable, his mouth turned down and his eyes sad. "That's great. You don't seem too happy about it. Is she...married?" She dropped her voice to a whisper.

His jaw dropped. "No! Gwen is not married. I would never date a married woman."

"Then what's the prob—"

130

"She lives in Seattle." Her father's words came out in a rush. "She's a friend of your aunt. Gwen is a wonderful woman. She's also a widow. Two children, both sons. They're in college."

Madison couldn't remember her father ever going out on a date the entire time she'd been growing up. He'd once said her mother was the love of his life. She had to remind herself that her father was still young, not quite sixty. He'd been alone a long time and deserved to find happiness again.

"I'm happy for you, Dad. That's why you've been spending so much time there isn't it?"

"Yes. I'm sorry I didn't tell you before now." He was staring into his cup, which made her think there was more to this story.

"You're in love aren't you, and you think I'll be upset?" She grabbed her father's hand. "Dad, I'm happy for you, really. You deserve this. Will Gwen be moving here soon? I can move out."

Madison didn't relish becoming a third wheel. She was used to living on her own anyway. If anything, it had been an adjustment moving back to her childhood home.

Red stained her father's cheeks. "That's just it, honey. Gwen isn't moving here. I'm moving to Seattle."

She blinked. "You're going to Seattle?"

He ran his hand down his face. "Honey, I'm so sorry. I convinced you to move back here to take over the practice when I retire, and now I feel like a heel. I had no idea I'd be moving when we started talking about this."

She didn't doubt his word. They'd been discussing this for almost a year. "It's okay, Dad."

She rubbed her temples, her head starting to pound. She'd left Chicago to come home to Montana and now her only family was planning to leave.

Greg Shay looked like he rather be any place but sitting at the kitchen table with her at the moment. Madison loved her dad and she needed to let him off the hook.

"I understand if you're angry, sweetheart." Her father jumped up from the table and began to pace. "I begged you to come home and now you probably feel like I'm abandoning you."

"I'm thirty years old. I can hardly call it abandonment," she protested.

His shoulders slumped and he turned his back to her, his hands gripping the edge of the sink. "I just love Gwen so much. She has her own catering business in Seattle. I'd be asking her to pick up and start all over again if she moved here." He swung around. "Gwen and I want you to move to Seattle with us. She can't wait to meet you and I can't wait for you to meet her."

Madison got out of her chair and walked over to her father, wrapping her arms around him for a hug. "I'd love to meet her. As for moving to Seattle, I don't see that happening, Dad."

Her father started to speak but she held up her hand. "I wouldn't know anyone there except you two. Trust me when I tell you moving to a new city is hard. I've done it and it wasn't easy."

"Will you move back to Chicago?"

She shook her head. "No, I like being home. Chicago was good but Springwood is more."

Greg Shay sighed. "I'm so sorry I brought you back only to pick up and leave. You're being more understanding than I deserve."

"What I remember is a man who put me before himself the entire time I was growing up. You never dated—heck, I don't think you even saw a movie without me until I was in high school. I'm grateful for that, Dad. Now it's your time. I'm happy for you. Really, I am."

He crushed her in his embrace. "How did I get so lucky? I love you, Madison Eloise Shay."

"If you love me, you won't mention my middle name. And I love you, too."

"Your grandmother insisted on that middle name." Her father chuckled. "Your mother and I agreed to it to keep the peace."

"I've forgiven you for that because you were a terrific parent. Now let's drink our hot chocolate and you can tell me all about Gwen. What is she like?" They sat back at the table and her father's body language was completely different. He was leaning forward, his eyes twinkling. Her father was in love, and Madison recognized the signs. It was exactly what she saw when she looked in a mirror.

Chapter Fourteen

Sara, Madison's receptionist, stuck her head around the door to the kitchen where Madison was trying to gulp down lunch in record time. She was running behind today and she hated that. She didn't like to keep sick people waiting, especially in their tiny waiting room.

"Can you squeeze in one more patient?" Sara grimaced. "Sandy Donovan's toddler has a fever and she's worried."

Madison tried to chew and swallow her sandwich. "Is she already here?"

"She is." Sara nodded. "What should I tell her?"

There was no way Madison was turning away a sick toddler and a concerned mother.

"Put her in room two and give me a minute. I'll be right there."

There were only two examining rooms luckily, and there had been a steady stream of patients in them today. Madison tossed the remainder of her sandwich in the trash and gulped down half a glass of iced tea in one shot. She checked her teeth in the mirror, popped a breath mint and headed to the exam room, knocking on the door.

"Hello, I'm Dr. Madison Shay. What can I do for you today?"

Madison clearly remembered Sandy Donovan from school but the woman in front of her barely resembled the girl. It struck her that Tanner was right when he'd said that life had been hard on some of Madison's classmates. Sandy looked older and sad, almost humbled. Her shoulders were hunched and she was staring at the floor intently. It was a far cry from the girl with fancy clothes and perfect hair who had made Madison's life such a misery.

Sandy looked up and tried to smile. She held a tiny blonde-haired girl in her arms who had a very red nose and glassy eyes. She was clutching a stuffed dog to her chest and staring at Madison with a dubious expression.

"Hello. Kylie seems to be running a fever."

Madison headed to the small sink and washed her hands. "Well, let's take a look then. Can you set her on the table? You can sit with her there if you like."

Sandy looked dead on her feet, with purple smudges under her eyes. The woman hesitated for a second but then sat down on the table with Kylie next to her.

Madison smiled at the lovely little girl. "My name is Dr. Madison. What's your name?"

The child's blue eyes were like saucers and she took her thumb out of her mouth long enough to answer. "Kylie Marie." Back went the thumb.

"That's a very pretty name, just like you. I'm just going to check a few things, okay? I'll tell you everything I'm going to do before I do it and you can ask me anything you want."

The girl nodded solemnly and Madison started her examination. Kylie sat still for having her ears checked but wasn't as happy about having her throat examined. She was downright upset when Madison looked up her nostrils but calmed down when Madison listened to her heart and lungs. She completed the exam as quickly and efficiently as she could, knowing a sick child could be unpredictable. Happy one second and crying the next.

"Kylie has an ear infection in her right ear. That's why her temperature is elevated and she feels crabby. According to her records, she gets these quite often. Have you talked to an ENT about possibly putting tubes in her ears?"

Sandy looked like she might cry. She scooped Kylie up in her arms and cradled the child. "No. I don't get insurance where I work and there's no money for a specialist. Gary got hurt and he hasn't been able to work for almost a year. Your dad's taken good care of Kylie since she was born."

"Gary Howard?" Madison remembered him as a handsome jock who had helped the basketball team go to State their senior year.

Sandy nodded and looked down at the floor again. "He's a good dad. We've been planning to get married but haven't had the money to do it yet."

"Well, congratulations on your engagement and this sweet little one. She's absolutely beautiful, Sandy."

Sandy raised her eyes, her forehead wrinkling. "How come you're being so nice to me? I was never nice to you. I was one of those mean girls, you know, like in the movie."

Madison exhaled slowly. Tanner was right about how things had changed. It was time to put the past firmly behind her. "Yes, I remember. But I've learned since coming back to town that people change. You're not being mean to me now, so why would I be mean to you?"

Sandy's mouth turned up. "She is pretty, isn't she? She's a good girl."

"I can see that. She's been such a quiet, good girl since you got here. Very well-behaved."

Beaming, Sandy placed Kylie on the table where she could play with her stuffed dog. "I want to say I'm sorry about how I treated you in school."

Madison didn't want to think about those years at all. "Apology accepted."

Sandy put her hand on Madison's arm. "I was real insecure, and I know this sounds bad but it made me feel better about myself to tear other people down. I'm not excusing what I did." Sandy shook her head. "I'm simply trying to explain it. I wanted people to like me."

Madison turned back to Kylie's folder. "So did I," Madison said quietly. "I understand."

"Thank you. I'm grateful that you were able to see us today." Sandy lifted Kylie into her arms and slung her purse over her shoulder. Madison reviewed treatment for Kylie and mother and daughter left the office.

Madison handed the file to Sara. "Sandy said she doesn't have any insurance. What does my dad normally do with their bills?"

Sara sighed. "He puts it on account. Sandy tries to pay some but that poor girl has had a run of bad luck you wouldn't believe. She lost her father in a ranch accident and her mother has Alzheimer's. Then she gets pregnant with Kylie and Gary has a car accident on some black ice. She's due for some good things."

"Let's see that she gets some then. Let's write off her bill. It's the last thing she needs to worry about."

Sara looked unsure. "Sandy has some pride, Madison. She may think this is charity. It makes her feel better about herself to try and pay when she can."

Madison scratched her chin. "Yes, you're right. How about we forget to send her a monthly bill for awhile?"

Sara nodded. "Now that I can do." She tipped her head. "I wasn't in the same year at school as you were but I know that the kids were hard on you. You're a good person to forgive."

"No, it's normal to forgive." Madison shook her head. "It would be petty and crappy to hold on to the past. I did for a long time and let me tell you it's no fun. It ends up hurting you more than any one else. Kids can be cruel at times. The one thing I've learned is it wasn't personal."

"I bet it felt personal."

"Man, did it ever." Madison sighed. "But strangely, it wasn't. It was about them and their issues. I'm certainly not going to hate them because of it. Doesn't mean I'm looking to invite them over for dinner either." She laughed and headed to exam room one.

"You just wait. By this time next year, you'll be the entire town's best friend. Your dad certainly is."

Madison was already feeling as if these people were her responsibility. As a doctor, she wanted to take care of them and make sure they were healthy. It probably wasn't a long stretch to be their friends as well.

* * * *

Tanner was having a crappy Monday. First, all hell broke loose the minute he stepped into the station. Sam had arrested a prominent citizen over the weekend for violence against his spouse. A blustering high-priced lawyer had shown up this morning before Tanner had even had a cup of coffee. The attorney wanted his client released immediately and made noises about false arrest and police brutality.

It had taken close to an hour, but Tanner had finally evicted the blowhard from the station, basically telling him he needed to talk to the judge at the arraignment which would be held at ten o'clock in Courtroom A.

It had been call after call all day long capped off with an AA meeting where Chris attended. That was a win. But he was clearly hung-over. That was a loss. By the time Tanner headed down the library steps to his truck, he was ready for something good. He was ready to see Madison. He'd missed her all day long. A hastily sent text before his meeting asking her to dinner had been answered in the affirmative. Maybe the day wouldn't be a total loss after all.

Out of the corner of his eye, Tanner saw Chris heading down the sidewalk. Jogging to catch up with him, Tanner put his hand on Chris's shoulder.

"Chris, got a minute?"

His son whirled around, his jaw jutted out as if ready for a punch. For the life of him, Tanner didn't know how Chris had bottled up all this anger.

"A minute. What do you want? I came to the stupid meeting, didn't I?"

Tanner muffled a heavy sigh. "You did and I'm glad. I saw Harvey talking to you before the meeting. Did he offer to be your sponsor? He's a good man."

Chris shrugged. "He said something about it. But I told him I'm not an alcoholic. I mean, I like to drink, but I could quit anytime I want. I'm just coming to the meetings so Stacey will let me see Annie."

There were worse reasons to go to an AA meeting, but Tanner couldn't think of any at the moment. Chris was deeply in denial about having a problem, which Tanner understood. He hadn't been happy about admitting it either. Arguing about it, however, would get him nowhere.

138

"Listen, I wanted to ask you to have dinner with me one night soon. I'm going to ask Emily, too. I want you both to meet someone."

Chris's eyes narrowed. "I heard you were seeing Madison Shay. Is that who you want me to meet?"

"It is." Tanner nodded. "Will you do it?"

He held his breath as his son seemed to consider the offer. "I guess. I haven't seen Emily in awhile."

Tanner ignored the barely concealed barb from his only son. "Good. I'll get with you and we can decide on a day and time. Thanks."

Chris turned his back and headed down the sidewalk without another word. Tanner was still standing there, his heart aching for his boy, when his phone rang.

"Tanner."

"Vegas, huh? Did you do anything you're ashamed of?" Logan's voice was full of amusement.

Tanner sighed and started to walk back to his truck. "How did you know I was in Vegas this weekend?"

"I must have seen it on Facebook."

"I don't have a Facebook account, asshole."

"Twitter then?"

"Try again."

Logan laughed. "I talked to your Deputy Sam on Saturday. Listen, can you meet at the roadhouse tomorrow? Nine in the morning. Marshal Davis wants to talk to us and go over the assignment and get a plan together."

"I'll be there. We're finally going to hear the details? It must be close then."

"I think so. Within a week or so."

Tanner made a decision then and there. "I got some information about Fenton from that DEA agent."

"None of it good from the sound of your voice."

"It's not. Do you have a minute? I need to talk to someone about this." Tanner swung into his vehicle and started the engine, cranking the heat full blast.

"I'm on duty but nothing is happening. Shoot." Tanner could picture Logan in his office, his feet propped up on his desk, lounging back in his chair.

"I need to get my family away from Fenton," Tanner began, filling Logan in on everything. If Tanner had to, he'd get all the guys together and they could brainstorm ways to keep everyone safe. With or without Fenton, their towns were in the middle of a deadly drug war.

* * * *

Tanner kissed her lips lightly before sitting down at the table. Madison hadn't stopped smiling since they returned from Las Vegas the day before. Being with Tanner made her happy. He seemed to feel likewise, although he'd had a moment of dark clouds right as they were boarding their plane. It had quickly dissipated and he'd been acting normally since.

"I'm sorry I'm late. I had to talk to Chris after the meeting. Have you been waiting long?" Tanner asked.

She shook her head. "Just long enough to get settled and get a hot cup of cocoa. It's freezing out there today." Madison shivered, even in the warm restaurant. It had been cold in Chicago, but she'd spent most of her time in the hospital so it rarely mattered. Here in Springwood she had more of a personal life. Not that it was easy having one when it was around zero degrees with a couple of feet of snow on the ground.

The waitress came to take Tanner's drink order and then bustled away. "You look tired, Maddie. Hard day?"

She smiled remembering the long list of patients she'd seen. "More like long day. I saw my last patient less than an hour ago. Tina Sands brought her eleven year old in today. He'd broken his arm playing King of the Mountain on a fifteen-foot snowbank. Up until then I was running on time. After that, I was late all day."

Tanner thanked the waitress for his coffee. "That's right. School was out today for some teacher thing. I take it he took a tumble down that snowbank? Hell, I remember doing the same thing when I was his age. Lucky I ever made it to twelve."

"I'm very glad you did. That reminds me, Sheriff. What are we going to do for your birthday?"

Since finding out his birthday was this week, she'd been trying to think of a present or something special they could do. The problem was he seemed to be a man who had everything. Or at least everything he needed. She couldn't even think of something he didn't need but would like to have, other than to have a better relationship with his son. She wasn't sure she could do anything there, and she wasn't one to stick her nose where it didn't belong. If he wanted her help with it, he'd ask. Until then, she planned to butt out.

Tanner winced. "Ignore it and maybe it will go away? Honey, I'm going to be forty-five. I outgrew balloons and ponies a long time ago. Maybe we can just have a nice dinner or something." His smile grew. "I can think of a few 'or somethings' we can do. If you're game."

Madison pretended to pout. "You have to have cake. And ice cream. If not for yourself, think of others. Like me, for instance."

"How about if I eat the cake off of you?"

That sounded like a good idea. Maybe they could get some dessert to go from the restaurant tonight. If something was worth doing, it was worth doing more than once. Right?

"I can see you have a one track mind tonight." She didn't mind. She liked the fact that he wanted her all the time. She sure as hell wanted him.

Tanner laughed, the sound rich and deep. "I guess I do. I promise to behave." He leaned forward. "How about I call a few friends of mine and we can all go out to dinner and maybe some dancing on Friday night? Will that ease your guilty conscious about my birthday?"

"Sort of. It sounds fun and I'd like to meet some of your friends. You've met most of mine." She picked up her menu. "Do we have to wait for Friday to do the cake thing?"

"Aw, honey. We can do it after dinner." Tanner was grinning. "Your place or mine?"

"Yours. My dad doesn't leave for Seattle until tomorrow." The waitress appeared at their table to take their order. Tanner ordered the rib eye medium with a baked potato. Madison ordered the trout with a side of grilled vegetables.

"Always so healthy. I admire your restraint. This place has the best steak in town." Tanner sipped his coffee. "I assure you my cholesterol is under control. I promise. How long will your dad be in Seattle?"

Madison played with the handle of her cup. "About that. Dad told me yesterday he's met a woman in Seattle. He's in love."

Tanner's smile was immediately wiped away. "Is that good or bad?"

"It's good. I'm happy for him. Really," she assured Tanner. "I'm just going to miss him. He's decided to move to Seattle. She has a business there she can't leave."

"Didn't your dad ask you to come back to Montana?" Tanner was looking less happy by the minute.

"He did. He feels badly that he had me move back and now he's leaving. He and I have been talking about this forever so I understand he couldn't predict how he was going to feel about someone."

There was a long stretch of silence before Tanner spoke. "I'll just ask this straight out. Are you planning to go back to Chicago, Maddie?"

Two salads slid in front of them, and the waitress offered fresh ground black pepper, which they both declined. Madison picked up her fork and dug into the fresh greens.

142

"No."

Barely glancing down at the plate, Tanner sat back as if to take in her answer. "No? That was very simple and straightforward. Was the decision difficult?"

Madison finished chewing and swallowed. "No." Did she look like she was ready to bolt? She'd never been happier in her life.

Irritation flashed across his features. "Dammit, Maddie. You're being kind of cruel here."

Madison frowned. "How am I being cruel? I answered your direct question with a direct answer. What more do you want me to say? Do you want me to say you're the reason I'm staying?"

He opened his mouth then shut it just as quickly. It was clear from the sheepish look on his face that was exactly what he'd wanted her to say. She felt a rush of emotion and something akin to relief. She wasn't out on this limb all by herself. He was traversing it right along with her.

"I was just wondering the reasons," he finally answered. "You must have had friends in Chicago. A life that you enjoyed."

She shook her head. "Not much of one actually. I worked. All the time. Seventy or eighty hours a week. And don't get me wrong. I loved it. I had a few friends but rarely went out. My friends were other doctors and they worked the same crazy schedules. When I wasn't working, I was tired." She placed her fork on the plate. "I admit I wasn't sure about coming back to Springwood. I had some pretty crappy memories of how other kids treated me. But since I've been back, well, I've realized that people can change and grow. I've made new friends and reconnected with others. I don't want to leave. This is home. And yes, part of the reason this feels like home is you. I'm happy. You make me happy, Tanner."

His expression softened. "You make me happy, too, Maddie. Happier than I've been in years, if I were honest. I'm not sure what you see in this old lawman but whatever it is, I'm grateful."

She swallowed the lump that had formed in her throat. "I don't think you're old. I think you're wonderful."

Tanner shook his head and picked up his fork. "This is what's so great about you. You simply say what you feel. No beating around the bush. No head games. Just straight up truth."

Madison felt a twinge of guilt. She hadn't told him the whole truth about starting to fall in love with him.

"I think we're both past playing games," was all she said. "Now tell me about these friends we're going to have dinner with on Friday."

"Wait until you meet Seth and Presley." Tanner laughed. "Presley runs circles around Seth, and all he can do is sit back and enjoy the show. I'd like to invite Logan as well."

Tanner described his friends over dinner and Madison breathed a sigh of relief at just how close she had been to revealing her feelings for this man. She wasn't quite ready yet. There was still that niggling corner of her heart holding back. It was the same part of her that still felt like that tall, gangly kid with braces and glasses.

She really needed to get that girl under control. She was starting to be a real pain in the butt.

Chapter Fifteen

Tanner filled his travel mug, yawning and stretching despite a shower and a fresh uniform. After dinner last night, he'd convinced Maddie to come back to his place and share the dessert they'd ordered to go. He'd ended up licking that chocolate cake off her belly and breasts, which had led to even more pleasant pursuits for a few more hours. He made a mental note to toss those chocolate covered sheets into the washer.

He had been unable to persuade her to join him in the shower. Instead she'd headed out before the sun was up like a guilty teenager sneaking home past curfew. Maybe he could talk to her about moving in with him.

Consequently he was ass-dragging today. Getting old was hell. He remembered a time when he'd drink and party until three in the morning and get up at sunrise the same day back to work.

He waited for the fear and trepidation to settle in his gut but they didn't come. Being with Maddie was good and right. He was grown up enough to know what he wanted and that was Maddie. In his bed, in his life, and in his heart. It was that simple.

When she'd told him her father was moving to Seattle last night, for a moment he hadn't been able to breathe. He'd been paralyzed with fear she would leave Springwood. He'd just found her, but there was no way he could let her go. He'd been about to declare he would move to Chicago when she'd calmly and succinctly told him she wasn't leaving. So damn matter-of-fact. But that was his Maddie and he wouldn't have her any other way.

He twisted the lid on the mug, shoved his keys in his pocket and looked for his hat. Maddie had sent it flying last night as they'd left a trail of clothes all the way to the bedroom. For someone who didn't have much experience, she was adventurous now that she was comfortable with him. She'd also been the recipient of a stinging spanking that had turned her curvy bottom a pretty pink. After that, he'd only had to touch her and she'd exploded.

He found his hat tossed behind the couch and his coat on the chair. Shrugging into the warm fleece, he pulled open the door and stopped in his tracks. Chris's beat up old truck was pulling into his driveway. Either Chris hadn't gotten drunk last night or he'd never gone to bed after the bars closed. Peering closely at his son as he made his way out of the vehicle and up the driveway, Tanner decided that thankfully it was the former, although Chris didn't look too damn happy about being sober. In fact, he looked downright miserable.

"Son? Is everything okay?" He doubted Chris would talk honestly with him, but Tanner would never give up on having a relationship with his progeny.

Chris stopped on the front porch, misery written in every line. "Stacey filed for divorce." His voice was choked, and he pulled a thick set of papers from his pocket, shoving them at Tanner. "She's done. She said she can't take anymore."

A sinking feeling in his stomach, he opened the door wider. "I'm sorry, Chris. You better come in out of the cold."

"I've fucked everything up, Dad. I don't know what to do." His son's voice was filled with anguish and every parental instinct inside of Tanner reared up, wrapping a tight band around his heart. He'd bear this pain if only his son didn't have to go through it. He'd tried so hard to protect his children from the world, but every parent finds out that same thing. For the most part, they're powerless.

"Come in. We'll have some coffee and we'll figure out what to do."

This time Chris came inside, his shoulders hunched, his head hung down. He followed Tanner into the kitchen and sat at the table, defeated. This wasn't the same young man Tanner had raised. Chris had been a star football player, popular in school, just as Tanner had been. Perhaps Chris was too much like Tanner. Chris had become rudderless after high school. Hesitant to join the military with so much going on in the Middle East, he had wandered from job to job, eventually getting Stacey pregnant. Tanner had hoped marrying Stacey would help, but the partying and drinking had only gotten worse.

He poured two cups of coffee and sat down at the table with Chris waiting for him to speak.

"You probably think I deserve this. That I'm a lousy husband and father." Chris didn't look at him when he spoke, simply picking up his coffee cup.

"Chris, you're a grown man. It no longer matters what I think. It only matters what you think."

Chris finally looked up, his chin trembling. "I think I fucked up. I don't want to lose Stacey and Annie. I love them." He looked away for a moment and then back. "Did you ever get scared you might lose us?"

Fathers were supposed to be pillars of strength for their children. How could Tanner even begin to explain the fear that had plagued him the lion's share of his life? The fear of never being good enough. It was that fear that drove him to be a star quarterback, a star soldier, a star deputy. It was only when he faced that fear he'd been able to stop drinking.

He didn't worry about being good enough anymore. Whatever he was, it would have to be good enough for the people around him. That was what was so special about Maddie. She never left him in any doubt he was enough for her.

"I did lose you, Chris. Every time you turned away with scorn, disgust, and even hate, I died a little inside. The pain of losing your respect will never go away. I'm sorry I failed you, son."

It was hard to get the last words out through the lump in his throat. He would probably never get another chance to talk to Chris this openly. He wouldn't waste it.

To Tanner's surprise, Chris's eyes were bright with tears. "I don't hate you. I'm mad at you."

A shudder of relief ran through Tanner. "Well, that's a start. What are you mad about?"

A few tears spilled over. "You didn't love us enough to stop drinking. By the time you did, it seemed like you didn't do it for us. You did it for you."

He put his hands on his son's shoulders, shaking him a little. He'd stopped drinking for a myriad of reasons, and yes, one of them was for himself. But his family had always been uppermost in his mind.

"My drinking never had anything to do with how much I loved you. I'd give my life for you, Chris."

He shrugged. "Sure, now that you're sober."

"Then," Tanner insisted. "You're still drinking. Think you'll love Annie more when you don't? Alcoholism doesn't have anything to do with how much I loved you, Chris. It had to do with my own demons."

Chris's gaze met Tanner's. "How do I get rid of my demons? Why do I drink to feel better, but then I only feel better for awhile? Then I drink again. Fuck, I don't want to do this anymore. I need help. I need Stacey and Annie back."

"You have to show them you're serious about getting sober. Can you do that, son?"

Tanner held his breath, his heart beating fast. More than anything, he wanted to heal the wounds Chris kept inflicting on himself and make him a happy person again. Tanner needed his children to lead a life with joy. There would be hurt and disappointment. He couldn't protect them from everything, but he could help get them on the right road.

Chris nodded. "I want to. More than anything. I don't want to live like this."

I don't want to live like this.

Tanner remembered those very same words coming out of his own mouth ten years ago. He swallowed hard and gave Chris's shoulder a squeeze.

"First we'll get you a sponsor in AA. Someone to help you. Then we'll drive over to Stacey's parents and talk to her about what you're doing to put your life together. Speak from the heart and she'll know you're sincere."

148

Chris shook his head. "She's not there. I called her cell. She's in Arizona with Grandma and Grandpa."

While Stacey had not gotten along with Abbey, Tanner's parents were another story. They loved Stacey like their own granddaughter and Annie was their treasure. It was no surprise Stacey had gone to them when the going got tough.

Suddenly he remembered a conversation with his father about a drug and alcohol rehabilitation center near their winter home. They'd even discussed sending Chris there to dry out. Tanner took a deep breath, hesitant to bring it up, but knowing it would accomplish two goals.

One, Chris would be getting the help he needed.

Two, he would be out of Springwood and Fenton's influence.

"You know, your grandpa mentioned they have a day program at a nearby rehab center. Would you consider going down there, staying with your grandparents, and attending the program?"

"I can't," Chris replied, shaking his head. "I can't lose another job. Besides, those programs cost money. I sure as hell don't have any."

Tanner scraped a hand down his face. "I'll pay for it. As for your job, honestly, I don't like you working for Fenton. When you were a kid, you said you wanted to be a deputy. Were you just kidding or is that something you still want? I have an opening and if you get straight and sober, I'll give you a chance."

Tanner wasn't made of money, but if he had to work an extra year before he retired it would be completely worth it. Fuck, he'd work until he dropped for his children.

Chris's eyes widened. "You mean it? Really, Dad? I never thought you'd give me a chance."

"If you don't want to work for me, and I could understand why you wouldn't," Tanner replied, "I can talk to some of my sheriff friends in nearby towns. They might be able to hire you. Keeping a good deputy is tough."

"I'll work hard, Dad. I promise." For the first time in a long while Tanner saw hope in his son's expression.

"First thing, I'll call your grandpa. Then you can talk to Stacey. Tell her what we've talked about and see if she's open to you coming down there for a month or two."

"That long? What about everything here?"

"What's here that's more important than your family and your health?"

Chris straightened up. "Nothing, I guess, when you say it like that. It just seems too easy."

"It won't be." Tanner shook his head. "It will be the hardest thing you've ever done, getting sober and building back the trust you've lost with Stacey. It will be work and it will take time. It won't happen in a few weeks or even a few months."

"What if I drink again?" Chris's lips were turned down and he looked so much like the little boy Tanner remembered.

"You might. But you are in charge, Chris. If you drink again, then you start your sobriety all over. And you keep doing that until one day you get ready for bed and realize you didn't crave a drink that day. Those are the good days. The bad days are going to be hell. But if you slip, you just get back on that horse. Just like when you were a kid and you would fall off of Lightning."

His son smiled. "I never fell off of Lightning. That was the meanest damn horse that ever lived. He would throw us off and then laugh about it."

Tanner laughed. "He was an ornery thing. He did seem to take too much pleasure when anyone flew over his head. But the point is you didn't let him win, did you? You got right back up on him and rode him."

"Do you ever want to drink, Dad? Do you still think about it after all this time?"

Tanner knew what Chris wanted to hear, but lying wasn't something Tanner did with a clear conscience.

150

"Every now and then when life seems to be tough, I think about taking a drink." He exhaled slowly, wanting to make sure he said this just right. "But then I remember what alcohol did to my life and how much better it is now. I don't even like the smell of booze anymore. It makes me physically ill. I doubt I could even keep a drink down after all these years. In my mind I've associated it with everything bad in my life. So the answer is every now and then. But as time passes it's less and less. Shit, it was probably over a year ago the last time I thought about it, and then only for a minute. I want to live more than I want to drink."

Chris nodded, apparently accepting Tanner's answer. "What do I do now?"

He reached for the phone in his pocket. "Let's call your grandparents. Make arrangements for you. Then you can call your mom and let her know you're going to Arizona."

Chris was clearly relieved, the color coming back into his skin. "Thank you, Dad."

"You're welcome, son." Tanner choked out the words, the love he felt squeezing his heart. His own father had told him but it was really brought home at this moment. You never stop being a parent no matter how old your children are.

Tanner dialed his parents and felt a sprout of happiness inside him start to grow. Emily was in Billings, Chris would be going to Arizona. Now the only issue was Abby.

How would he get Abby away from Fenton?

* * * *

Madison bustled into the coffee shop and hurried toward the table where Sherry was waiting. She and Madison were going to catch up since they hadn't seen each other since Sunday before their flights. Madison's father was taking the patients this morning since he was leaving for Seattle in the afternoon.

Madison shrugged off her coat, draping it over an empty chair. "I just need to order my coffee."

"I already did." Sherry pointed to a large steaming cup that was wafting a heavenly aroma. "I'm way ahead of you. As usual."

Madison laughed and sat down, stuffing her gloves and scarf into her coat pockets. "Can't disagree with you there. I'm always trying to catch up with everything that needs to be done. No rest for the weary."

Sherry cocked her head to the side and gave Madison a mischievous grin. "A great sex life will play havoc with your rest."

Madison didn't even try to pretend. Instead she nodded solemnly. "You're right. Totally worth it."

Sherry cracked up laughing. "I want to hear every dirty detail, especially any extra special sinning you may have done in Sin City."

Madison snorted. "You were the one on your honeymoon."

Sherry waggled her eyebrows. "Yes, we were. And can I say that Dan was *up* to the task, so to speak? I never knew what a freak my husband was. He'd always been good before, but he was positively inspired in Vegas." She leaned forward, her eyes sparkling. "I loved it. Married sex will never get boring, that's for sure. We'll be swinging from the chandelier when we're eighty."

A picture of a scantily clad Sherry and Dan hanging off a crystal chandelier flashed through Madison's mind. She scrubbed at it with some mental bleach, determined not to dwell on such disturbing images.

"The really big news is my dad is in love and is moving to Seattle."

Sherry's mouth fell open. "Zowie, I didn't see that coming. I don't think I've ever even seen your father go out on a date. Are you okay with this?"

"I want him to be happy." Madison sipped her hot coffee. "He's sacrificed so much for me, especially after Mom died. He deserves this. I will miss him, though. It's been strange and nice at the same time to live under the same roof again."

"You could always Skype and stuff." Sherry's eyes went wide. "Unless you're thinking of moving back to Chicago. Say no. Say no," she begged.

"No," Madison said firmly. "I'm not entertaining any such thought. I'm glad I came home. It's really made me realize how cold and sterile my life was there. I'm not going anywhere." Madison paused. "Tanner was worried I was planning to leave, too."

"Of course, he was," Sherry exclaimed. "He's in love with you."

Madison shook her head but her insides quaked. She wanted Tanner to be in love with her, but it scared her, too. Being with him was changing her whole life– it was changing her. She liked this new, more confident person but she was out of her comfort zone.

"He's never said he's in love with me."

"Please," Sherry scoffed. "I saw the way he looked at you in Las Vegas. He worships you. A man like Tanner Marks isn't going to go on and on about his feelings. He's going to show you."

Remembering the sensual foray of his tongue across her flesh as he'd licked off the chocolate made her flush with heat. He'd shown her a thing or two that night. Could he have made love to her that way but not feel anything? Madison didn't know enough about men to be able to answer that question.

"I have no complaints about how he treats me. He's caring and respectful."

"Geez, he's caring and respectful with everyone, Madison. When a man is in love, especially at the beginning, they're proud of their woman. They want to show her off and tell the world what they have. Tanner had his arm around you like you were solid gold."

"I'm not sure how I feel about being his trophy," Madison replied.

"I didn't say trophy." Sherry wagged a finger at her. "I said gold. Something precious. That's a pretty good sign."

Madison sighed. "Let's face it. I've never been good at reading a man's signs. He may have to rent a billboard for me to get it."

153

"I can suggest it, if you like." Sherry's eyes lit up, her mouth curved in an evil grin.

"Don't. You. Dare. I mean it. I'll deal with this on my own. Maybe I'll just tell him I've fallen in love and see what he says."

"No! You can't do that." Sherry smacked her forehead. "You have to let him be the one. If you say it first, you're handing over all the power in the relationship."

Exasperated, Madison drank the last of her coffee. Love had too many damn rules. She'd never learn them all. "And power is important?"

"Of course it's important. He needs to feel like he's won your love. You can't just hand it over like it's nothing."

"Fine. I won't say anything." Madison pushed away the empty cup. "Is it okay to invite him over for dinner tonight or will that be seen as needy or pushy?"

"The more regularly he sees you the better. Then he won't like when you're not there. Yes, invite him." Sherry's smile died. "Um, you're not planning to cook are you?"

"I'm not planning to poison him," Madison retorted. "My cooking skills have really improved."

"I'm sure they have." Sherry patted Madison's hand. "But…well, don't you want to put your best foot forward? You don't want Tanner to see any weaknesses this early, do you?"

She was pretty sure Tanner had already seen some but she didn't want to upset Sherry by saying so. "I can grill a couple of steaks. How bad can that be?"

Sherry wrinkled her nose. "Remember when you fixed dinner for your dad and the meat was charred on the outside and frozen in the middle?"

That hadn't been one of Madison's finest moments, but she'd been sixteen at the time.

"I know to defrost now. It'll be fine."

154

"Or the time you cooked a turkey on Thanksgiving and didn't take out all the giblets and stuff inside of it first?"

"That was a mistake anyone could have made," Madison protested. "The labeling on the turkey is deceptive."

Sherry started to dig in her handbag. "I think I might have a pizza coupon in here."

"Your confidence in me is overwhelming. With friends like you..."

Sherry held out a piece of paper triumphantly. "Here it is. Take it. You know, just in case."

Madison plucked it from her best friend's fingers and stuck out her tongue. "Fine, but I won't need it. You're worrying for nothing."

A couple of steaks and a salad. She had this completely under control.

Chapter Sixteen

"Thanks for coming. I really appreciate you doing this on short notice." Marshal Evan Davis stood at the front of the group, all meeting at the roadhouse.

Tanner had made it with minutes to spare after his morning with Chris, who was currently being driven to the Billings airport by Deputy Sam. Tanner had wanted to take his son to the airport, but he was already committed to being here for this meeting.

He'd been about to call Logan and tell him when Chris had shaken his head and told him it would be easier if someone else drove him. No long goodbyes, no emotional crap. He was, after all, heading into a delicate situation with Stacey and his addiction treatment. A no-pressure drive with Sam would give Chris time to clear his head.

Tanner had reluctantly agreed, and Sam assured him he'd make sure Chris got to the plane on time and sober. Chris, for his part, would be texting Tanner when he landed in Arizona. Tanner's dad would be picking Chris up at the airport.

"Are we finally going to hear about this super secret assignment?" Logan grinned.

"You are." The Marshal smiled and pulled a stack of papers from his briefcase. "I'll hand these out, but I'll be taking them back at the end of our meeting. I can't have any of these floating around. Not that I don't trust you. I do. That's why I asked for your assistance."

Stapled packets were handed down to each man. Tanner flipped through his quickly, noticing all the men were doing the same. Evan seemed content for them to peruse the papers for the moment as he'd paused his presentation.

Griffin Sawyer, the quietest of the group, opened to the last page. A map of Montana, Wyoming, and Colorado. "Can we assume this is a prisoner transport to Florence?"

Evan nodded. "It is. I figured you would know what was up even before I told you. I'll just preface all remarks by saying everything today is confidential. You aren't to tell anyone. Not your mother, brother, or..." Evan looked directly at Seth, "...your wife. No matter how beguiling she may be. If this has any chance at all of working, absolute secrecy is a must."

Seth raised his eyebrows. "I get what you're saying. So say it."

"I will. A high-ranking member of the Jackson drug cartel has been captured in Canada after breaking out of prison. He snuck onto a vendor's truck and rode right out of there. He's been sitting in jail awaiting extradition to the States. It's been months of paperwork, but we finally have clearance to bring him back to this country."

Reed stroked his chin. "He went to Canada? Why not the Caymans? Or Central America?"

"He had a girlfriend there. And for awhile it worked. He blended in like he was just another ordinary guy."

Logan grinned. "Let me guess. It was his girlfriend who turned him in? A woman scorned and all that shit."

Evan chuckled. "Bingo. Apparently this guy, Howard Kerr, was doing the neighbor and the girlfriend found out. She didn't get mad. She got even. She called the authorities and he was arrested shortly thereafter."

Jared laughed. "And that, gentlemen, is why I'm still single. Women are crazy."

Seth's expression softened. "They're not all crazy. You have to find the right one."

"That is not so easy to do," replied Tanner. "If you find a good one, hold on."

"I intend to. Go on, Evan," Seth urged.

"Kerr is now at a prison near the border of Canada. On Saturday, Canadian officials will release him into our custody. Our mission, should you accept it, is to escort him down to Florence where he will be kept in a supermax environment. We won't make the same mistake with him twice."

Tanner paged through the booklet, scanning the dossier on Kerr. Mid-thirties, non-descript, which probably was to his advantage when he was hiding out. He was a high-level moneyman for the cartel, which didn't exactly scream violent felon. The guy looked like an accountant or maybe an actuarial.

"Do you think he'll try to bust out in transit?" Tanner asked.

"No. We think the Jackson cartel will try and bust him out. As best as we can tell, Kerr knows the whereabouts of laundered drug money."

Reed slowly smiled. "And only he knows the location. Nice life insurance policy."

"He's smart. You got to give him that," Logan said. He looked up at Evan. "How smart is he? Or the better question is, how smart is the cartel?"

"Smart isn't the question." Tanner shook his head. "How deadly is the question. We're dealing with the Warner cartel trying to take over a drug route and the body count keeps going up."

Evan's head swiveled to Tanner. "Warner? Are you sure?"

Tanner nodded. "We're working with the DEA." He exhaled slowly. The story was going to come out sooner or later, so it might as well be now. "I've already told Logan this, but since this meeting is confidential, I'll tell all of you. I had a conversation with DEA Agent Anderson on Sunday. You know that Fenton guy who's marrying my ex-wife?"

Tanner quickly recounted the tale. By the time he was done, there were several jaws hanging. Including Evan Davis's. Evan slapped the papers on the desk.

"Fuck. This is not good. The Warner cartel is in direct competition with the Jackson cartel. They rule that drug route. If Warner wants it, driving a Jackson member right through that territory could be deadly."

"Then we'll fly him," Seth suggested.

Evan shook his head. "They expect us to fly him. They'll be waiting at the airport. The reason I chose driving is that it would be a surprise."

Tanner tapped his fingers on the table. "We simply have to be smarter than they are. We can make them think we flew the guy. Then confuse them if they figure out we've driven him."

Evan pursed his lips. "I was planning multiple vehicles anyway, but I could get a decoy transport to the airport. Also have a decoy team waiting on the airfield near Florence."

Jared nodded. "We could have vehicles taking different routes so even if they find us, they'll have to split up to follow all of us. It shrinks their numbers and helps us keep the advantage."

"I was planning on at least one other decoy vehicle but we may need to think bigger. We need to diagram it all out. Step by step. Every move. I don't want to leave anything to chance," Evan replied.

Seth stood up and grabbed an armful of soda cans from the bar. Only water and soda could be served when the roadhouse was closed.

"Here. We may be here for awhile." Seth handed out the cans to each of the lawmen. Tanner popped the top on his root beer.

"Is it just us or will there be other marshals?" Griffin asked.

"I can get as many men as we think we need," answered Evan. "This is an important assignment, which is why I was able to bring all of you in."

Tanner leaned forward, his arms resting on the table. "So no one knows this is happening? What about Kerr himself?"

Evan shook his head. "He has no idea when or where."

Reed tapped his chin. "If anyone was going to break him out while in transit, he would be watching the prison then. Maybe someone inside as well."

Evan sighed. "That's my fear. We've done everything we can to keep this a secret, but one person could blow it all sky high. Make no mistake. This will be dangerous. I'll understand if anyone wants to back out now that they know what they would be signing up for."

The men at the table all grinned and chuckled. Logan took a long drink of his soda. "Shit, Evan. This is what a lawman lives for. Most of us spend our days chasing cattle thieves and wife beaters. Pushing paper and filling out forms. I, for one, wouldn't miss this for the world."

Tanner nodded along with his friends. He could feel the adrenaline pumping and his excitement sharpen. There was nothing like facing danger to make you feel vibrantly alive.

Evan slapped another stack of papers onto the table. "Then let's get to work. I'll go through what I had originally planned and we can make changes wherever needed."

* * * *

Madison had just slid the broiler pan into the oven when Tanner knocked on her front door. One look at his face and she knew he'd had a hard day. His shoulders drooped a little as he walked into the living room, and she helped him off with his coat and hat, placing the latter on top of the table in the foyer.

She put her hands on her hips and looked him up and down. "Do you want to talk about it?"

Tanner smiled. "As a matter of fact, I do. Is your dad here?"

"Nope. He left for the airport right after lunch."

"Good. Then I can do this." Tanner pulled her into his arms and pressed her against his hard, warm body. She didn't resist, instead melting into him, her face tucked into his shoulder. She breathed his clean, male scent and felt her entire body relax. She never felt more safe than when she was with this man.

She lifted her face and he didn't need any more encouragement. Their kiss was like their relationship. Hot, sensual, yet comfortable at the same time. It wasn't their first time. They knew each other's sensitive spots and they explored them, delighted when a new one was found and cataloged for the next time.

160

When they broke apart, her face was hot and her breath ragged. "You are way too good at that, cowboy."

He touched her lips with his briefly once more. "Thank you kindly, ma'am. I aim to please. Coming home to your arms after a long day is just what the doctor ordered."

She giggled and snuggled deeper into his embrace. "Why don't you tell me about your day? You look tired."

"I am tired. It's been a helluva day, Maddie." He sighed and loosened his hold, taking a step back. "Why don't we sit down? I've got a lot to tell, actually."

She made a move toward the kitchen. "Can I get you something to drink? Dinner's in the oven so we have a few minutes."

"Not right now." He pulled her to the couch and they sat down. She waited for him to collect his thoughts. "You know that I had a drinking problem, and I think you know my son Chris also has one."

She nodded. She'd heard that from Sherry, and Tanner had mentioned the tension between father and son. "Is Chris okay? Has something happened?"

Tanner leaned forward and rested his elbows on his knees. "Chris came to see me this morning. Stacey served him with divorce papers. He was devastated."

After what Sherry had told Madison she wasn't surprised, but she was sad. They had a small child that would be caught in the middle.

"I'm so sorry." She put her hand on Tanner's. "But it's good you were there for him."

"For the first time, Chris was open to getting treatment. His plane should be touching down in Arizona any time now. He's going to stay with my parents and go into a day treatment program."

"That's wonderful." Madison knew there was more. If everything looked positive, Tanner wouldn't be this exhausted. "Or is it?"

He leaned back on the couch and wrapped an arm around her shoulders. "It is. You see, Stacey and Annie went to stay with my parents."

"Is she okay with Chris coming down there?"

"Once we talked to her and told her Chris was coming for treatment, she was very happy. They love each other. If my son can get sober, I think they have a real chance of making their marriage work."

"That's the good news. What's the bad news?"

The corners of Tanner's mouth tipped up. "How do you know I have bad news as well?"

"Because you wouldn't look like you've been rode hard and put up wet if the only thing you had to tell me was about Chris."

"Smart lady. There is more, actually. I'll start with Saturday. I'm leaving early on Saturday morning after my birthday celebration. Me and some law enforcement buddies are helping a Federal Marshal with a little job. I'll probably be gone until sometime Sunday."

"A little job? Is that code for 'If I told you, I'd have to kill you'?"

"Kind of. Suffice it to say I'll be on the road most of Saturday night heading to Colorado. Once we make it to our destination they'll fly us back."

"I didn't know that local law enforcement worked with the federal government like this."

"Evan Davis is a Federal Marshal which means he can deputize local law or even a private citizen."

"You mean I could become a deputy?" Madison laughed. "That would be cool. I could arrest somebody."

"You might want to start with your friend, Sherry. She's got a lead foot. She races up and down Maple like it's her own private speedway while talking on her cell."

"Sherry would tell you she's completely in control."

"Maybe we should invite Sherry and Dan to dinner, then afterward have a private showing of *Blood on the Highway*?"

162

Madison made a face. "She and I both saw it in high school. Grisly movie. Sherry puked in a trash can, if I remember correctly."

"What about you?" Tanner pressed a kiss to her temple. "Did it bother the future doctor?"

Madison shrugged. "Not really. I have a cast iron stomach."

Tanner sniffed the air. "Speaking of cast iron stomach...honey, is something burning?"

Oh shit. The steaks.

Chapter Seventeen

Tanner dumped the charred meat into the trashcan, trying hard not to burst into laughter.

"I wanted to cook you dinner," Madison sniffed.

"I like my steak medium." Madison's chin began to wobble. He pulled her into his arms and stroked her hair. "Hey, it was my fault. I knew you'd put the steaks on but I didn't pay attention and kept talking until they were burnt."

She looked up at him, clearly not buying his argument. "It was my job to watch the steaks, not yours." She chewed on her bottom lip. "I think you should know this is not the first meal I've cooked that's ended up in the trash."

Tanner quirked an eyebrow, happy to see her expression clear. "How many have there been?"

Madison sighed. "Too many to count. I'm a terrible cook," she pronounced, as if daring him to say something about it.

He wasn't that stupid.

"Honey, I'll just check the refrigerator. Maybe I can whip us up some scrambled eggs or something."

She shook her head. "No need. Sherry gave me a pizza coupon today when I told her I was going to fix you dinner. I'll give them a call now. What do you want on your pizza?"

This time he couldn't hold back the laughter. "Sherry gave you a coupon?"

"She did. And I'll thank you not to tell her what happened here tonight."

"Honey, your secret is safe with me. And I'm not picky about my pizza. Whatever you want, I'll eat."

Within minutes the pizza was ordered and they both had glasses of iced tea. There was still one more thing he needed to tell her. He simply could not keep this secret from her, and in truth he wanted her advice. They settled in front of the fire while they waited for their dinner to be delivered.

"There is more to tell you," he said.

"You've had a busy day, apparently." Madison stretched out next to him and rested her head on his shoulder. "I'm listening."

"First, I'd prefer if you didn't mention this to Sherry, or anyone. I'd like to keep this quiet."

"Okay. I'm a doctor, Tanner, I can keep a secret."

"Yes, I bet you can. That's why I'm mentioning this. This needs to stay confidential. But I don't like keeping secrets from you." Tanner shifted restlessly. He was threading the needle here, but the need to protect those he loved was strong. "What if the DEA is in the middle of an investigation in this area? What if two rival drug cartels are fighting over a drug route to Canada?"

Madison sat up, her brows knitted. "I'd say that would be dangerous. For everyone in Springwood."

She was quick and smart. "If such a thing were to happen, hypothetically speaking, the DEA might be looking at people who came to town right before all the violence broke out six months ago."

She looked confused for a moment, and then her expression cleared. "There is such a person."

"Hypothetically there is. If they were looking at this person, it would probably mean he or she has a potential to be dangerous."

She nodded. "That's why you sent Chris to Arizona."

"I would have sent him either way, but it was great timing."

"What about Emily and Abby?"

"Emily will be in Billings for the time being. Abby is another story."

Madison was quiet for a long moment. "What are you going to do?"

That was the million-dollar question.

"I don't know. The one thing I do know is that you need to be careful. Be cautious as to who you spend your time with and try not to be alone when you go places."

He knew that would frustrate her. She made a face and pulled her knees in, wrapping her arms around them. "I'm not sure I like this pretend situation."

"I don't like it much myself, but if anything happened to you, I'd like it even less. Can you do that for me, Maddie? Will you be careful?"

"I will," she agreed. "I'm not too concerned for myself. You're the law in this town. I'm worried about you."

"Don't. Hypothetically speaking, no one knows I'm aware of any investigations that might or might not be ongoing."

Madison sighed. "Will you let me know when this hypothetical situation is over?"

The doorbell sounded before he could answer. Madison hopped up but he held her back, going to the door himself. He paid for the pizza and led her into the kitchen.

"I'm not trying to scare you. I just want you to be on your guard, that's all. You're very trusting, Maddie. I need you to be just a little less for awhile."

"I will, but I doubt you need to worry about me in the least. I'm sure I'm off anyone's radar."

"I just want you to be careful and aware."

He felt better that he'd said something to Madison. He couldn't ship her out of town as he could his children, but he needed to make sure she was safe.

She placed two plates on the table and he flipped open the box, the aroma of garlic and tomatoes making his stomach growl. He'd barely eaten today and he was starving. Within half an hour the cardboard box was empty and his stomach was full. He pushed back his plate with a sigh.

"That was good. I really needed a good meal after today."

Madison reached for their plates and popped them in the dishwasher. "I want you to let me spoil you tonight."

Tanner wasn't sure what that entailed but he was completely on board with the idea. He couldn't remember the last time someone had wanted to spoil him. If ever.

"Yes, ma'am. I'm putty in your hands."

Madison rolled her eyes. "You are far too alpha for that to ever happen." She folded the pizza box and shoved it into the large trashcan right outside the door to the garage. "Why don't you go sit by the fire? I just need to get a few things."

He didn't argue. Instead he found several cushions and stretched out in front of the warm fire. It might be March but spring came late to Montana. He was lost in the flickering orange and red flames when Madison sat next to him. Her floral scent mixed with the oak from the fire and swirled around him, making him think of all the decadent things they could do to one another. Her skin and hair would be magnificent by firelight and he reached for her, unwilling to wait another second.

"Not yet." Madison placed her hands over his. "I want to take care of you."

"I can think of a few things that would do just that."

He brushed her soft lips with his and they parted, inviting him inside. He could feel the blood pumping through his veins, roaring in his ears. The kiss was searing hot, branding his heart and soul. This woman had become everything in such a short time. He pulled away reluctantly, hesitant to break the spell but needing to be closer. He reached under her sweater but she smiled and twisted away.

"Not yet. Take off your shirt and pants and lie down."

Her tone was commanding without being overbearing. She probably used it on naughty children who wouldn't sit still for a flu shot. Unfortunately for her, he wasn't a kid anymore.

"Why would I be doing that? Are you going to get undressed, too?"

She sighed. "You're going to be difficult, aren't you? I told you I want to spoil you. Help you relax." Her hand went behind her back and brought back a heating pad, a towel, and a bottle of lotion. "I want to give you a back rub."

He literally could not remember the last time a woman had massaged his aching shoulders. It had probably been in the early days of his marriage but those memories had dimmed over the years, some by accident and some by design.

"Honey, you don't have to do that."

Why in the fuck was he arguing? He wanted to feel her hands on him, but he felt guilty. She worked as hard as he did. He should be spoiling her. After all, Madison could have any man she wanted. A beautiful doctor could do a lot better than a middle-aged sheriff, complete with his own deluxe set of personal baggage.

"I want to. Will you please?" Her lower lip was protruding in a cute little pout. He couldn't say no. He stripped off his shirt and pants and settled his torso on the towel she had laid down on the rug. He rested his head on his crossed arms and tried to relax, but just the anticipation of her hands running all over him had his pulse jumping.

He heard the lotion top flip open and then she was rubbing her hands together. She straddled his hips and leaned over him, her breath warm and soft against his neck. At the first touch of her warm palms, he had to bite back a groan. Her hands worked up and down his back, stroking and kneading the tight muscles until they were soft and pliant. He exhaled slowly, feeling any residual tension from the day drift away. Now the only tension he felt was created by Madison herself.

He was hot and hard, fighting his instincts to roll over and take control. Tanner wanted to strip the clothes from her body and have her here and now, burying himself deep inside of her.

He didn't do any of those things. Instead he allowed her to massage his aching body, her fingers working on an especially tight area around his shoulders. It was heaven and hell as her hands glided across his back. She hummed softly as she worked. A song he'd never heard of but would always now attach to this moment. He tried to concentrate on anything but the feelings she was evoking with her touch.

He closed his eyes as Madison placed the heating pad on his back and began working on his thighs. This time he did groan when her fingers brushed near his groin. He was throbbing and the pleasure was painful. He had to grit his teeth to fight his natural urges.

"You're tensing up. I can feel it." Her voice was soft in the dim light of the room.

He lifted his head slightly. "Honey, a man can only stand so much torture. I'm hot, hard, and horny. It's all I can do not to rip the clothes from your body and take you right here in front of the fire."

There was silence and then the heating pad was lifted from his back. "Okay, that sounds good."

He didn't need a second invitation. He rolled over and immediately started tugging her sweater over her head. She giggled and slapped his hands away, pulling it off herself. Her jeans, bra, and panties followed until she was sitting in front of him in nothing but her socks. Her creamy skin glowed in the firelight, beckoning to his fingers.

Tanner grinned. "You going to leave those socks on, honey?"

She gave him a shy smile despite her state of undress. "My feet are cold."

He stripped them off her feet quickly. "Let's see what I can do about that."

He placed her feet in his hands and started working on the arches and heels. She moaned and fell onto her elbows, her head thrown back, long hair in a pool on the rug. He rubbed her ankles and worked his way down to her toes before leaning down to press a kiss to each dainty instep.

"Warmer?"

"Much," she gasped. "Nobody warned me that the foot is an erogenous zone."

Tanner hadn't known himself but one look told him the tale. Her chest was rising and falling, her breath coming in pants. Her skin had turned a warm, rosy glow and her eyes were closed as if she wanted to savor every caress.

He kissed a trail up her calves, over her thighs, hips, and belly, until he was hovering over her breasts. He traced a circle around her nipple leaving it wet and shiny, and then blew on it gently, watching it pucker from the sensation. He repeated his ministrations on the opposite side. Madison's back was arched and her lips parted.

He couldn't resist and swooped in for a long kiss, taking his time and exploring his woman's mouth. He wanted to kiss and love her all night but his cock ached and the blood pounded in his veins. He needed her now. He couldn't remember wanting anyone this badly.

He trailed a hand down her body and watched her squirm at the contact. He cupped her mound and pressed a finger inside, testing her readiness. He slid in and she surrounded him, slick and hot. Her fingers clutched his shoulders, digging in as he swirled his digit around while his thumb brushed her pearl button.

She gasped and opened her eyes. "Now, Tanner. I need you now."

He loved her unashamed response. She made him feel more of a man than he'd ever dreamed. He kicked off his jockey shorts and donned a condom, his fingers clumsy with haste. He might be in a hurry to be inside her, but once he was he intended to take his time.

He hovered over her, slowing the pace despite his cock screaming for satisfaction. Luckily he was no longer a schoolboy, at the whims of his overactive libido. He was a grown man and he was in control. He stopped to look at her gorgeous body, her long red hair in disarray. Every curve and slope of her flesh called to him, enticing him to kiss or touch it.

He pressed his lips to her abdomen, dipping his tongue in her belly button. Madison's fingers curled into his hair and he heard the soft intake of her breath.

170

He positioned his cock between her thighs and put his weight on his forearms. Her long legs wrapped around his middle and he slowly, inexorably, pushed forward.

She was warm and welcoming, her pussy stretching to accommodate him. The vaginal walls hugged him tightly and he gulped for air, dragging it into his starved lungs. Every nerve ending on his cock was alive and pulsing. It felt as if they were one human being. So closely tuned, he could feel her heartbeat next to his as they marched in time.

"Open your eyes." His voice sounded like gravel on an old dirt road, but she must have understood. Her eyelids fluttered open and their gazes locked. He never looked away as he started to move in and out of her–each stroke suffused his body with pleasure. He fucked her slow and thoroughly, never hurrying his pace, until they both were frantic with need.

Her nails dug into his back and her thighs tightened on his hips. Tanner could feel her legs start to tremble and knew she was close. He pressed his forehead to hers and began to speed up his thrusts. The pressure built in his lower back and his balls tightened.

Madison was whispering his name over and over in his ear, urging him to keep going, fuck her harder. In this he was her willing slave. His eyes never leaving her, he reached between their bodies and found her swollen clit. His thumb rubbed circles around it and she closed her eyes and cried out as her climax overtook her. Her pussy clamped down on his cock, and he groaned his own release. His dick seemed to swell and jerk as he pumped his hot seed into the condom. He watched her orgasm play out, the expressions on her face changing from joy to pain, and then back to joy. Her lips were curved into a smile as she relaxed back onto the rug. The perfume of their lovemaking hung heavy in the air. The only sound was her soft breathing, synchronized to his own.

Dear God, she was beautiful. His heart ached in his chest. She was everything.

He was humbled by her sweet response and empowered at the same time. This was more than fucking. She was more than simply a woman he was falling for.

He'd fallen. He loved her.

His soul felt renewed, as if he'd taken a healing potion. He still had his baggage but suddenly it seemed a lighter burden.

Anything was possible if Madison loved him.

Chapter Eighteen

Tanner pushed open the door to the coffee shop Wednesday morning, but stopped short when he heard shouting voices. He went on alert, used to domestic disturbances in his line of work. His ears rang and a shudder ran down his spine at the din. He'd heard one of those angry voices before. Many, many times in fact.

His gaze swept the room and came to rest on Abby standing over a purple-faced Fenton, shaking her finger at him. For once, Fenton didn't look so smug. She had him backed into a chair, but he looked like he still had some fight left him in.

Tanner could attest that Abby in full-frontal attack was a sight to behold. Her face was red, her jaw clenched. Her dark hair was wild around her face and her brown eyes looked like black marbles. He remembered those eyes vividly. He'd called it her "zombie stare", although he'd never said it out loud. He'd had some sense of self-preservation.

"You asshole," Abby groused. "Can't keep it in your pants can you? I can't believe this."

Trouble in paradise. Tanner hadn't known Fenton had some action on the side, but he wasn't surprised. The guy was sleaze personified.

It appeared Fenton hadn't expected to be found out. He shook his head as if to shake off his shock, and he patted Abby on the shoulder.

Dude, you are so fucked.

"You're misunderstanding the entire situation. Sherilynn is just a friend."

"A friend you fuck? I talked to her when she called today, Fenton. She said you were her boyfriend. She said you've been seeing her for over three months. She was very surprised to hear I was your fiancée."

Abby's lips were trembling but her voice was strong. Fenton tried to hold her hand but she knocked his arm away.

"You heard wrong. It wasn't what you think. Sherilynn was joking with you," Fenton cajoled. He gave Abby his very best sincere look. To Tanner, he just looked slimy.

Her lips twisted. "I know what a joke is, and this isn't one. Don't lie to me anymore. At least man up enough to tell me the truth."

Fenton's face turned from charming to cold in an instant. "You drove me to it. Always bitching and complaining about my work. I needed a way to relax."

Apparently Fenton had decided a good offense was the best defense. He was trying to turn it all around on Abby. Tanner almost laughed at the poor bastard's efforts. He of all people should know Abby was too savvy to fall for it. She was like a bulldozer, plowing through anyone that got in her way.

"Relax!" Abby screeched. "Don't make me the bad guy here. You're the one at fault. It's over. I'm taking my stuff and going to my mother's house. Don't call me, Fenton. Don't send me emails or texts." Abby ripped the ring off her left hand and threw it at him. It bounced off his forehead and onto the table, leaving a red mark on the skin. "Don't even think about me. Forget I ever existed."

Abby spun on her heel and marched toward the door. Tanner opened the door for her and she breezed by him. He followed her out, catching her elbow in his hand.

"Abby, are you okay? Can I help you?"

She whirled around, her breathing fast and irregular. "I suppose you're happy about this? I know you never liked Fenton."

Tanner couldn't deny he was happy about this turn of events. He'd been flummoxed as to how to get Abby away from Fenton, and here she'd gone and done it herself.

"You're right. I never thought Fenton was good enough for you. You deserve better, Abby."

She exhaled slowly, the fight going out of her. "He's a jerk."

174

Her eyes were bright with tears and he squeezed her shoulder. "He is. You need to find a man who appreciates you. Someone who will treat you the way you deserve to be treated."

A few tears fell. "I thought he was the one," she sniffled. "I thought he loved me."

"I doubt Fenton loves anyone but himself. Don't forgive him and give him another chance, okay?"

Her shoulders straightened. "I may be dumb, but I'm not a pushover. I don't give second chances on something like this."

"Good. Are you really packing your things and moving to your mother's?" He held his breath.

"I am. Can you keep him here until I get my things? I don't want him to come to the house and try and talk me out of this."

Tanner nodded. "Leave it to me. How long do you need?"

Abby chewed her bottom lip. "An hour?"

Tanner grinned. "Since when have you been able to pack in an hour? When we would go on vacation it would take you days."

The corners of her mouth turned up. "I'm very motivated to get out of that house. How about an hour and a half?"

"Deal. You go on and get packed up. I'll handle things here. Text me when you leave the house."

Abby turned to go, and then turned back. "Thank you, Tanner. And thank you for getting Chris some help. I should have thanked you for that before now."

"I figure I owe you."

"You weren't a terrible husband, Tanner." Her expression softened. "You were a hard worker and you cared for us. You just drank too much."

"I'm sorry about that." He truly was. He wished he'd stopped drinking years earlier than he had.

"I think maybe it's time you stopped apologizing. Neither one of us was perfect."

Shock ran through Tanner's body, but it was followed by a peaceful feeling. "Maybe you're right. Now go before Fenton gets other ideas."

Abby turned and headed down the sidewalk. Tanner watched her until she was in her car and driving away. He turned and walked back into the coffee shop almost running into Fenton. Tanner placed his hand on Fenton's chest.

"You're not going anywhere. Abby wants some space to pack her things."

At some point Fenton had gathered his wits and he was in fighting mode. "Fuck you, Tanner. This is none of your business." He tried to push past Tanner, but Fenton only found resistance.

"I'm the law in this town and that makes it my damn business." Tanner leaned forward and got into Fenton's personal space. He had to look up and Tanner used his height advantage to his benefit. He crowded Fenton so the man was forced to take a few steps back.

"You can't keep me from leaving." Fenton's face was starting to get red again.

"Yes, I can, and yes, I will." Tanner turned to the staff behind the counter. They'd been watching the entire soap opera intently and he had no doubt rumors would be swirling before dinnertime tonight. Not much happened in a small town that was kept a secret. "Dana, will you fix my friend and I a couple of coffees and maybe some of those fresh bear claws?"

Dana, the manager, smiled. "Sure will, Sheriff. Here or to go?"

"Here, thank you. I think Fenton and I are going to sit a spell and enjoy our break."

Fenton's eyes narrowed. "I don't think I will."

Tanner couldn't stand this fucking piece of shit, but years of training came to the fore just in time. He would have liked to take Fenton out back and beat

176

the shit out of him, but that wasn't going to solve anything except lower Tanner's blood pressure.

"Sit." Tanner pounded his finger on Fenton's chest. "Sit the fuck down before I run you in."

"For what?" Fenton's voice was soft, but menacing. Tanner could see why some people might be afraid of him. Too bad for him Tanner wasn't one of them.

"I don't fucking need a reason for twenty-four hours, but we can call it obstructing an officer of the law. How does that sound? If I arrest you I can take your fingerprints. I wonder what I'll find if I do that?"

Tanner rubbed his chin thoughtfully and watched fury practically vibrate out of Fenton Jacks. Eventually the man got himself under control. He straightened his tie and smoothed his hair. Clearly he didn't want to have his fingerprints taken. Instead he turned and stomped back to his table where Dana was slipping two cups of coffee and a couple of bear claws at each chair.

"Thanks, Dana. Put it on my tab, okay?'

"Will do, Sheriff." Dana winked at him and gave Fenton a sour look. The town was none too fond of the man it turned out. He'd pissed off too many people in the eight months he'd been here.

Tanner pulled the chair out, the legs scraping the old wood floors. "Now we're going to sit here and be cordial until Abby is done packing her things, understand?"

"I understand." Fenton practically spat out the words. "Did you do this? You're a son of a bitch, you know that, Marks? I fucking hate cops."

"What else do you hate? Abiding by the law?" Tanner leaned back in his chair, stretching out his legs. "Seems to me you only like what you can control. Just so we're clear here, Abby isn't someone who can be moved around like a pawn on a chessboard. You're lucky she didn't shoot you when she found out. I applaud her restraint."

"You've poisoned Abby's mind against me. And what have you done with Chris and Emily?"

"Chris and Emily are somewhere safe. From you. I don't want you around my family, Fenton. I don't like you. As for poisoning Abby's mind, she makes her own decisions. Always has. If she thinks you're slime, she came to that conclusion on her own. Not that I disagree."

Fenton's lips were thin and his skin looked like it was stretched tightly over his features. No one would call him even remotely handsome at the moment. "Prick. You think you're some badass sheriff, running your little chicken shit town. You're nothing. Do you hear me, Marks? You're a speck of lint on my jacket." Fenton kept his voice low and flicked at his lapel. "That's how easily I can get rid of you. I hope your affairs are in order."

"Are you threatening me?" Tanner was unmoved by Fenton's demeanor. He'd faced much worse in the Middle East.

"I don't make threats. I make promises."

Tanner chuckled. "Did Clint Eastwood or Charles Bronson say that?" He leaned forward, his hands on the table. "Or maybe it was Tony Montana?"

Fenton's jaw tightened. It was obvious he wanted to rise to the bait, but instead he lifted his coffee to his lips, taking a drink before answering. "I don't know who Tony Montana is. Is he some sort of local hero?"

"For some I imagine he is. Drink your coffee, Fenton. You're not going anywhere until I hear from Abby."

Tanner sat there babysitting Fenton. He should have been out on patrol but he wanted to make sure she got away from Fenton's house. By the time the text arrived, the silence had stretched on for almost an hour. Tanner had chatted with townsfolk as they came in to the coffee shop, but Fenton never said a word.

"You're free to go, Fenton. Just stay away from Abby. Am I clear?" Tanner stood and Fenton followed suit, pulling on his coat.

178

"As crystal, Sheriff." Fenton turned to Tanner and moved close. "Let me make myself clear. I know you came between me and Abby. I won't forget it. You'll be sorry you fucked with me."

Tanner straightened and tipped his hat to the biggest bastard he'd ever met. "I already am. I mean it. Stay away from Abby. And my kids. In fact, just stay away from everyone in this town."

"I can't wait to leave this backwater turd," Fenton said, his lips curling.

"Don't let the door hit you in the ass on the way out."

Fenton turned and strode out of the coffee shop. Dana came up beside him and started to wipe down the table. "Good riddance to trash, I say. That man is just unpleasant."

She didn't know the half of it. He was also dangerous and ambitious. Two things that were a deadly combination.

"Feel free to refuse service to him, Dana. Thanks for the coffee."

Tanner left the coffee shop and headed down the sidewalk to the station. He needed to call Jason Anderson and tell him Fenton was looking to leave Springwood. That would mean he thought whatever his job was to do was almost done.

Tanner wasn't going to let him finish.

* * * *

Fenton paced the expensive maple hardwood floor of his office. Talking to his boss, Lionel Warner, was always frustrating. He wasn't interested in hearing about what an asshole Tanner Marks was. No, Warner was firmly concentrating on the job at hand. He didn't give a shit about Fenton's personal crap.

"Stay fucking focused," Warner ground out. "Stay the fuck away from Tanner Marks. I told you that he's not to be underestimated."

"I want him dead, goddammit. He's interfering in my life." Fenton snarled into the phone. He'd already thought of at least three different scenarios where he killed Marks. Slowly. Painfully. Maybe he'd even get his wimpy-ass son and bitchy ex-wife to watch. There was nothing Fenton loved more than to use his long Bowie knife. He could filet Tanner Marks, keeping him alive for a long time. The man would beg for death.

Fenton could already hear the pleading, see the pain etched on Marks's face. But Warner was being a total asshole as usual.

"You aren't going to do a goddamn thing, Jacks. Jesus, if a sheriff goes missing or turns up dead now we'll have the Feds all over the fucking place. If you fuck this up, I'll make sure you are so gone Google won't be able to fucking find you. Do you understand what I'm saying? Am I making myself clear?"

Fenton pulled the phone from his ear and swore under his breath, resisting the urge to throw it against the wall. As soon as this job was done, he was going to take out Warner and his cronies. It was simply the next step in Fenton's campaign for power. The fact that he hated Warner's fucking guts would make it enjoyable.

"You're clear. I got it." Fenton's anger simmered, but he pushed it down into his churning gut.

"Good. Now fucking listen to me. You know what to do tonight, right? You take this last cartel guy out and we've got this route. The cartel is on the fucking run and I don't want any fucking mistakes. Your ass in on the line for this, Jacks."

No, your ass in on the line, old man. If I fail, I'll be out of here and in the Caymans with all the money I've stolen from you over the years. You'll never find me, you son of a bitch.

First, I'll kill Marks.

"There won't be any screw ups. The plan is in place. It's foolproof."

Warner snorted. "There's no such thing. Make sure this happens. You only have a few more days there. When you're done, I'm sending you down to our Central American operation. Be ready to leave at a moment's notice."

There was no fucking way Fenton was going to the hot, humid, deadly jungles of Central America. Warner might think that's where he was going, but Fenton didn't intend for Warner to be the boss much longer anyway.

"Don't worry. I'll be ready." *To slit you open like a fish, and watch your guts spill out on to your carpet.*

"And stay the fuck away from that sheriff, do you understand? I'm only going to say this once more, dammit. I don't want you anywhere near him. The last thing we need is a local fucking hero sniffing around in our business. Shit, the DEA is bad enough."

"Got it," Fenton bit out. He was ready to blow. This job couldn't be done fast enough. "I'll call you when it's done."

"Don't fucking bother. I'll know when it's done." Warner hung up as abruptly as usual. Fenton slammed his phone down on his desk and took several deep breaths. He ran his fingers though his hair and looked out his office window.

Abby was gone. She'd taken everything she owned including all the gifts Fenton had given her. It was probably just as well. Thinking she might be okay with his somewhat shady business was a pipe dream. She may not be the sheriff's wife any longer, but her sense of right and wrong was as strong as ever. She could consider the clothes, handbags, shoes, and jewelry payment for services rendered. It was easier that way. Make the deal up front. Let the woman know you weren't in it for the long haul but you would be generous along the way.

Tonight Fenton would close the deal on the drug route. Only one other man stood in his way and he didn't know it yet, but he was as good as dead. Once that was done, there was only the one other job and he was gone.

But he would definitely send Marks a message tonight. A harbinger of things to come, so to speak. Before Fenton left town, he would take great pleasure in killing Tanner Marks.

* * * *

Madison and Tanner were heading home after dinner out when his cell phone rang. His expression grew darker and darker as the conversation went on.

"I'm heading there now." Tanner ended the call and shoved the phone back in his pocket. He leaned forward and turned on the sirens and lights before making a U-turn and heading out of town. The needle on the speedometer was up around a hundred when he turned to her. "Honey, we're going on a little field trip. I hate to make you go, but you live in the opposite direction and I want to get to the scene as quickly as possible. I'll have a deputy drive you home, okay?"

Tanner didn't wait for Madison's answer. His foot pushed more firmly to the floor and she felt the powerful engine growl as it built speed. The sirens were wailing and the lights whirling as people pulled over to let them by. She held onto the armrest as he navigated a turn at way too high of a speed.

"These lights and sirens would have come in handy in Chicago. Traffic is terrible there."

He nodded grimly. "I admit they do help." He returned to concentrating and she stayed quiet while he drove. The last thing he needed was a bunch of questions distracting him.

Tanner slowed the vehicle down and pulled into a field. The truck bounced on the rough dirt road until they pulled up beside an old building. She peered into the darkness and squinted, trying to read the weathered sign on the side of the gray concrete building. There were several other cop cars already there and one officer was stretching yellow crime scene tape around the perimeter.

"What is this place?" she asked. "I've driven by it but never knew what it was."

"It's an old meat packing plant that hasn't been used since the seventies." Tanner reached under the seat and pulled out a long flashlight. "I'll leave the truck running and the heat on. I'm sorry about this, honey. I really am."

He pushed open the door and she made a quick decision. Staying in the vehicle sucked. She wanted to go with him. She hopped out and made it to the front of the truck just as he did.

Tanner scowled. "You can't come in with me. You need to stay in the truck, Maddie."

"Why?"

"It's a murder scene. I don't want you to see it. You'll have nightmares for the rest of your life."

She started walking toward the building. "You have to be kidding. I've cut up cadavers. I've stitched together kids who have been blown apart by automatic rifles. Do you think I'm going to get sick at a little blood?"

He grabbed her elbow, spinning her around. "Maddie, I mean it. You can't go in there."

"I want to see what you do."

Tanner sighed as if she was trying his patience. "I don't come barging in when you're seeing patients, do I? Besides, it's a crime scene."

"I took a forensics medicine course in school. I know what to do to keep from contaminating a scene." She looked around. "I don't see the coroner here yet. Maybe I can look at things until he gets here? Just look, not touch."

"You want to see a murder?" Tanner's eyebrows shot up. "Maddie, you never cease to amaze me."

Deputy Sam walked up to them. "Boss." He nodded to Madison. "Dr. Shay."

"Call me Madison, Sam. Everybody does."

Sam smiled. "Thanks, I will." He turned back to Tanner. "It's around this way." He pointed to the side of the building with his flashlight.

"It's not inside?" Tanner craned his neck to see.

"No. I've got a couple of guys looking for evidence inside but the scene is out here. Follow me."

Because they were outside the tape, Madison was able to tag along. Tanner didn't say anything to her until they were right up on it. Someone, possibly Sam, had placed a couple of spotlights on the body. What was left of it, anyway.

Tanner stopped and turned to her. "You stay outside this yellow tape. Dammit, Maddie, I mean it."

She was deeply curious about what this amazing man did for a living but she wouldn't jeopardize his investigation. "I promise I'll stay on this side."

Tanner nodded then ducked under the tape, followed by Sam. It gave Madison a chance to really examine the sight before her.

Grisly.

The man had been murdered but it hadn't happened quickly. He appeared to be cut in dozens of places and allowed to bleed to death. Some of the wounds were shallow and some appeared deep, although it was hard to tell from this distance. The man's mouth was open in a silent scream and his eyes were fixed in a stare as if he still bore witness to the atrocities committed upon him.

The copper smell of blood was thick in the air and the white snow was colored pink with pools of red, dotted here and there, where the liquid had ran into a low spot.

Tanner was speaking in a low voice to Sam and another deputy. He was pointing to various areas around the body, and his expression was tense. She didn't know how long she stood there in the cold watching him as he directed the gathering of evidence but she was startled to hear the sounds of an approaching helicopter.

She covered her ears as it landed a few hundred feet away. A tall man with dark hair exited the chopper followed by another man in a beige jumpsuit carrying a square case. They hurried up to the yellow tape, brushing by her. Tanner turned and waved them in.

"Hey, Anderson. Glad you could get here. We've been working the crime scene. Looks like another drug route murder."

The man peered at the deceased and nodded. "That's Jerome Allen. He's in the Jackson cartel. He's in charge of transport, shall we say."

Sam shook his head. "Not anymore. He took an early retirement."

The man named Anderson wore a grim expression, lines deeply grooved in his forehead. "This is the final stake in the heart to the Jackson cartel. It looks like Warner won the war."

Tanner crossed his arms over his chest. "Will Jackson give up?"

"No. He'll regroup and strike back. Eventually."

Tanner looked up and suddenly seemed to notice Madison standing there. She'd been quiet and observant. Watching this intense man work had been riveting. He gave everything to whatever he was doing whether it was work or play. If anything, she was falling further in love with him with each passing day. She couldn't even begin to express how much she respected him. The way he dealt with his job and with his family spoke of bone-deep integrity. In that way he reminded her of her father.

Tanner motioned to one of his deputies and ducked under the tape. "Maddie, I'm going to have Deputy Leo here take you home. I'm sorry I had to drag you out here."

"It was interesting to watch you work." She looked down at the body. "Will the coroner get here soon?" The man in the jumpsuit was taking pictures and talking to the other deputies that had begun to gather evidence.

"He's on his way. I'll walk you to the cruiser."

Tanner and Madison, followed at a discreet distance by Deputy Leo, walked through the snow toward the vehicle. They paused and the deputy walked around them, starting the car and turning on the headlights illuminating the snow. She caught something out of the corner of her eye.

A coffee cup, exactly the same as the to-go cups at the coffee shop, was dropped in the snow. She turned and reached for it.

"One of your deputies dropped his coffee cu—."

Tanner grabbed her arm, holding it in place. "Don't touch that." His voice came out raspy, but she could hear the urgency in his tone.

She pulled her hand back. "Um, okay. It's just garbage. People shouldn't litter."

Tanner walked closer and knelt down, shining his flashlight on the paper cup, the black marker more easily seen under the light. It looked like the person who had thrown it down was partial to a Sumatra blend with shots of vanilla, cinnamon, and caramel.

He cursed and stood before yelling at the agent. Agent Anderson ran over, his breath making vapor in the Montana cold.

"What's wrong?"

Tanner pointed his flashlight at the cup. "I think that's evidence."

The agent quirked an eyebrow. "Then we'll gather it. May I ask why you think it's evidence?"

"Because Fenton Jacks was drinking that very cup of coffee earlier today."

Chapter Nineteen

The steakhouse in Billings was quiet and upscale; only the murmur of voices could be heard. Madison took in the dark wood and leather furnishings as the hostess led them to their table. The aromas wafting from the kitchen were tantalizing and the trays of food passing them appetizing. Madison's father had been right in recommending this restaurant. It was the perfect place to celebrate Tanner's birthday.

Madison sunk down into the chair covered in a red and gold brocade on the seat and arms and the hostess handed her an oversized menu. Tanner sat to her left, and on her other side was Presley Reilly, a pretty brunette and wife of Sheriff Seth Reilly from a neighboring town. So far Presley was an absolute hoot. Constantly smiling, she was lively and entertaining, and just plain nice. She reminded Madison of Sherry in a way. Both women had never met a stranger in their lives.

Next to Presley was Seth, then Sheriff Logan Wright and his date, a gorgeous young blonde woman named Christina. She was quiet and more subdued than Presley but seemed to be just as friendly. Christina's hand was on Logan's arm and she lit up whenever he looked at her.

The waiter approached their table with a smile. "Good evening. I'm Charles and I'll be your waiter this evening. Can I start you out with something from the bar or perhaps bring the wine list?"

Madison tensed, wondering if Seth and Logan knew that Tanner didn't drink. Logan laughed and waved his hand. "We men are the designated drivers tonight, but the ladies might like something."

Madison shook her head and Presley also demurred, turning a pretty shade of pink. Seeing that no one else was drinking, Christina also declined. The waiter took their drink orders and bustled away. Madison relaxed back and Tanner threaded their fingers together under the table. She liked how he didn't make a production about their feelings, but he always let her know he cared.

Seth sat back in his chair. "Well, happy birthday, old man. You seem to be holding together pretty well for someone of your...advanced age."

A smile played around Seth's mouth. He seemed like a good man and he obviously adored Presley. He hung on her every word and his gaze constantly sought hers.

Logan, obviously the jokester of the group, grinned. "Shit, you're lucky you can still walk at your age." He looked around the table. "Excuse my language, ladies. I'll try and behave myself tonight."

Madison had a feeling Logan didn't behave himself very often. His tousled dark blond hair, twinkling blue eyes, and mischievous grin spoke of a man who liked to have fun. A lot of it. He laughed easily and had turned almost every female head in the restaurant with his easy self-confident air and movie star looks.

It was clear, however, that Christina was out of her league with Logan. Her eyes had a hungry look in them, but Logan didn't seem engaged. Unlike Seth with Presley, Logan didn't lean closer to her when she spoke, nor did his eyes follow her around a room. There was a detached air about him. It was like a part of him was here with them, but another part far away.

"He never behaves." Seth grinned. The waiter placed their drinks down in front of them and Seth cleared his throat. "Actually, Presley and I have some news." Seth looked down at his wife, his gaze tender and loving.

Presley was practically bouncing in her chair, her face alight. "We're pregnant," she announced with glee. "We're having a baby."

Seth looked every inch the proud father as they accepted everyone's congratulations. He wrapped an arm around Presley and she looked up at him with such love it made Madison's heart ache. She wanted what they had.

Logan slapped him on the back. "I don't have any cigars to hand out."

"You don't hand out cigars when it's announced. You hand them out when the baby's born. And the father does it," Christina said. "You're not a father. Not yet anyway."

188

"I'm not ready for fatherhood." Logan grinned. "I'm happy the way I am."

Christina's mouth drooped slightly and Tanner must have noticed. He lifted his glass in a toast. "Congratulations to the new parents. May your children be healthy and happy."

They all clinked glasses and the waiter came back to take their order. Since it was a special occasion, Madison ordered a filet mignon with the potatoes au gratin. Tanner ordered the same in a larger cut and added an order of grilled shrimp. When the waiter headed back to the kitchen, Seth turned to Tanner, his expression now sober.

"Any more on the coffee cup found at the scene?"

Tanner's lips tightened. "It will take a few weeks, maybe more, to put the cup through the FBI lab. But I know it belongs to Fenton."

Logan stroked his chin. "Is he that careless? Did he think it was far enough away from the actual crime no one would notice? It seems like a bonehead move."

"He meant for it to be found, of that I'm sure. He's taunting me. Letting me know it doesn't matter what we do, he's untouchable."

Madison frowned. "If the DNA or fingerprints come back as his, he'll be arrested. That's hardly untouchable."

"Assuming he hasn't disappeared," Tanner answered. "By the time we get a result, he could have vanished from the face of the earth."

"A person can't really just disappear," Madison protested.

Presley pressed her face into her palms and groaned. "Do I have a story to tell you."

Seth chuckled and put his arm around her shoulders. "That is a good story. My favorite, in fact."

Presley began recounting how she walked out of a restaurant and her car blew up. Next thing she knew, she was being whisked away by Feds and put in witness protection. That's where she'd met Seth and he'd protected her until her would-be killer was apprehended.

Madison was wide-eyed. "Wow, that's some story. Thank goodness you're okay. It must have been scary as hell to have to start a new life with a new name and everything."

Presley gazed up at her husband. "It had its perks. I kept the name and the new life. Honestly, it was better than my old one."

They all laughed as Logan told a story about working on a cattle rustling case with Tanner. Each story led to another one and before she knew it the waiter was clearing away the dessert dishes. They had all ordered a decadent chocolate mousse that had managed to be light and rich at the same time. It was the house specialty.

As they drank their after-dinner coffee, Madison was feeling happy and comfortable. She'd never been big on socializing but it felt easy with these people. She liked Tanner's friends and hopefully they liked her.

Logan put down his coffee cup with a flourish. "Are we ready to have some fun? I know a country-western bar not far from here where we can kick up our heels and the ladies can let down their hair."

Madison wasn't sure she had ever let down her hair one night in her life. She wasn't sure she could do it, but trying was going to be fun. Presley beamed and leaned forward. "I can't wait to get Seth out on the dance floor. Soon we'll be parents and will probably hardly ever get a night out on the town."

They paid the check and headed to a place a few miles away. The parking lot was packed and that only hinted at how many people were crammed into the building. The bar had been built in an old warehouse but it still didn't seem large enough. There was a crush of bodies on the dance floor dancing to the latest Kenny Chesney song. Music was blaring from the speakers, the lights were dim, and the smell of sweat and beer was strong.

190

The DJ announced a line dance and suddenly the crowd formed neat rows of at least a dozen people. Presley grabbed Madison and Christina and tugged them toward the dance floor.

"Come on. If we go, the men will follow."

Her words turned out to be prophetic. Madison danced shoulder to shoulder with Tanner and Presley for several songs. The steps weren't hard and soon they were all hot and thirsty from their efforts. Logan jerked a thumb toward the bar.

"How about we get some sodas and some air?"

Madison nodded gratefully and lifted her long hair to cool off her neck. Someone had opened the back door and a chilling breeze blew over her flesh, raising goosebumps. Presley pointed to the ladies room.

"I need to visit the restroom and repair my lipstick."

"Me too," Madison agreed. "Christina?"

Despite Logan being a perfect gentleman all evening, Christina looked down. She'd probably figured out Logan wasn't as in to her as she was with him, and it had to hurt. Madison felt a little guilty thinking it, but Christina should probably cut bait and find another guy. Whatever issues Logan had, it was clear he wasn't looking to pair up. At least not with the pretty blonde.

Christina followed Madison and Presley to the ladies room. They repaired their melted makeup and Madison tried to tame her wild hair.

Christina applied some lipstick. "You have the most beautiful hair, Madison. Maybe I should go red."

Presley shook her head. "You have gorgeous blonde hair. Why would you want to do that?"

Christina shrugged nonchalantly. "Something different. Something more exciting maybe."

"Is this about Logan? Do you think he'll like you better with red hair?" Presley asked bluntly.

Madison admired Presley's ability to cut through the bullshit and get to the heart of a matter. Christina looked shocked for a moment and then her expression crumpled, her eyes watery.

"I just love him so much."

Her tone was filled with emotion, and Presley put her arm around the woman. "Why don't you tell us all about it?"

In a halting voice, Christina told them about meeting Logan one night a few months ago when she and some friends had car trouble. He'd rescued them and her world had never been the same.

Her eyes lit up. "You know how it is when you meet the one? The man that's going to change your world and rescue you from being alone? That's how I felt when I met him."

Madison's eyes met Presley's. Madison had never in her life thought about a man rescuing her from anything. Even when she thought about Tanner, it was how they could build a life together. It wasn't about him building one for her.

Presley patted Christina's shoulder. "I don't think Logan is looking to settle down. He's got bad boy written all over him."

"But a good woman could change him," Christina argued.

"You know," Madison began. "I have a good friend named Sherry. She always says that men are capable of change. For the worse. Her motto is that men don't change unless they damn well want to. I'm not sure Logan is looking to change."

Christina pressed her lips together. "But I love him."

Presley shook her head. "You can't make someone love you back whether it's your family or a man. I learned that one the hard way. You want someone who will give you love without you having to beg for it."

Christina nodded. "I know you're right, it's just that he's so wonderful. He's handsome, charming, funny."

192

"Have you told him how you feel?" Madison asked, pretty sure of the answer. If Logan knew how Christina felt, he'd be gone so fast he'd leave skid marks on the floor.

"No. I don't know how to tell him or if I even should."

"Don't tell him," Presley replied. "Logan's the kind of man who needs to feel like he has space around him. Freedom." She sighed. "I think you should know he's said, on more than one occasion, he's never getting married or having children. I think it has something to do with his childhood, although I couldn't get the whole story out of Seth. Damn lawmen are so close-mouthed."

Christina's expression turned to dismay. "Never?" She tossed a tissue into the trash. "I might as well hang it up. He'll never be serious about me. I'm wasting my time. I always pick the emotionally unavailable men. "

"You're beautiful. You won't be alone long," Madison said. "Find another guy who adores you."

Christina sniffed. "I just want what you both have. A man who worships me." She turned to face them. "How did you do it?"

Presley laughed. "Well, I got blown up in a car. I'm not sure about Madison."

"I put stitches in Tanner's forehead after he got beat up in a bar fight."

"I mean how did you make them fall in love with you? Great sex?" Christina asked.

"Great sex is a byproduct of love," Presley replies. "Although we do have a great sex life. I remember this one time in the cab of his truck after we went turkey hunting. Or even better, I did a striptease for him one night. That knocked his socks off, let me tell you. Holy hell, that was hotter than fire."

Presley looked far away, reliving her past glory moments with Seth. A smile was playing on her lips and her cheeks were a becoming pink. The memories must be pretty darn good.

Madison felt heat flood her face when the other two women looked at her. "Um, we have a good sex life."

Presley grinned. "Relax. You're private about it. Nothing wrong with that. I guess my whole point here, before I digressed, is that sex is great but it's not why we fell in love."

"That's true. That's not why I fell for Tanner. He's simply a wonderful man."

Madison hadn't even told Tanner she loved him yet. Honestly, she was chicken shit to say it. She'd be devastated if he didn't say it back. Secretly she wanted him to say it first.

Presley looked at her watch and grimaced. "If we don't get out there, the men are going to send in a posse after us."

The three women headed into the main room to look for their men. Madison craned her neck, but the crowd blocked anything more than three feet in front of her. She sighed and turned to Presley and Christina.

"Maybe we should just stay put and have them find us. They're taller and can see over the crowd."

Before anyone could respond a large hand clamped onto Madison's shoulder and squeezed hard. She jumped in her high heels and forced herself to relax. It was only Tanner messing around, she was sure. She whirled around, ready to give him a rash for scaring her and instead looked into the face of a stranger.

"Can I help you?" Madison tried to take a step back but his hand held her firmly, making her distinctly uncomfortable. She didn't like being manhandled in the least.

The man grinned, showing off white teeth that reminded her of a shark she'd seen when she was on vacation in Florida. Luckily it had been on the other side of three foot thick glass. This one, on the other hand, was breathing down on her and smelled like whisky.

"I love your hair." He leaned forward and sniffed near her ear and she almost fell off her shoes trying to scramble away. She liked being smelled by strangers less than she liked being touched. "It's so long, shiny, and red. You wanna dance, babe?"

"Uh, no thanks. I'm here with someone." She managed to move enough that it dislodged his hand but he simply slid it down and grasped her arm.

Well, crap.

"I don't see anyone." The man's head swiveled like a bobble head doll. "Seems to me you're alone. Come on. I won't bite. Just a dance."

In her years as a doctor, Madison had handled some ornery people. She lifted her arm so he could see he was holding it and then jerked it hard so his hand fell away. Pulling herself up to her five feet seven height plus her three-inch heels, she gave him her best pissed off physician look.

"No." She put just the right amount of displeasure in her tone. "Leave me alone. I'm with someone."

The man's friends started to laugh at him and that's when things started to go down hill. His face turned purple and his lips curled back.

"Cunt. You're probably a big dyke anyway."

Madison was about to tell him off, but Presley stepped up and shoved her finger in front of the man's face, shaking it. Her face was red with rage, her mouth a thin line.

"And you're an asshole. A big one. Do you kiss your momma with that mouth?"

The jerk's friends laughed some more and Madison distinctly heard the words "ball buster." Christina pulled Presley back and tried to soothe everyone's exposed nerves.

"Listen, just leave us alone. We're only trying to find our men."

"You ain't got no men. You're three bitches, that's what ya are." A little spit came out of his mouth, his anger and humiliation spilling off of him. The situation had escalated quickly and if something wasn't done soon could fly out of control. Somebody might get seriously hurt. With Presley in a delicate condition, Madison couldn't let that happen.

Madison took a step in retreat, holding on to Christina and Presley's arms so they were forced to move with her.

"We're turning and walking away. We don't want to argue with you."

Madison congratulated herself on her voice not wavering. Her heart was pounding and her adrenaline was racing but she couldn't let it show. Men like this preyed on any sign of weakness.

The man lunged and grabbed Madison's hair, wrapping his fingers into the long strands so if she moved an inch it was going to hurt like hell. She yelped as his hand tightened and then another hand, a large and familiar one, was on his arm, squeezing. The knuckles turned white with the effort and Madison felt the grip on her hair loosen and then fall away.

She looked up and Tanner was there, his expression a mask of fury. He hadn't let go of the man's arm, his fingers still tightening until her attacker was almost on his knees.

"Don't you know better than to touch a woman?" Tanner's voice was cold and deadly. Madison felt a shiver go up her spine and hoped his icy cold anger was never directed at her. He wasn't even out of control. His eyes had turned into black stones, his jaw flexing with tension.

"I— I—. Shit, let me go, man. I was just playing."

The man's voice was thin and desperate. Tanner let go but didn't retreat, staying eye to eye with the bully. The man rubbed his arm, his eyes darting from Tanner, to Logan, to Seth, and back again.

"Funny way of playing. Didn't look fun for anyone but you. Do you get your kicks out of terrorizing defenseless women? How about taking on someone your own size? Let's make it fair."

This time it was the jerk who took a step back, almost running into his two friends. His eyes were wide with panic as Tanner, Logan, and Seth made an impressive man-wall between the bullies and Madison, Presley, and Christina. Their men had stepped in front of them so all the women could see were their muscular backs.

"Hey, man. We were just having fun. That's all. No harm, no foul. Ya know?"

Madison peered around Tanner in time to see the three men hoof it through the crowd and head straight for the front door. Tanner, Logan, and Seth turned around in unison. Tanner pulled Madison close.

"Are you okay, Maddie? Did he hurt you?" Tanner's voice was laced with anger and tension, his arms like steel bands around her.

"I'm okay. He simply scared us, that's all. You got here just in time." She kept her voice soft, hoping to soothe his obvious worry.

"No." Tanner shook his head, a muscle jumping above his eye. "It looked like we got here a few minutes late actually. If we'd been earlier, he wouldn't have touched you."

She couldn't argue with that logic. She was just grateful he'd shown up at all. How he'd seen her in the crowd was a mystery.

Seth tilted Presley's chin up with his hand.

"I'm afraid to ask what you said, wife of mine. I know your sassy mouth."

Presley smiled. "I called him an asshole and asked him if he kissed his momma with that mouth." Her lips tightened in a sign of distaste. "He called Madison a cunt. Only women can use that word. Men aren't allowed to."

Tanner's expression still hadn't relaxed. His shoulders were set and his jaw was tight. "Did he really call you that?"

Madison put her hand on his arm, the muscles a tight knot under her palm. "He did, but it doesn't matter. I don't care, okay? I just want us to have some fun tonight."

Logan exhaled and put his arm around Christina. "You okay, Chrissie? You look pale, babe."

Christina pressed against Logan's side. "It was a little scary. That guy was drunk, I think."

Presley snorted. "God, I hope he doesn't behave that way without booze. What a loser."

Tanner straightened, but fury was still written in every line of his body. "I think we've had enough fun for one night. How about we start for home?"

No one objected and the three couples gathered their coats from the coat check and went out into the cold evening. Not one word was spoken between Madison and Tanner as they headed to the SUV parked at the very edge of the parking lot, with Seth and Logan's trucks parked on either side.

A flurry of footsteps behind them had Tanner freezing in place. He whirled around and pushed Madison so he was standing between her and whoever had followed them. She stiffened in shock when she realized it was the jerk from earlier and this time he and his two friends had brought in a couple more men for reinforcements.

The man hit his palm with his fist. "I don't think we finished our conversation."

Tanner didn't even turn his head. He pressed his car keys in her hand. "Maddie, get in the truck with Presley and Christina."

"But—"

"Now, Maddie."

Madison's heart accelerated but his tone brooked no refusal. She looked at the drunk jerk with a sort of pity. Tanner, Logan, and Seth were going to kick their asses from here to Bozeman and back.

The idiots should have left when their men gave them a chance.

Chapter Twenty

Tanner had had about enough of this guy's shit. He was drunk, belligerent, and apparently needed at least four friends to help him fight his battles.

"Brought some of your friends? Let's settle this man to man," Tanner said.

He had no doubt the three of them could easily take on five drunks, but it was his fucking birthday and he was wearing his good suit. He looked at Logan out of the corner of his eye, and Seth sidled up so he was shoulder to shoulder with Tanner. Logan nodded, indicating the women were safely locked in the SUV. Tanner appreciated Madison's reluctance to leave him, but he needed to know she was out of harm's way. He wanted to end this with as little fanfare as possible.

"I'm going to kick your ass," the drunk snarled. "You embarrassed me in front of my friends, you motherfucking cocksucker."

Seth grinned. "Looks like Presley was right. He's got a nasty mouth on him. How do you want to do this?"

"Please, oh please, let me have the two guys on the right. The ones with the confused expressions. My birthday's coming up." Logan laughed.

"I want to take them down with little fuss and no blood or broken bones," Tanner said. "Should we identify ourselves to these gentlemen?"

Seth took a step forward. "Before you kick our asses, we think you should know all three of us are officers of the law and trained to kill and maim."

One of the men with the confused expressions sniffed the air. "I thought I smelled bacon." He spat on the ground. "Shit, I hate cops."

"That went well." Logan chuckled. "What do you think they're waiting for? They're just standing there. We don't have all damn night here."

Tanner, Seth, and Logan knew better than to make the first move. They would wait out these yahoos and hope they changed their minds.

"I dunno." Seth shrugged. "Maybe we should insult their sister or something. This is getting old."

The main drunk asswipe stepped forward, his fists up and ready. "Time to beg like a girl, cop. Come here and get it."

Tanner didn't move, but he didn't have to. The jerk charged him and Tanner feinted one way and went the other. He grabbed the man's arm and bent it behind his back, hooking his leg around the man's ankle. Tanner pushed him to the icy concrete without trouble. Since the man had had several too many, Tanner was able to use the drunk's own body weight against him. He sank to the pavement with only a howl of protest. With Tanner's knee lodged in the man's lower back, he pulled his cuffs from his back pocket and quickly snapped them on the man's wrists.

Tanner sprang up to help Seth and Logan but they clearly had the upper hand with the thug's friends. The two "extra" men had fled and were running across the parking lot as if the hounds of hell were on their heels. The other more loyal friends both had their arms bent back behind them until they were bent over so far they could lick their knees.

The bully tried to get to his feet but slipped on the ice. The fight was out of him. Tanner could see it ebbing and reality setting in. The bully was finally sobering up and realizing he'd done something incredibly dumb.

"Now, are you finished?" Tanner hated violence but this was just fucking stupid. The man was lucky Tanner wasn't a different kind of cop. He knew of a few who would have beat the ever loving shit out of this guy. The man nodded and Seth and Logan loosened their holds on the friends, letting them stand up straight.

Logan grinned. "You carry cuffs?"

Seth dug in his back pocket and pulled out a pair, holding them up. "I was ready as well."

Seth was also carrying a pistol and maybe a knife in those fancy cowboy boots. Tanner didn't know what Logan was packing, but there was no doubt he was heavily armed, too. Tanner himself only had a knife in his boot and a shotgun in the truck.

Tanner helped the drunk to his feet. "If I take these off, are you going to behave?"

The drunk ass nodded, his head down. The man's body language spoke of defeat so Tanner didn't feel any fear as he took off the cuffs. The guy rubbed his wrists but didn't look up.

"Listen, take this as a lesson learned. Don't mess with women that don't want to be messed with. There are too many willing ones in this world to worry about the others. Do you want me to call you a cab?"

One of the friends shook his head. "Naw, I haven't been drinking tonight. I can drive."

Logan sighed and pointed to the man. "Then you damn well should have known better than this shit. What if one of us had drawn a fucking gun on you? What would you have done?"

Red stained the man's face. "Shit, I don't know. We were just bored and wanted to stir something up."

Seth shook his head. "Bored? They can put that on your fucking tombstone. 'Someone shot his ass because he was fucking bored.'"

The main drunk finally looked up but didn't look Tanner in the eye. "Can we go now? Are you going to arrest us?" he asked gruffly.

"Yes and no. We don't have jurisdiction here. It's your lucky night." Tanner stepped back to give the man room and the two friends escorted him across the parking lot. Tanner flexed his shoulder. "I'm getting too old for this shit. Next time you ask me if I want to have fun, the answer is hell no."

Seth rubbed his temples. "I agree. I could do with less fun. This was supposed to be my night out and here I am keeping the peace. As usual."

"Well excuse the hell out of me." Logan shook his head, but he was smiling. "I'll never ask you anywhere again."

"Good." Tanner turned and headed for the truck where the women waited. "Anyone in the mood for a burger?"

"I could eat," Seth replied with a smile.

Logan picked up his cowboy hat that had fallen off in the shuffle. "I can always eat. There's a little dive down the road..."

"Holy shit, I'll pick the place," Tanner said. "Just follow me."

It was shaping up to be quite a birthday, but Tanner hoped it wasn't done yet. He had plans for Madison tonight that didn't include any of his friends.

It would be just the two of them.

* * * *

"Do you want me to rub your shoulder?" Madison asked as they entered Tanner's dark home. He flipped on the lights and Scout bounded down the stairs to greet them, his paws sliding on the smooth tile. When the dog realized there were two people to welcome, his tail went into overdrive and he gave them both a thorough sniffing.

Tanner laughed. "He thinks every time I leave the house, I go pet other dogs. He's mighty jealous."

Scout gave Madison's hand a lick and he sat quietly, love in his brown doggy eyes when she scratched behind his soft, furry ears.

"I think I made a friend for life." Madison giggled. "He's not much of a watchdog, though. I thought he might bark or growl when we came in."

"We came in through the garage, plus I think he recognizes the sound of my truck. If anyone else tried to come in through the front door or a window, hell, he would have greeted us with one of their limbs in his mouth."

"Good dog, Scout," Madison crooned. "Very good dog."

"And my shoulder is fine, but I sure as hell am not going to turn down a back rub from you."

"It never occurred to me that you would," Madison answered tartly. "Besides, it's my fault all of that happened back at the bar."

202

Tanner helped her off with her coat. "No, ma'am. It was that drunk's fault. He was acting like a stupid asshole. This wasn't any of your doing."

"I guess I haven't really thanked you for protecting me." Madison pushed to her feet.

Tanner, Seth, and Logan had shrugged off what happened quickly. Clearly drunks bent on violence didn't faze the men in the least. They'd strolled back to their vehicles, cool as you please, and driven to the nearest burger joint where they'd eaten their second dinner of the night while the females looked on, amused but awed at the amount of food these men could pack away. All three of them had eaten a double cheeseburger with a large order of fries. Madison had felt her arteries harden as the men had tucked into their meal.

Tanner looked down at her, his expression solemn. "It's my job to protect you. One I take very seriously. Nothing will ever happen to you when I'm around, Maddie. I will always take care of you."

"It's not really your job." Even as she said it, warmth was spreading from her heart to the rest of her body. Other than her father, she'd never had a man with Tanner's protective instincts. She was a modern woman and shouldn't enjoy the feeling. But she did.

Tanner chuckled and walked into the kitchen. "You sound like it's a burden. It's a privilege, honey." He pulled two water bottles from the refrigerator. "I guess I'm old-fashioned. Does it piss you off?"

"No." Madison shook her head. "I'm ashamed to say I like that about you."

"Why ashamed?" Tanner frowned, his brows drawn together in a line.

"I'm not supposed to want a man to take care of me. I'm supposed to be a self-sufficient woman who can do anything that needs done all by herself."

"Sounds lonely." Tanner's lips twisted. "The best part of a relationship is that you're there for each other."

"I've never really been in one." Madison shrugged.

Tanner handed her a water bottle and smiled. "News flash. You're in one now. How does it feel?"

"Pretty good, actually. But it could feel better."

"I'm listening." Tanner's smile was sexy and her heart started beating faster. There was something about this man that got to her every single time.

"I was thinking we should do something special for your birthday. Something sexy." She screwed up her courage. "Presley said she did a striptease for Seth."

An eyebrow quirked. "You want me to do a striptease? I guess I could give it a shot."

Tanner looked like he was trying not to laugh. She sighed and rolled her eyes. "No, I meant me. I was thinking maybe I should do a striptease for you. Or something. It's your birthday."

She sounded so freakin' lame.

"Should? Do you want to do a striptease for me, honey? I want you no matter what."

She set the bottle on the kitchen table. "I'm not Presley, I guess."

Tanner slid his arms around her. "Thank God. I love Presley. She's a wonderful woman and she makes Seth very happy. However, she would run me into an early grave. He has his hands full twenty-four seven with her. I'm happy with you. In fact, I think you're the sexiest woman I've ever seen. Hands down." He set his own water bottle down and walked over to the clock radio on the windowsill. He switched it on, finding a soft, instrumental song. "I think I have an idea. How about we dance together and do a mutual strip?"

"A mutual strip?" A lump had formed in Madison's throat and the blood in her veins was starting to sing. "I don't think I've ever done that before."

Tanner flicked open the top button on her black wool pencil skirt, his fingers brushing the bare skin of her midriff. She quivered at the feeling of his callused hands.

"Follow my lead."

His voice was deep and promised pleasure with a touch of sin. She'd follow him anywhere.

Raising his hands, he shrugged off his suit coat and tossed it on a kitchen chair. His fingers played with the buttons in his shirt before plucking them open, leaving it gaping. A white ribbed undershirt peeked out from under the snow white button-down.

"Your turn," he said. A smile played around his lips and his eyes glowed a dark blue. He was enjoying this by the look of the bulge beneath his zipper. "Unbutton the sweater, Maddie. I want to see what's underneath."

He'd already seen everything but it didn't stop her from feeling compelled to follow his command. Her clumsy fingers unfastened her cardigan and slid it off her shoulders so it fell heedlessly somewhere on the floor. She'd worn a pink camisole under the sweater but no bra. Her nipples rubbed against the lace as he inspected what she'd revealed.

"Your turn."

The words almost caught in her throat but he seemed to understand. Tanner pulled the shirt from his waistband and made short work of the buttons. He shrugged it off and then peeled the undershirt from his body, revealing his hard muscular chest. Something fluttered in her stomach and her insides seem to turn to molten liquid. She reached out to touch him but his hands caught her wrist.

"Not yet. Now you again."

Madison lowered her hands to the zipper on her skirt. Tanner had already unbuttoned it, so she slowly slid the zipper down until the skirt pooled at her feet. She stepped out of it and kicked it away. She should have felt chilly standing there in only a camisole, panties and her garters and stockings. Instead, she was on fire from the inside out. She licked her dry lips and his gaze zeroed in on her movement.

"You." She swallowed hard. "Next."

His expression was tense but he reached for the fastening of his pants and popped them open before pushing the zipper down. The metal teeth sounded loud in the silence and the anticipation made her tremble in her heels. He shoved them down his thighs and soon they were tossed carelessly across the room. His erection was bold and proud, tenting his boxers. She dropped to her knees and reached for his cock.

Tanner stepped back quickly. "We're not naked yet."

His voice sounded raw with need, and she had more than enough of her own.

"I need you now. I can't wait."

This time he didn't pull away when she lowered his boxers, letting his hard cock spring free. She wrapped her fingers around it, wrenching a tortured groan from Tanner's lips.

"Aww fuck, honey. That feels so good."

"It's going to feel better, cowboy. Just stay still."

Madison knew her man well enough to know he wasn't in the mood to be teased. Instead of lightly licking him all over, she took him into her mouth as far as she could. His fingers tangled in her hair and she sucked and laved her tongue on the underside until his balls had drawn up close to his body. She pulled off with a pop and looked up at him. He'd closed his eyes, but now he opened them. His hands caressed her face, cupping the jaw and rubbing his thumb over her lips. She marveled for the hundredth time how a man so big and strong could be so gentle.

Tanner bent down and lifted her to her feet. "You're a dangerous woman, Madison Shay."

She smiled and ran her arms around his lean middle. "How so? I'm perfectly innocent of any crime, Sheriff. Butter wouldn't melt in my mouth."

"I can say with certainty it would." Tanner chuckled. "Your mouth is hot and lethal. Not to mention this sexy underwear you've got on. If I'd known you had that on all evening, we wouldn't have made it through dinner."

He was fingering the delicate lace on the garter belt Sherry had convinced Madison to buy that first day she'd taken her shopping. At the time she couldn't have imagined standing here in front of Tanner wearing nothing but garters, stocking, a camisole, and a scrap of panties.

"You have Sherry to thank for this. I never would have bought it by myself."

Tanner knelt down and tugged on the sides of her panties until they were around her ankles.

"I'll send her a handwritten thank you note. Now off with that thing." He pointed to her camisole and she pulled it over her head, leaving nothing but the garters and stockings. He stood and grinned stepping out of his boxers and kicking them behind him.

"I think I need to show you what those garter things do to me."

He picked her up and swung her onto the gleaming wood of the kitchen table, spreading her thighs until his hard cock was nestled right against her clit. Madison sat back on her elbows and let her gaze drift over Tanner. Every inch of him was beautiful, from the sculpted muscles to his square jaw that spoke of his integrity. She'd had a crush on him as a girl, but she now loved him as a woman. She opened her mouth to tell him, but the words caught in her throat. She was terrified he didn't feel the same.

He leaned over her, balancing on his palms and captured a nipple between his lips, nipping and licking until she was squirming on the smooth surface of the table. He repeated the process on the other side then kissed a wet trail down her abdomen straight to where she needed him the most. He sat down in a chair, his breath on her wide-open pussy, his fingers playing with the garter buckles. She hooked her high heels on the backs of the kitchen chairs on either side of him and lay back on the table.

"You're going to scream my name, Maddie."

His wicked tongue made her moan, tremble, and groan. He explored every inch of her cunt and teased her clit until she was begging for release.

Her fingers clawed at the table but there was nothing to hold on to. When his mouth closed over the swollen pearl, she did scream his name.

"Tanner!"

The world seemed to tip and spin as the waves ran through her. She heard him rummage in his pants, and then the snap of elastic. His cock pressed into her welcoming pussy and his arms lifted her up so she was in a sitting position.

"I want to fuck you and look into your eyes. I'm fucking you, Maddie. Me. No one else."

No one else existed on the planet besides the two of them. Tanner pulled from her pussy and she whimpered, needing to be filled again. He thrust hard and her head fell back as pleasure filled her to her core.

"Yes," she hissed. "More."

He gave her everything she asked for. He fucked her hard and fast, one arm behind her and one wound in her hair. She wrapped her legs around his waist to keep up with the rhythm he set. Every powerful thrust of his body sent her closer and closer to another climax.

"Come with me, Maddie."

Tanner's voice was a whisper in her ear but her body responded. She was already going over when he reached between them and rubbed her clit. She cried out at the sensations colliding inside of her so overwhelming it took her breath away.

Thrusting one more time, Tanner froze, his expression a mask of pain, pleasure, and then something like serenity. He held her close for a long time, his lips brushing hers over and over before trailing across her jaw and down her neck.

She leaned against him, letting her body relax and come down from the heights he'd sent them both to. Finally she pressed a kiss to his chest and looked up into his eyes, so soft and warm.

"Happy birthday, cowboy."

Tanner kissed her slow and sweet, taking his time. When he lifted his head, she was sure she saw love in his expression.

"Best damn birthday I've ever had, Maddie. You're the best thing in my life."

Chapter Twenty-One

The bed felt too warm and comfortable. Madison was pressed up against Tanner, one arm thrown over his chest and a leg thrown over his thigh. The insistent ringing of his cell phone wasn't going to let him go back to sleep, though. Someone wanted to talk to him right now.

He peeked open an eye and saw it was eight in the morning. It wasn't an ungodly time to call considering Tanner was a morning person. He was usually up long before now even on his days off. However, most days he hadn't spent the night making love to a fiery red haired witch.

After they'd finished on the kitchen table, they'd gathered up their scattered clothes and taken the party into the bedroom. Considering he turned forty-five yesterday, Tanner couldn't complain about his stamina last night. He couldn't do that every single day, of course. Shit, that would put him in the hospital. But once in awhile was still doable.

Tanner groaned and rolled over carefully, trying not to wake Madison. He should have known her years of being on call would make her sleep with one eye open. She sat up in bed, practically wide awake in seconds.

"What? What's that noise?"

"My phone."

Tanner reached for his pants on the chair and pulled out his cell.

Chris.

He swiped the screen and put it to his ear, settling back on the pillows while Madison padded to the bathroom wearing nothing but a smile. Despite last night's debauchery, his cock, already hard with morning wood, twitched with interest.

"Uh, yeah son. How are you?"

Tanner hadn't heard from Chris in a few days but so far so good.

"Good, Dad. I called to wish you a happy birthday. I'm sorry I didn't call yesterday but I was in meetings all day and then the program had a dinner for the families. Stacey got to meet my counselor and some of the other people in the group."

"Don't worry about it, Chris. When you get to be my age, you don't care as much about your birthday."

"Annie drew you a picture and it's in the mail. Of course, it's really just a blue blob made with crayon."

Tanner chuckled. "I'll put it on the refrigerator. How are Stacey and Annie?"

"They're good. Stacey's been great and so have Grandma and Grandpa. Things are good, Dad. Thanks for sending me here."

Tanner cleared his throat, a lump lodged there made it hard to speak. "Thank you for going. I know it isn't easy."

Chris blew out a breath. "It isn't. I'm struggling, but I want this to work. You're right. Being with Stacey and Annie is better than being drunk. But I still crave it. If I was in Springwood right now, I know I'd go drinking with my friends."

"You will want to drink for a long time, son. But it gets better. I promise you. Keep focusing on the things you want to do that alcohol gets in the way of. After some time, you'll find the craving to drink wasn't about the booze. It was about whatever reason you drank. Once you get to the bottom of it, the urge to drink, well, it won't control you anymore. "

Madison came back and slid into the bed next to him, cuddling close. He gave her the thumbs up sign which drew a smile from her.

"Chris?" she mouthed silently.

Tanner nodded. "You stay there as long as you need to, Chris. Don't rush back here before you feel up to it. Old habits will be easy to fall in to."

"Thanks, Dad. Listen, I talked to Mom and she said she isn't with Fenton anymore. She didn't want to talk about it. Do you know what happened?"

Fenton's a fucking idiot, that's what happened.

"I don't think it would be right for me to comment on it. When your mother's ready, she'll talk about it. Until then, just be supportive of her decision."

"I will. I need to get going. Annie wants her breakfast and then I need to get to a group meeting."

"Give her a kiss from me and call me in a few days. Love you, son."

"I love you too, Dad."

Tanner felt like a hammer pounded his chest. It had been too long since he'd heard those words. He would love his children until his last dying breath.

"Talk to you soon."

Chris hung up and Tanner put the phone on the end table, and then pulled Madison closer. She settled her head on his chest.

"Chris is doing better?"

"He is. It's going to be hard and he may still have some setbacks, but at least he's realized he has a problem. That's the biggest step."

Madison traced hearts on his skin sending tingles straight to his cock. "If he has half your strength, he'll be okay."

Tanner rubbed his stubbly chin on the top of her head. "You're good for my ego."

She looked pointedly at the tent his dick had made under the sheet. "I'm good for more than that, apparently. Do we have time before you have to catch that flight for your super secret spy adventure?"

Tanner was flying out of the secret airfield where Marshal Evan Davis had brought in Presley last fall. Tanner and the other lawmen would be taking a charter flight to the prison on the Canadian border where they would be picking up the prisoner for transport. They'd escort him to Florence outside of Denver, then fly back to the airfield sometime Sunday. The approximately twelve-hour drive would take place tonight under the cover of darkness when the roads weren't as crowded. It would be easier to spot a tail that way.

212

"Very funny. It's not a spy adventure. Just a field trip of sorts. And the flight doesn't leave until noon. We have time for some fun and some breakfast."

"A field trip you can't tell me about." Madison sighed dramatically.

"I'll tell you all about it when I get back." Tanner paused. "I'd like you to take Scout with you to your house tonight."

Maddie frowned. "I've already invited Sherry to spend the night because you didn't want me to be alone. Are you that worried?"

Tanner rubbed his chin. He didn't want to scare her, but she needed to take this seriously. "Yes, I am. Someone needs to watch Scout anyway. Normally Sam watches him for me, but he's in charge while I'm doing this. I'll feel secure knowing Scout is with you. He'll keep you safe."

"Then I'll take Scout with me. He's such a good dog. He'll be a pleasure to have around. I'm more worried about you, Tanner. If that coffee cup really belongs to Fenton, won't he be trying to hurt you?"

He wants me dead. Period.

"I'll be heavily armed. That reminds me. Does your father have a gun?"

Madison levered up on her elbows. "You really are worried, aren't you? What's going on tonight?"

"Let's just say I'm helping transport something that Fenton would like to have. In fact, many people would like to have it."

"Then they'll be going after you, not me." Madison poked a finger in his chest. "Maybe you should take Scout."

Tanner shook his head. "Scout is retired from real police work. I'll be with several heavily armed and well trained men. You will be here. Now do you have a gun, Maddie?"

Madison exhaled slowly. "Yes. Dad has a shotgun in the hall closet outside the exam rooms."

Dr. Greg Shay wasn't as much of a pacifist as he put on.

"Loaded?"

Madison nodded warily. "You're not going to tell me to keep it next to me are you? I couldn't shoot that thing if my life depended on it."

Someone unfamiliar with firearms shouldn't handle guns. Tanner shook his head. "No. Does Sherry know about guns?"

"She's gone hunting with her dad." Madison was looking at him like he was crazy. "Tanner, I'm not going to need a damn gun."

"As long as you have Scout, I'm sure you won't. Put the gun in your bedroom though, okay? It will make me feel better if you do."

Madison gave him a put upon expression. "Fine. Why don't you just post an armed guard at my door? Wouldn't it be easier?"

"Now that, Madison Shay, isn't a bad idea. Let me call Sam and see if any deputy wants some overtime. If I don't have any men, I can at least have a deputy drive by there every few minutes or so."

With a deputy watching the neighborhood and Scout inside the house, Tanner wouldn't have to worry about Madison at all. He could concentrate on the job he had to do tonight. He would need to be completely focused just in case the worst happened.

"My boyfriend has gone completely insane." Madison pouted.

"Humor me. Call it my birthday present, okay?"

Madison's eyes went wide. "Shit, I forgot to give you your present. Dammit, it's at my house." She slapped her forehead. "How could I forget something like that? It was those damn garters cutting off the oxygen to my brain."

"Totally worth it." Tanner grinned. "I'll come by when I get back into town and you can give me my present then. In the meantime, this will be my gift."

Her lips twisted. "Okay, cowboy. You win. I'll pretend to be Fort Knox tonight. But you're going to feel pretty silly when nothing happens."

Tanner hoped with all his heart that would be the case.

* * * *

Tanner leaned back against the armored truck and squinted up at the sky where the sun was already starting to set. It had been a long afternoon of preparations, but the Canadian authorities should be here any minute with the prisoner, Howard Kerr.

They were on the American side of the Canadian-U.S. border and within an hour or so of Highway 191, which they would take south toward Billings. At Billings they would pick up US 90 and then on to US 25 to Denver. Florence was located just outside of Denver and the drive should take about twelve hours. Once they turned Kerr over to his new home, they would fly a charter back to Montana.

They'd planned every stop for fuel so that nothing was left to chance. Every man had an assignment and a place to be, along with some heavy government issue artillery. The Marshal Service had assigned eighteen men to this detail along with the six sheriffs Evan Davis had deputized today. With two motorcades, that made twelve men for each.

Two cars, each with two men, would be in front of the armored vehicle, and then two cars to the rear. One would have two men and the other would have three men. The extra man was designated as a communication hub. He would keep in contact with every other vehicle in his motorcade in addition to the other communication hub with the other team.

Two men would ride in the front seat of the armored truck and one in the back with the prisoner. The Federal Marshals had insisted that they ride in the very front and rear chase cars as it was their mission. Consequently Tanner, Reed, and Logan would be directly behind the armored vehicle and Jared and Griffin would be directly in front.

One motorcade, Red Team, would take the back roads and the other, Blue Team, would keep more to the main. Marshal Evan also had a crew at an airfield about fifteen miles from their location as a decoy. Opposing force expected Kerr to be flown to Florence. Tanner and the other sheriffs, along with Marshal Davis, had planned a little "now you see him, now you don't" for the Jackson and Warner cartels. If everything went according to plan, they would never know which motorcade Kerr was in.

"It's getting fucking cold out here. Shit." Logan stuck his hands in his pockets, his rifle slung over his shoulder.

Jared pulled up his collar. "Damn straight. The sun isn't even down yet. Let's get this show on the road."

Tanner chuckled inwardly at their impatience. He'd taught two teenagers algebra and how to drive a stick shift. He had patience to spare.

Reed laughed. "Welcome to Canada. It's colder than a brass witch's tit, but hey, they've got hockey."

Evan shook his head and smiled. "Technically we're still in the U.S. and Montana is just as cold."

"No way," Griffin replied. "This is colder. I didn't think it could get any colder, but hell if it isn't."

Seth grinned. "You asked for them, Ev. I guess I should have told you they whine a little."

Marshal Harry Morey stepped out of one of the vehicles, his lips a grim line. Tanner had met him on the plane and so far the dour man hadn't cracked a smile once. Morey kept talking into his cell phone and scowling. Apparently he wasn't happy about being assigned here or that Evan was in charge. When they'd gone over the plans on the flight up here, Morey kept interrupting Evan trying to make changes. Finally, Evan had to basically tell the guy to shut the fuck up. No modifications were going to be made this late in the game unless warranted.

"They're late," Morey said flatly. "Call them."

Evan, to his credit, didn't bat an eye at the other man's gruff command. He simply shook his head. "They're on their way."

"You can't know that unless you call them." Morey had a mutinous expression.

216

Evan leaned against the truck. "They'll be here."

Morey turned on his heel and walked several paces away pulling out his phone. Again.

"What crawled up that guy's ass?" Logan asked with a grimace. "I think someone pissed in his Wheaties this morning. Everyone else doesn't seem to have an issue."

That was true. The other Federal Marshals were milling around, talking and drinking coffee from styrofoam cups. They all seemed as relaxed as they could be in the circumstances.

"Let's just say I'm not Harry Morey's favorite person. We could also say that unless something is Harry's idea, he doesn't think much of it."

"Charming," Jared said. "Likes to be in charge, huh?"

"Too much," Evan agreed. "He likes being in charge more than doing a good job. He's ambitious though. I probably should watch my back."

Evan was grinning though, so it didn't appear that he was worried. The government was sometimes a very fucked up place and guys like Morey could be promoted to the level of their incompetence. Tanner had seen it in the military. Some of the biggest assholes seemed to gravitate toward positions of power.

Evan straightened and nodded toward a man in uniform walking toward them.

"Marshal Davis?" The man looked them over, his features bland.

"I'm Marshal Evan Davis."

Evan stepped forward and showed his badge to the man who nodded and looked down at his clipboard.

"Are you prepared to take custody of one Howard Kerr?" the man asked.

"I am. I have the paperwork right here."

The man took the thick set of papers and quickly scanned them. "Wait here."

The man turned and headed back into the border office building. Tanner was instantly on alert, his adrenaline pumping. He hated to admit it, but he loved the rush right before doing something ever so slightly dangerous. It was stupid and kind of immature, but fuck, he felt so alive at moments like this. One look at the expressions of his friends and he knew they felt the same way. He couldn't have explained it to a civilian, but these men were the closest thing he had to brothers. They understood what he didn't even have words to describe.

Four uniformed men came out of the building leading a man in an orange jumpsuit. The man's hair was clipped short, almost military style, and he was shackled hand and foot. His head was down and Tanner scanned the sky and rooftops looking for anyone who might be looking to take Kerr out. From all the intel they'd been privy to, Kerr would be wanted alive and kicking, but that didn't mean someone might not want to take out a few Canadian Mounties in the meantime.

Logan sidled up to Tanner and looked back at the building the men had just walked out of. "I don't like this at all. We need to get out of here. There are too many fucking people here."

Jared joined them, leaning in so he wouldn't be overheard. "I'm with you on this. I know that protocol states we meet them at the border but shit, he could get taken out by a sniper."

"Then let's get him in the wagon," Tanner said. "You're right. This is way too open."

Morey took the prisoner by the arm and led him to one of two armored trucks, opening the steel doors and escorting him in. Kerr was quickly cuffed to the bench and his feet shackled to the metal floor. The bench opposite would be for the Marshal who drew the short straw and had to ride with the prisoner. It wouldn't be pleasant or fun in the least. The seats were hard metal and there were no windows to watch the passing scenery. The two men would basically be staring at each other for the next twelve hours.

Evan handed Morey a coffee can. "If he needs to take a piss."

Morey's mouth gaped open and his face turned purple. "What do you mean? I'm not riding with him in there."

"Yes, you are. I need a Marshal to do this." Evan's voice was even and calm in contrast to a decidedly honked off Morey.

"Fuck you. Get Hampson or Thompson. I'm not doing it." Morey poked Evan in the chest.

Evan looked down at Morey's finger. "Hampson and Thompson will be on the Blue Team. And don't ever do that again or you'll be pulling back a stump." Evan's tone was dangerously soft and menacing. Morey took a step back.

"I'm going to call Staley. He won't let you do this," Morey blustered.

Evan smiled slowly. "Go ahead. Call him." He crossed his arms over his chest and waited.

Morey looked unsure as to whether Evan was bluffing, but eventually he pulled his cell from his pocket and punched in a few numbers. He barked into the phone and his face grew redder with each passing minute. He finally shoved the phone back in his pants with a growl.

"Fuck you, Davis. You haven't heard the last of this."

Evan smiled. "Now that I believe. You can lodge a formal complaint when this is over. Get in. We need to get on the road. We have a long drive ahead of us." Evan took a few steps away and then turned back. "I'll need your phone."

Morey's eyes went wide. "Why? It's untraceable. It's the service's standard issue."

"You know the rules. No cell phones in the truck. And your piece as well. All of them."

Morey muttered and bitched but handed over his phone and his handgun. Evan lifted an eyebrow.

"Is that it?"

"Fuck you."

Evan laughed. "I'll take that as a yes." He turned to the rest of them who were watching the sideshow with interest. "Saddle up. Let's get this parade in motion."

Everyone knew his position. Evan was driving the armored car with Kerr inside and Seth was riding shotgun. Jared and Griffin were in the front of the armored vehicle and Logan, Reed, and Tanner to the rear. Reed was playing communication hub. The front and rear chase cars completed their motorcade.

Just before the motorcade was about to leave Evan walked to the back of the decoy armored truck and removed the license plate. Tanner immediately picked up on what Evan was doing and did the same on the vehicle with Kerr inside, then handed it to Evan. He gave Tanner his plate and Tanner affixed it to the spot where he'd removed the original.

The decoy motorcade pulled out and theirs followed suit. At the five mile mark the other motorcade split apart and headed to more rural back roads. Evan's motorcade would stick to main arteries. It would be easier to see a tail in a more wide-open space, and the better roads would give them room to maneuver if the need arose. The sky was clear of any aircraft and the roads pretty much deserted. Evan had said that the FAA was clearing the airspace above them for security purposes.

They hadn't gone more than fifty miles when Evan came on the radio. "Good news. I just got word from the decoy team at the airport. They've got the crew the Jackson cartel sent to break out Kerr. That only leaves the Warner men who we need to worry about."

"The decoy worked then," Logan said. "They thought we would fly him."

Tanner nodded but kept his concentration on the road. "Warner's men are still plenty dangerous."

"Everybody wants this guy," Reed observed. "When they get what they're after, he's a dead man."

"If he talks," Logan countered.

"He'll talk," Reed said grimly. "Death will seem like a vacation for him if the Warner cartel gets their hands on him. He'll beg to die before it's all over."

Tanner remembered the grisly scene at the packing plant and couldn't argue with Reed.

"We don't let Warner's crew get anywhere near Kerr." Tanner shook his head. "He's going to be a guest of the U.S. government at Florence for a very long time."

"I think I'd rather die than sit and rot in Florence for the rest of my damn life." Logan looked out the bulletproof glass, leaning back against the headrest. "Caged up like a fucking animal. That's no way to live. Just put a fucking bullet in my brain and let me die."

"I don't know about that. The survival instinct is strong. I saw it when I was in the Middle East. You'd think you'd want to check out, but there's something inside of us that's stronger. The will to live is overpowering." Tanner sipped at his coffee and made a face. He handed the coffee thermos to Logan. "Can you pour me one? My cup's gone cold."

"Me too?" Reed held out his styrofoam cup.

"Yeah, yeah, I'm the damn waitress around here," Logan groused, but good-naturedly. "All I'm saying is I couldn't be locked up like that. No way, no how."

They drove for awhile, the silence only broken every ten minutes by the regular comm checks. Reed sighed and rubbed his temples.

"It's quiet. Too quiet."

"I thought it was just me thinking that," Tanner said. "It's going too smoothly."

Logan groaned. "Jesus H. Christ, how can things go too smoothly? You know what your problem is? You both are pessimists. You expect shit to go wrong and then you just wait for bad things to happen. Then when they do, as shit eventually will, you point to it and act all smug and shit. Well, fuck

221

you. I'm not going to get all pissy because shit is just going too damn good. Son of a fucking bitch. Do you get upset when your girlfriend has an orgasm too? Do you think next time she won't? Fuck."

Laughter bubbled up and Tanner couldn't hold it back. Logan was a fucking piece of work, but Tanner had never met a better lawmen or a more true friend.

"Just for the record, Maddie comes every damn time. Most times more than once." Tanner grinned.

Reed shook his head. "I don't want to hear that shit. I haven't been laid in weeks."

"What are you waiting for?" Logan laughed. "Your dick out of commission or something?"

"I'm no man-whore like you." Reed pelted Logan with a wadded up napkin. "I'm particular as to where I stick my cock, thank you very much."

"That's enough. We're working, not comparing sex lives," Tanner interceded. Logan and Reed could go at it all night if Tanner let them, and he wasn't in the mood. "Location check."

Logan consulted the GPS. "We'll be changing roads here soon. Keep an eye out."

That was exactly what Tanner planned to do. He wanted to get home–alive–to Madison.

Chapter Twenty-Two

Kerr should be on the plane by now.

Fenton leaned back in the leather chair and looked out his office window. The sun was starting to set and the night was going to be fucking freezing. Again. He couldn't wait to get to New York where it might be cold but there were plenty of women to keep him warm.

He hadn't bothered to call Abby. There was no point. He had enjoyed her company but it was over. He would be moving on and she would be staying in this backwater shithole. Now her ex-husband Tanner Marks was another matter. Fenton had plans for him. As soon as this job was done, he and Marks would be having some quality time together. They'd find his body in a field outside of town.

Fenton wouldn't be hanging around for the funeral.

By Monday morning he'd be in New York with a new identity. By Monday afternoon, he'd be checked into a private plastic surgery clinic. It wouldn't be perfect, but it would be enough to make facial recognition just a little more difficult. This surgeon was supposed to be the best.

Of course this was all predicated on the job going well. If he fucked it up, Fenton only had one choice. Disappear somewhere Warner couldn't find him. Fenton had enough money in the Caymans to live very well for the rest of his life.

If it went well, then Fenton would have the information he needed to tap unknown amounts of Jackson cartel wealth. He would be able to buy the loyalty and manpower he needed to knock off Warner and take over the organization. It was what he'd worked for all these years and it was almost within his grasp.

Fenton's phone went off and he smiled. This was the call he'd been waiting for. His informant inside the prison had called this morning and said Kerr was being prepared to travel today. Fenton's team would have extricated the man from federal custody by now and be on their way to a neutral location that had been scouted weeks ago. Fenton, personally, would lead the interrogation. He was looking forward to it.

He lifted the phone to his ear. "Jacks."

"Mr. Jacks, this is John Bilson."

Fenton sat up in his chair. Bilson's voice was soft as if he was afraid of being overheard. John Bilson worked for the Canadian Border Patrol. For a hefty fee he helped the Warner cartel, allowing them to move drugs through the checkpoints he monitored. Fenton also had a Border Patrol cop on the payroll at the airport. It should be that man calling him, not Bilson.

Every hair stood up on the back of Fenton's neck. He didn't like surprises and his intuition was telling him something had gone very wrong.

"Why are you calling me?"

"Your prisoner? That Kerr guy? He's not on the airplane. They just loaded him into an armored truck here at the border."

Fenton jumped up from his chair. "Son of a fucking bitch. Are you sure? It sounds like they're using decoys."

He paced the office, muttering expletives under his breath.

"I'm sure it was him. I saw the picture you sent Terry." Terry was the Border Patrol agent at the airport. He'd been recruited on Bilson's recommendation. "They had two large motorcades with two armored cars. They loaded two armed Federal Marshals into the back of one and the prisoner and a Marshal in the other. They drove out of here together, but I overheard them say they were taking different routes. So I got the plate number of the truck they loaded him into."

At least one person was on the job in the organization. "How many cars? How many agents? What were they armed with?" Fenton peppered the agent with questions.

He had to react quickly or lose their quarry. Bilson rattled off the information and Fenton scratched some notes on a piece of paper, already making plans in his head. There would be more collateral damage this way but it wasn't his fault. The government had decided how Fenton would play it. The blood would be on their hands.

"You did good, Bilson. Expect a bonus. I always appreciate loyalty in my organization. Call me if you hear anything more."

Fenton hung up the phone and quickly made a list of everyone he needed to contact. Nothing could go wrong the second time. He wanted Kerr and he would get him.

Fenton picked up the phone to call his second in command. He wished he could call his lead man at the airport but the fact was he might not even be alive. If he had been captured by authorities, Fenton didn't want to call the burner cell phone the operative would be carrying. At this point, the man and his team were dead to him. At least for now.

"Carl? Where the fuck are you? Billings? Good. Get the team, get the chopper. Once you do that, call me back and I'll tell you the plan. And Carl? You have about ten minutes."

* * * *

The motorcade stopped for gas about three hours later. They were north of Billings and the traffic had been few and far between. They pretty much owned the road. Even the few houses they passed were dark, the residents asleep.

Tanner got out of the car and stretched his legs, the cold wind whipping around his body and sending a chill through him. He'd much rather be in bed, curled around Madison but there was a job that needed doing. It was too bad Evan wasn't transferring Kerr in July.

"Damn thing's a gas guzzler. I think it gets like seven miles to the gallon, for fuck's sake. We'll be stopping for gas constantly." Reed jerked his thumb toward the armored vehicle which was still locked. Kerr and Morey wouldn't be getting out to stretch their legs. Evan would get them a snack and might even let Morey out for a bathroom break, but that was it.

Logan laughed. "You don't buy an armored truck for the gas mileage. Damn thing probably weighs ten tons with all that steel and bullet proof glass."

Tanner scanned the area, his rifle at the ready. It appeared to be completely deserted but looks could be deceiving. The front chase car had already checked out the area before they'd stopped, but Tanner couldn't stop the feeling of unease that had built with every passing mile. Two dangerous drug cartels wanted this guy, but so far they'd driven peacefully down the state of Montana. In a few hours they'd be in Wyoming and Evan had already told them a group of local sheriffs from that state would be joining them when they crossed over the state line.

Evan nodded toward the attached convenience store. "It's your turn."

They'd planned ahead and the team would go to the bathroom and grab a coffee in shifts, no shift lasting more than five minutes. With three shifts they should be back on the road in fifteen minutes. Tanner always felt better when they were moving. Standing still he felt like a sitting duck.

Logan walked with Tanner inside the store. "You've had a sour look on your face for the last hundred miles or so. What's up?"

"I'm worried about Maddie. This has gone too smoothly. If they're not targeting us, are they targeting people we care about? I wouldn't put it past Fenton to go after her."

Logan shrugged and looked away. "Lucky me, there isn't anyone I care about. Didn't you leave Scout with her and have a deputy driving by every ten minutes? You can't do much more than that, man."

Tanner had never delved into Logan's past. The man had no family to speak of, or at least Tanner had never heard about any. But Logan wasn't a man to discuss his past. His eye was always firmly on the present. He lived in the moment, enjoying life to the fullest whether it was climbing a mountain

226

or romancing a pretty young thing. Logan only knew how to live life one way. Full speed ahead and have a ball doing it.

"I just wish I was there, that's all." Tanner pulled his cell from his pocket, saw the time, and put it away. It was almost eleven and Maddie was an early riser. She'd definitely be asleep or as good as, even with Sherry there with her.

Logan glanced at his watch. "You will be in about twelve hours, give or take. I know you don't want to hear this, but shit, you need to keep your mind on the job. Stay focused, Tanner."

Logan was right. The reason he'd left Scout with Maddie and posted that guard was so he wouldn't worry. Now here he was...worrying. He needed to keep his head in the game or risk getting it blown off.

"I will. You're right. I've protected Maddie. Now we just need to get this guy to Florence."

Tanner hit the bathroom and grabbed a coffee and a snack on the way out. The motorcade was gassed up and ready to go. One leg of the journey down and only three more to go.

* * * *

Madison poured the microwave popcorn from the bag into a large bowl. She and Sherry were watching movies and talking. Sherry was telling about the latest wedding she was planning and how the bride was a complete Bridezilla.

Taking the popcorn back into the living room, Madison had to chuckle at how Scout and Sherry were sprawled on the couch. Woman and dog had bonded instantly. Sherry adored animals and Scout was no exception. The dog was half reclined on Sherry eating pieces of cubed cheese. Tanner was going to kill Madison. By the time he got his dog back, he'd be completely spoiled. Tanner didn't allow Scout on the furniture, and she was pretty sure he didn't get cheese cubes either.

"Watch what Scout can do." Sherry balanced a piece of cheese on Scout's nose. "Wait for it. Wait for it. Get it, Scout!"

The dog moved its long snout and snatched the cheese right out of the air. Sherry clapped and praised the canine, ruffling its fur and scratching his ears. Scout stuck his nose right into the bag of snacks and smacked it with his paw, indicating more.

"You've turned Tanner's police dog into a circus animal." Madison groaned. "He's going to be livid."

"He's still ferocious. Aren't you, Scout? You'll rip some poor man's leg off, won't you? Good boy." Sherry crooned, nuzzling the dog with her cheek. The dog's ears perked up and he nudged the bag with his nose again.

"Have some popcorn and no, don't give it to Scout. I don't think Tanner lets him have popcorn slathered in butter."

Sherry laughed and dug into the bowl after tossing Scout another cube. "All I hear you talk about these days is 'Tanner this' and 'Tanner that'. When am I going to get a 'You were right, Sherry' or 'Thank you, Sherry'?"

"Thank you, Sherry."

Sherry tossed a few kernels of popcorn at Madison. "Once more with feeling, please. I managed to get this entire town working together so you and Tanner could fall in love."

"They'll build a statue in your honor in the park." Madison giggled, picturing it in her mind. Sherry would have her iPad and her cell phone, complete with headset.

"It is love, isn't it? Do you think he'll propose soon? I totally cannot wait to organize your wedding. I think a mermaid silhouette would be the perfect wedding gown for you."

Madison wasn't sure what to say. She absolutely loved Tanner, more than she had ever thought possible. But he had never mentioned the word love.

"I don't even know if Tanner wants to get married again. I mean, we've never discussed it. We haven't been going out all that long, you know."

228

"True." Sherry tapped her chin. "But you're both adults, not kids. I can tell you're both in love."

"Do you think so?" Madison chewed her bottom lip. She wanted to believe Sherry.

Sherry smacked her forehead. "You haven't told him?"

Madison shook her head.

"And he hasn't said it either?"

Madison shook her head, again, heat suffusing her cheeks. She was a relationship idiot.

"May I ask what you are waiting for?"

"For him to say it first? Isn't that what you told me to do?" Madison asked indignantly. She'd been following orders, for heaven's sake.

"Well yes, I did say that. But once you could tell, it's okay to say it."

"Now you tell me. Honestly, I've been scared to death to do it. What if he doesn't say it back? What do I do then?"

The mere thought he might not say it back had Madison shaking in her favorite boots.

"He'll say it. He loves you. Everything is working out for you, Madison. I know you weren't sure about moving back home."

Madison hadn't been sure at all, but she'd promised her father she would someday come back and join him. When he'd called, she hadn't been able to think of a single reason to stay in Chicago. She had thought of several reasons not to come back to Springwood. It had been the home of too many unpleasant childhood memories.

But coming home had taught her more than how to be in a relationship with a man. It had taught her that time marches on even when you're not watching. She'd been in Chicago, maturing and changing, building her career. The people in town had been doing that exact same thing.

For Madison, Springwood had remained frozen in time. It was an unchanging memory. Coming back showed her that wasn't the case.

Everyone had moved on with their lives, sparing little thought to the freckled, red-haired girl they had tormented.

And that was how it should be. Her classmates grew up and were smacked sideways by adulthood, as most young people are. They'd been busy falling in love, marrying, having children, and working at jobs. It made those years in school seem very far away and kind of unimportant. Tanner's words that day in the coffee shop had given her a perspective she'd lacked in Chicago.

"I wasn't sure, but I'm glad I came back. I missed you and well, Springwood is home. Chicago was great, but it would never have been the place I wanted to settle down."

"With two kids and a dog?" Sherry grinned.

"Honestly, you just won't let anything go will you? Even if Tanner does love me—"

"He does," interjected Sherry.

"Even if he does love me," Madison began again. "It doesn't mean he wants to get married or have children. He's already done that."

Sherry wrinkled her nose. "You two should talk about this. What if he doesn't want to get married or have kids? Are you okay with that?"

"I've never dreamed of a big, fancy wedding." Madison shrugged. "As for children, I haven't given them much thought either. I've been too busy working. I guess I always thought I would have one or two, but I think I would be okay if I didn't."

"As long as you had Tanner?"

Madison nodded. "I could be okay with him, married or not. I don't need a piece of paper to feel committed to him."

Sherry laughed. "You're the original modern woman. I wanted a marriage license, Dan's last name, and now we're working on the kids. Call me old-fashioned, but I want the dream."

Madison could only smile at her best friend. Tanner all by himself was more than anything Madison had ever dreamed of.

She yawned and tried to hide it by turning away.

"You're not fooling anyone. Go to bed," Sherry ordered, but she was smiling.

"You wanted to watch this movie."

Sherry was mad for old films and one of the movie channels was showing Casablanca.

"I'm still planning to. Scout can keep me company. Won't you, Scout?"

The dog wagged its tail and was given another cheese cube as a reward. Madison was exhausted and decided to give in gracefully.

"Okay, I'll see you in the morning." Madison got up and headed for the bedroom.

"I'll be quiet when I come to bed," Sherry called out. Sherry was sleeping on a rollaway bed in Madison's room. She'd tried to convince Sherry to stay in her dad's room but Sherry wouldn't do it. She said it would feel weird and disrespectful. Madison didn't push the subject as she didn't want to sleep in the bedroom alone with a gun. Besides, Madison's bedroom was huge, taking up almost the entire top floor of the house. Her father had renovated the second floor when she was a teenager giving her the bedroom of her dreams.

"Don't worry about it. I can get back to sleep easily if I wake up."

Madison had learned to sleep anywhere at anytime when she'd been a resident. She took one last look over her shoulder and smiled at the picture of Sherry eating popcorn and Scout cuddled as close as he could get. By tomorrow morning, Tanner would probably call her and she could tell him that nothing bad had happened except his dog was now addicted to cheese cubes.

* * * *

Fenton was sitting in an SUV just south of Billings in the middle of a deserted field. When he'd received the call from his informant on the Canadian Border Patrol he'd sent out two teams to find the motorcades. A large one for the motorcade that contained Kerr and a small one for the decoy.

Fenton wasn't sure what made him do that, but he wanted all his bases covered. He'd learned you could never be too careful.

He stared into the darkness as he waited for his cell to ring. The other team should be dealing with the motorcade at this very moment. A helicopter would take out the first chase car and an RPG would blow up the rear, leaving the middle vehicles boxed in. His team would blow the doors of the armored truck with a shape charge and extricate Kerr, flying him to this location where they would change to a nondescript vehicle. He would then be driven to the designated location for interrogation.

The phone vibrated on his thigh.

"Jacks."

"He's not here. We were double-crossed or something. He's not here." The lead man, George Keene, was breathing hard and Fenton could hear gunfire in the background.

"What the fuck do you mean he's not there? We were told he was in that armored car."

"He's just not here. We've looked every—"

"Shut up. How many down?" he asked calmly while anger built in his gut. He'd kill Bilson for this.

"We've lost about half our numbers, but they've taken the worst hit. We've downed pretty much the entire group."

"Get out and get the bird over here. He's in the other motorcade, you fucking idiot."

Fenton gritted his teeth to keep the string of swear words from streaming out. This was not the time to lose control. He needed to stay calm and in control.

"Right. We should be there in twenty."

"Keene?"

"Yeah?" The man sounded anxious to be off the phone. He was probably ducked down in one of their ground vehicles for cover.

232

"No survivors."

Chapter Twenty-Three

Tanner stretched his arm over his head and rubbed his neck. Logan was driving this leg but Tanner was feeling antsy. He hated being cooped up in a car for hours on end. The scenery was the same blur of dark shadows with only the occasional car to break up the monotony.

"Hand me a soda, will you?" Reed asked from the back seat. "I need the caffeine to stay awake."

Tanner reached down to the small cooler situated between his legs on the floor and pulled out a can, tossing it to Reed.

"When's next check in?" Tanner asked.

Reed consulted his watch. "Three minutes. So far everything's been quiet. In about an hour we'll be in Wyoming and pick up the extra manpower."

"Tell me again why they're only helping us in two states instead of all three?" Logan asked with a sideways grin. "Do they have something against Montana?"

Tanner chuckled. "Not that I know of. It's to give some of us a break to catch an hour of sleep. These guys can drive and be on guard and the rest of us can rotate getting a quick nap. Evan's also thinking about letting Morey out of the back of the truck and putting another Marshal in for awhile."

"Evan's too nice of a guy," Reed observed.

The radio started to crackle. It was a Spearhead encrypted handheld that Tanner knew was fielded at first to military in Iraq. Reed frowned, glancing at his watch. It was too early for the check in from the other motorcade.

"Yes?" His voice was short and abrupt. Tanner and Logan were on alert the minute the radio started to go off. This was the first thing that hadn't gone like clockwork. The sound of gunfire and yelling came through the speakers loud and clear. The other motorcade was under fire.

"Echo-Two-Tango, here. We're under heavy fire." The man's voice was breathless. "They've got a chopper and they've blown the rear door of the truck. They took out the lead and rear chase cars."

The Blue Team was boxed in and practically helpless. To make matters worse, there weren't any agents in the vicinity to help them. The Red Team wouldn't be stopped for anything, even several agents being gunned down on the job.

"How many?" Reed asked.

More static and gunfire. "Two in the bird and about ten on the ground. We've taken out a few but I'm suffering heavy casualties here."

"Son of a fucking bitch. What a clusterfuck," Logan muttered under his breath. Tanner could see Logan's knuckles tighten on the wheel. When the bad guys realized Kerr wasn't there, they were going to be pissed the hell off.

"I'll relay to Echo-Three-Delta. Get the fuck out of there."

Reed ended the call with the Blue Team and immediately got Evan on the radio to relay what was happening less than a fifty miles away.

"Holy fuck." Evan growled.

Tanner could hear Evan telling Seth to get the Marshal Service on the phone and get some people there as soon as possible. Tanner remembered that DEA Agent Jason Anderson had people in this area and a helicopter to get there. He pulled the phone from his pocket and made a quick call, grateful when Jason answered on the second ring. As succinctly as he could, he outlined what was happening and luckily the agent got the drift right away. He'd head there with manpower and an ETA of thirty minutes.

That amount of time was an eternity when someone was under fire but it was the best they could do at the moment. It would take the Marshal Service time to get reinforcements. Every available man was being used for this transfer job.

Evan came over the radio. "We're increasing our speed. Shut off your lights. Stay in formation."

Logan pressed on the accelerator and the engine roared with power. Tanner kept looking up into the black night sky for signs of lights. He cracked the window to listen for any sounds of helicopters but there was nothing except the cold wind. If the Warner or Jackson cartel knew about the other motorcade, the chances were good they knew about this one as well. It didn't matter which cartel had hit them at this point. Both were well-armed and deadly.

The hum of the wheels against the road couldn't lull them into any sense of security. When the headlights of a car began to approach they all tensed, weapons ready, but it passed on by harmlessly into the night. Tanner turned and watched until the taillights disappeared in the distance.

There was nowhere to run or hide. Even if they found an abandoned building to hole up in, then they ran the risk of being surrounded and pinned down. Turning around and going back wasn't the answer either. The safest thing they could do was keep moving forward. They had reinforcements just over the border and Evan had already called them. The Wyoming men were moving northward and would hopefully meet up with the motorcade before anything happened.

"Fuck, I hate the waiting." Reed's head was looking from side to side, squinting at the inky blackness whenever he wasn't on the radio. They were all on edge, the minutes ticking by with an excruciating slowness. Their nerves were stretched to the brink of snapping. Tanner could feel the sweat beading underneath his bulletproof vest and he restlessly shifted in his seat. These feelings were familiar, and his mind and body went on autopilot, the rest of the world ceasing to exist. There was only this place and this moment.

His senses became sharper. He could hear every pump of his heart, the whoosh of blood in his veins. He could smell the leather of the seats and hear the tapping of Reed's fingers against the radio. Tanner let his instincts take over, gaining comfort from them. They'd never let him down before. Once a soldier, always a soldier.

236

Logan's face in the dim light looked carved from granite and Reed looked like a predator ready to pounce on its prey. It was almost a relief when they finally heard the sounds of a chopper in the sky.

* * * *

Fenton's adrenaline raced when the chopper hovered over the second motorcade. He hadn't known exactly what road they would be on, but this was southern Montana. There weren't too many to choose from unless they wanted to take twenty hours to get to Florence, zigzagging from country road to country road.

The headlights of each vehicle were turned off but the bird swept the spotlight over the motorcade from back to front. Six SUVs and the armored truck tucked in the middle. This wasn't going to be easy. He'd lost about half a dozen men taking out the first motorcade. He'd augmented with others from his organization but they weren't what he would describe as battle-ready. As it was, he'd be lucky to get Kerr out without losing most of his men.

It didn't matter in the long run. There were always men willing to do the dirty work if you paid them enough. Fenton had long since stopped being surprised by the lack of morals in the average man.

One of those men now had an M203 40mm grenade launcher mounted under his M16A2 held tight into his shoulder, pointing it at the lead car. Some sparks came from the High Explosive Dual Purpose shell and it flew straight down, eliminating the car in a fiery blast. The explosion illuminated the darkness and Fenton could see the shadows of his ground force heading in.

This time there would be no mistakes.

The next target was the last car in the motorcade. Then the middle cars would be trapped and he could pick off the Feds, one by one.

* * * *

The minute Tanner saw the explosion up ahead he knew what the cartel was planning. The convoy screeched to a stop, and Evan yelled over the radio to back up. Logan threw the SUV into reverse, but Tanner already knew the outcome.

He turned around in his seat and looked out the rear window as the last car in the motorcade was blown to smithereens by what could only be an RPG.

"Son of a bitch," Reed whispered under his breath at the yellow and orange light show. Tanner shook his head in disbelief. Four good Marshals were down and the rest of them were trapped in the kill box. They couldn't move forward or backward.

"Don't move!" Evan's voice came over the radio as Tanner watched the ground game begin. Surprisingly there were only about ten men and two of them were still in the chopper. They must have lost a large number when they ambushed the other team.

Tanner's heart galloped in his chest as he forced himself to stay in the bulletproof vehicle. He had to fight every instinct to jump out and start firing but that was a suicide mission. He'd wait until the cartel was distracted blowing the armored car door and then try and pick them off one at a time.

They'd discussed their positions if they were attacked. Tanner, Logan, and Reed were to focus on taking down as many men as possible from their location right behind the armored truck. Evan and Seth had the main responsibility of ensuring no one got Kerr, but ultimately that was everyone's job.

The headlights from the vehicles and the helicopter pierced the darkness, and Tanner could see the cartel men, dressed in dark clothing. They were huddled around the back of the armored truck with five men fanned around them keeping watch. The guards were armed with automatic rifles but one man looked uneasy, holding the firearm awkwardly, his gaze jumping nervously from side to side.

238

"Now." Evan's voice came over the radio and Tanner slid the passenger side door open, crouching behind it and pointing his rifle. He put the guard farthest to the right in his sight and squeezed the trigger. The man went down as the door blew, falling uselessly off its hinges. The two other guards began spraying bullets and Tanner was forced to take cover. His gaze sought Logan and Reed to make sure they were okay.

Logan had done the same as Tanner, and he was kneeling behind the driver's door firing shots when he had the opportunity. Reed was also ducked behind a car door, but Tanner could hear talking on the radio and Seth's voice. Reed was updating the armored car on what was happening behind them, which meant Evan was trying to put an offensive together with Griffin and Jared.

Tanner lifted his rifle to target another guard when he watched in horror as Morey pulled a small handgun from his boot, aiming and firing at Kerr. The prisoner must have been watching also because he managed to jerk away despite the chains holding him to the metal bench. A red stain was spreading across Kerr's leg and he was screaming in pain.

The man who blew the door lifted his rifle and double tapped Morey's forehead. The Marshal froze for a moment, his eyes wide open before falling to the floor of the truck. Tanner kept firing at the guards each time they paused their spray of bullets. Griffin, Jared, and Evan appeared on the roof of the truck shooting downward from their positions on their bellies. Two men went down and one jumped in the truck with bolt cutters, freeing Kerr.

A man streaked out of the chopper toward the truck and Tanner instantly recognized Fenton Jacks even in the dim light. Tanner tried to get a shot off but the spray from the automatic rifles held him until Jacks dove down under the vehicle. The man in the truck grabbed Kerr and pulled him out, tossing him on the ground next to Jacks.

"Jacks is going to get him on the bird. We need to take out the chopper," Tanner yelled, not sure he'd be heard over the gunfire. Reed relayed it to Seth, and Tanner watched as Seth stepped out of the armored car and started firing at the helicopter. Tanner gave him as much cover as he could but his stomach churned as Jacks and another man held Kerr and made a run for it. The men that had been spraying fire from behind the armored truck jumped between Jacks and Tanner and held the Marshals at bay.

Evan ran to the front of the roof and fired at Jacks. Jacks turned around and shot back, Evan jerking and then falling to the ground. Tanner and Logan fired into the mess of smoke and bullets but Jacks stuffed Kerr into the helicopter and used the other man as a human shield.

Tanner could swear he saw Jacks smile as the chopper began to lift from the ground. Tanner and Reed fired at the circling bird as it rose nose down clawing for more speed, and then it disappeared into the night sky leaving the rest of Jacks's men to fight it out.

Jared and Griffin took out a few more men and at that point the cartel was outnumbered. The last two started to make a run for it, but Tanner easily plugged one in the shoulder and Logan got the other in the leg. They would probably live, but they would sure as hell be able to talk.

Seth was kneeling next to Evan, and Tanner ran up and crouched next to him, the acrid smell of smoke and gunpowder in the air.

"How bad?" Tanner asked.

"He's alive," Seth replied. "He's got two slugs in his vest, one in his shoulder and one in his leg. Plus a big lump on his head from that fall."

Tanner looked down and Evan's eyes opened. His pupils were dilated and unfocused.

"Stay down. Reed's on the radio calling for help. You're going to live, man."

Evan licked his lips. "They got Kerr?" His voice was raspy and filled with pain.

"Yeah," Tanner nodded grimly. "We'll get him back. Kerr was shot by Morey so Jacks will have to get him medical attention."

"Morey?"

He was sure Evan already knew the answer–apparently he needed to hear it. "Dead. Two in the forehead."

Evan closed his eyes and tried to move. Seth put a hand on Evan's good shoulder and pushed him back. "Stay put. We'll have you terrorizing nurses as soon as we can."

The sound of sirens in the distance drew Tanner's attention. Logan was standing over them pointing north and then south. "Ambulances from Billings and the Wyoming guys."

Tanner scraped a hand down his face and stood. "A day late and a dollar short." He turned to see Reed still on the radio. "Who is he talking to?"

"Your DEA agent. We should hear the helicopter any minute."

Griffin and Jared had climbed down from the top of the truck and had joined them. Tanner slapped them on the back. "Good shooting today. You saved a few lives, not to mention my own."

Jared shook his head, a muscle working in his jaw. "It wasn't enough."

"Hey, we were boxed in. Shit, the odds of us even surviving weren't in our fucking favor. Yet we're standing here. Still breathing. We'll get Kerr back. It was Fenton Jacks who took him."

Griffin ran a hand through his hair. "And just how will we find him?"

Evan drew a loud breath from where he lay on the ground. "We have him chipped. We knew this was a possibility. We can GPS him."

Logan rubbed the back of his neck. "Fuck a duck, the government really does know where we are all times of the day and night. You fucking microchipped him? Shit."

"My bet is they'll dump the helicopter and move to a car," Seth said.

"I agree. Add in the fact that Kerr's bleeding pretty bad. Jacks is going to be desperate," Logan observed.

"That might be to Jacks's benefit. He may withhold medical attention until Kerr tells him what he wants to know," Jared offered.

241

Griffin snorted. "If Kerr tells him what Jacks wants, he'll never see a doctor ever again."

Tanner shrugged. "Stranger deals have been made. Jacks can't withhold medical attention forever or he'll lose his cash cow. Kerr will know that and use it to his advantage."

Two ambulances careened up on the shoulder of the road and came to a screeching halt. EMTs jumped out and ran a stretcher over to Evan while another chopper was closing in. Tanner tensed for a moment but then saw the familiar red and white paint job. DEA Agent Jason Anderson.

The man would have news of how badly the other motorcade had been hit. Tanner steeled himself for the news and the next phase of the job. They had to find Kerr and get him to Florence.

Personally, Tanner was going to take great pleasure in finding Fenton Jacks and book him an adjoining cell right next to Kerr's. Tonight Jacks would be stopped, once and for all.

Chapter Twenty-Four

Sherry yawned as the closing credits of the movie scrolled down the screen. It was late and she should probably crawl into bed. Madison would be up at the crack of dawn making pancakes and some of that supposedly healthy turkey bacon. Bacon in any form wasn't supposed to be good for you, it was simply supposed to be eaten.

Pushing up from the couch, Scout jumped down to the floor and ran straight to the front door. Sherry groaned in disbelief.

"Are you kidding? Now?" The dog pranced around, apparently needing a walk. "Well, shit. I shouldn't have fed you all that cheese. It made you thirsty. Hold on a minute."

She was in her pajamas but the chance of running in to anyone she knew at this hour was slim. She grabbed her boots and pulled them on, then shrugged into her coat, zipping it to her chin. It was colder than hell out there tonight. Her gloves and hat were in her pockets and they went on as well. She might as well give Scout a good walk so he would sleep in tomorrow. When she and Madison had walked him earlier, it had taken him forever to find a place to do his business so Sherry didn't expect this would be quick anyway.

Sherry lifted the leash off the hook by the door where Madison kept her car keys and smiled at Scout.

"Okay, sweetie. Aunt Sherry will take you for a little walk. How's that sound?"

Scout ran around in a few circles and then sat down to have his leash attached, his tail going a mile a minute. She pocketed Madison's keys. It wasn't Sherry's usual practice if she was only going to be gone for a few minutes, but the fact that Tanner had a deputy driving by the house every ten minutes or so spoke of a man who was concerned. About what she had no idea, and Madison was decidedly tight-lipped on the subject. Sherry assumed that Tanner had pissed someone off by arresting him and he was probably making empty threats.

The cold hit her the minute she opened the front door but Scout was already on the front porch looking at her with an expression of doggy disdain. She leaned down and ruffled his fur.

"You have a built in fur coat to keep you warm. I have to layer. All right. Let's get this show on the road."

She walked him down Fountain Street all the way to the cul de sac before turning around and heading back. Her breath made mist and her face was beginning to go numb, but Scout appeared determined to sniff every tree and bush between here and the house. As they neared the neighbor's bushes, Sherry stopped in her tracks and tugged on Scout's leash. She took a few steps back until she was partially obscured under some low hanging branches.

As she watched Madison's house, several men with flashlights splayed out around the outside. Two men, partially carrying a man in between them walked around toward the clinic side of the home. It looked like someone was injured and needed Madison's help. That wasn't all that unusual, but what was with the men stationed all around the house like guards?

Her heart started beating faster in her chest and the feminine intuition that Dan often made fun of reared its ugly head. This didn't look right at all. The men were looking around as if they were watching for someone. Trying to keep people out.

Or keep people in?

They reminded Sherry of the Secret Service men she'd seen on television, but the man they'd taken to the clinic probably wasn't the president. They'd shown up in two dark, nondescript sedans, not a mile long parade of limousines.

Scout whined and pulled on the leash and Sherry tugged him back until she could wrap her arms around him.

"I don't like the look of this, Scout. I think we need to find that deputy that's supposed to be patrolling the area."

Sherry's hand automatically went to her pocket for her phone, but she'd left it inside the house.

Craptastic.

Her phone was practically a third appendage and the one damn time she really needed it, she'd left it behind. She hated to leave Madison in that house with whomever had gone in there, but standing in the frigid cold freezing her ass off wasn't doing anyone any good. She turned and led Scout back down the street, taking a short cut through the Ames' back yard and over to Courtney Avenue. Luckily Madison lived close to downtown. If she cut through a few yards, she could come out right across the street from the sheriff's station.

She took off at a jog with Scout at her heels, adrenaline zipping through her body. Tanner might have been on to something when he had a deputy watch the house. Madison could be in real danger. Sherry had to sound the alarm.

* * * *

Evan was on his way to the hospital in Billings along with men from the other motorcade. Of the eleven Marshals, five had survived, three of which were critically injured. Tanner's team had taken less casualties. The four Marshals in the front and last cars were dead–of that there was no doubt. Evan would be fine but was going to be off duty for awhile healing. Of the deputized sheriffs, Jared and Griffin had both taken a slug in the vest that had knocked them backwards but were fine.

DEA Agent Jason Anderson had relayed that the first motorcade had thinned the cartels numbers by about half, which probably explained how their survival rate was better. The scene was crawling with DEA, Marshals, and state and local cops, the highway completely closed to traffic.

"We found the chopper abandoned in a field not far from here," Jason said, shoving his cell back in his pocket. "My team took pictures of the tire tracks and is running them right now to see if we can get a make and model."

"Government law enforcement sure is different than local. We'd put out roadblocks and a BOLO." Tanner slugged back the coffee that had somehow appeared. "Are your men at the hospitals yet? Kerr was bleeding out pretty bad."

"We've got every hospital in a three hundred mile radius covered. If they show up there, we'll get them," Jason affirmed.

Logan paced. "I feel so damn useless. What can we do?"

Jason shook his head. "Nothing at this point. You did the job Uncle Sam asked you to do. Let us do our job now."

Tanner scowled. "We didn't do it well enough. Kerr's gone."

Jason stroked his chin. "When someone is determined, it often doesn't matter what we do. You kept a lot of people alive, and you captured some of the henchmen. That's good work where I come from."

Logan stopped and crossed his arms over his chest. "They'd be crazy to go to a hospital, Anderson. Jacks has to know you've got this area crawling with agents. Where would he feel safe? Where can he get the help he needs?"

Son of a bitch.

"Maddie," Tanner growled. "Jacks feels safe in Springwood. He can take Kerr to Maddie. She has a clinic right in the house, for fuck's sake. We need to get there now!"

Tanner made to move but Jason caught his arm. "Hold on a minute. Who is Maddie and how would Jacks know to take Kerr there?"

"Everyone in town knows Maddie and her father have their medical office in their home. Everyone," Tanner grated, impatient to get out of there. "And she's my girlfriend. I'm going to marry her."

Jason's eyebrows shot up to his hairline. "Then we'd better go. You can explain it all to me in the chopper."

Tanner turned to Logan. "Get everybody together and get them staged down the street from my house. I'll call Deputy Sam and he'll meet you on Courtney Avenue. Got it? If Jacks has Maddie, I'll need all of you."

Logan nodded and headed to round up the other men. Tanner ran with Jason to the helicopter. They would radio Sam from there. If anything happened to Maddie, Tanner would kill Jacks. There wouldn't be a safe corner of the globe for that man to hide in. He'd hunt him down and make him wish he'd never been born.

* * * *

Madison was having a weird dream.

She and Tanner were back in Las Vegas but she couldn't find him anywhere. She looked and looked, walked all over the hotel and up and down the strip but couldn't see him. Somehow she knew he was there, but he was frustratingly out of sight.

A noise from downstairs brought her out of her deep sleep and she went completely still, trying to hear it again. Another bang and everything went silent. Madison sat up and saw that Sherry wasn't in her bed.

Probably still watching a movie, Sherry was known to stay up all night. Scout might as well come upstairs with Madison and get some rest. Either way, she needed to see what was going on. Knowing Sherry, she was making Scout a baked chicken dinner. When Scout never ate dog food again, Tanner would be livid.

Madison groaned and rolled out of bed, blinking the sleep from her eyes. She shoved her feet into slippers and pulled on a large sweatshirt over her T-shirt and sweats. Finger combing the tangles in her hair, she padded to the bedroom door and pulled it open, trudging downstairs. The television was still on but there was no sign of Sherry or Scout. A quick glance by the front door and Madison could see Sherry's coat and boots were gone, as was Scout's leash. She must have taken the dog for a walk.

Madison sighed and headed for the kitchen. Maybe some hot cocoa would help her and Sherry sleep. She opened the refrigerator door to get the milk when an arm wrapped around her body tightly and a hand clamped over her mouth. She was dragged into the center of the room and when the light flipped on, Fenton Jacks was standing in the middle of her kitchen holding a gun. Another man was sitting at her breakfast table, slumped over and pale. He was wearing an orange jumpsuit with a large bloodstain. His hands and feet were shackled.

Fear crawled up her spine and she struggled against the iron bands around her.

"I'm sorry to intrude on you at this late hour, Dr. Shay, but as you can see we are in need of medical assistance." Fenton nodded to his henchman. "You can let her go."

Madison swallowed the lump of fear lodged in her throat as the hands loosened and the man took a step back. In all her years in the Chicago ER, she'd never faced down a gun. She lifted her chin and prayed that Sherry stayed far away from the house. "I've never had a gun pointed at me before."

"I do apologize," Fenton said smoothly, but the gun pointed at her never wavered. "We don't have all day here, Dr. Shay. This man's life is very important to me."

"Bring him into the back of the house and into the room on the left."

Fenton waved her first, and she led the way into the medical office. The henchman helped the injured man, almost lifting him onto the table. The victim was breathing in pants, and his face contorted in agony.

She firmed her lips and looked up at Fenton Jacks. "What happened to this man?" She tried to keep her voice cool and controlled and her expression neutral.

Jacks gave her an appraising look. "He was shot, Dr. Shay. I need you to take out the bullet and sew him up."

248

Her stomach twisted into knots, her heart beating loudly in her chest. "He should be in a hospital. It looks like he's lost a lot of blood."

Laughing, Jacks pointed the gun at her chest. "I can't take him there as I'm sure you've figured out. We're on a tight schedule here, Dr. Shay. Fix him up and we'll walk out of here and you'll never see us again. Make a fuss…well, I don't want to hurt you."

Madison reached for her white coat and shrugged it on. "I doubt hurting me would bother you in the least, Mr. Jacks. Please stand back and give me some room to work here."

The other man who had yet to speak, drew his gun when she went to open a drawer. She lifted her eyebrow at Jacks. "Am I allowed to work? I need to cut off these pants to see the wound."

His lips twisted but he nodded. "Give her some space." Jacks smiled. "But not too much space."

Madison pulled on a pair of rubber gloves and retrieved the scissors from the drawer before beginning to cut through the blood-soaked material. She kept her eyes on her work and didn't spare the other two a glance. She was equipped to remove the bullet and sew this poor man up, but he'd lost so much blood she feared he might go into volume shock. She couldn't help him with that here. He could code on her at any moment.

That would probably make Fenton Jacks very upset indeed.

* * * *

Staged two blocks from Maddie's house, Tanner wanted to scream in frustration. He'd never felt fear like this before. Not in the Middle East. Not when Emily had pneumonia and had been hospitalized for a week. And not when Chris's appendix burst and they had to rush him to the emergency room.

"Tell me again what you saw, Sherry," Tanner asked.

Sherry was practically in tears. Her chin wobbled and her eyes were watery. "I was taking Scout for a walk before I went to bed. As I was walking back to the house, I saw a bunch of men surround it. Two men were helping a third around to the back door while the other seemed to stand guard."

"Are you sure there are four men outside?"

"I— I— think so." Tears started to escape Sherry's eyes. "I just don't remember. I'm sorry, Tanner."

He put his hand on her shoulder. "It's okay. You've done more than you know to help Maddie. You got Sam and now we're here to get her out, okay? I won't let anything happen to her. I promise."

Jason Anderson hung up his cell. "There are four heat signatures in the house and four outside of it." His expression was sober. "Listen, I know that's the woman you love in there. That's why I think you should stay here and let us get her out. You're too emotional, Tanner. And emotion is a luxury at a time like this that we can't afford."

Tanner was already shaking his head. "I can keep it under control. I need to do this, Jason. I don't expect you to understand it. I do expect you to respect it."

The man looked at Tanner for a long time and then slowly blew out a breath. "We better talk about strategy. Once your girlfriend patches Kerr up, Jacks will be wanting to tidy up any loose ends."

Maddie would be one of those loose ends. He had to get to her and soon.

The sound of approaching vehicles made Tanner turn on his heel but he breathed a sigh of relief when his friends spilled out of the two SUVs. Logan, Jared, Griffin, Reed, and Seth strode toward him and for the first time in close to an hour Tanner felt some hope. These men were like brothers and as he'd told Maddie, he trusted them with his and her life.

They all gathered around Tanner waiting for instructions, but Jason cleared his throat. "There appear to be four men stationed around the perimeter of the house. One on each side. There are also four people in the home. We know that one is Madison Shay. From the GPS chip we placed in Kerr, we also know he's in the house. We believe Fenton Jacks is also there.

The last person is probably a henchman of Jacks. Currently all four people are clustered in the back. Madison's friend identified that area as one of the examining rooms."

"Are there any weapons in the home that can be used against us?" Logan asked.

"We assume Jacks and the other man are armed. Madison also told me there is one gun in the house. I told her to put it in her bedroom, which is upstairs." Tanner replied. "As far as I know there aren't any more weapons."

"Does she listen to you?" Seth grinned.

"Sometimes, " Tanner answered grimly. "Let's hope today's the day."

Another truck pulled up and Sam alighted and headed for them, holding a large rolled up piece of paper.

"I got it." Sam handed it to him, and Tanner unrolled it on the hood of the vehicle. He'd sent Sam to wake up the county clerk to get the architectural plans for Maddie's home.

"This is the floor plan to Maddie's." Tanner shined a flashlight down and pointed to the rear of the home. "This is where the exam rooms are and here is where Maddie's bedroom and the lone spare weapon should be." Tanner pointed to the top floor of the house.

The men studied the drawing and Griffin stroked his chin. "Are you thinking what I'm thinking?"

Jason was leaning on the hood on his elbows, shaking his head. "I know what you're thinking and you're crazy. Let's call the house, set up a dialogue with Jacks. Once he knows he's surrounded, we can bargain for the hostages."

Tanner shook his head. "No way. Jacks won't hesitate to kill. He'll never give up. He'd die and take everybody with him first. He's an arrogant SOB who thinks he's smarter than everyone else. He'll never think he can't get out of the situation."

"You can't do shit until we take out the men surrounding the house," Jared scoffed. "Reed, Griffin, Seth, and I can take care of them. I assume you want them taken out of play but alive."

Jason nodded. "Preferably. I really don't want to explain a high body count to the brass. It's bad enough I've let you talk me into, well, whatever you're about to talk me into."

"I'm the law in this town. You can blame it on me." Tanner turned to Logan. "That leaves me and you going into the house."

Logan peered down at the drawing and pointed to the window of Maddie's father's bedroom on the ground floor at the front of the house. "Looks like a good entry point. It's the farthest room from where they are." He flicked a glance at Scout. "Are we taking Scout?"

Tanner scratched his faithful companion behind the ears. "What do you say, Scout? Want to come out of retirement tonight and help us get Maddie?"

At Maddie's name, the dog's ears perked up and his tail wagged.

"You're going to go in there?" Sherry asked incredulously. "You'll be killed."

Tanner put his arm around her shoulders. She was worried for Maddie, and she didn't need to be worried about them as well.

"It'll be okay. We know what we're doing."

"You're walking into your death," Sherry declared. "Can't you throw tear gas into the house or something?"

"Fenton will just shoot before it can take effect." Tanner shook his head. "This is the only way."

Sherry sighed. "Then I should tell you that the easiest way to get in and out of the house without anyone downstairs knowing is through Madison's bedroom window. Oh, and the third stair step from the top creaks."

Seth frowned and then smiled. "That's how she snuck out of the house as a teenager, isn't it?"

"We didn't do anything wild." Sherry bit her bottom lip. "We would just go driving around or hang out and talk somewhere. It was no big thing."

"So how did she get out of the window?" Tanner asked, although he had a pretty good idea what the answer was going to be.

"She climbed down the tree. Heck, her bedroom window is probably still unlocked. It's been unlocked since we were teenagers."

Tanner was going to have a long talk with Maddie about safety and security when this was all over.

Fuck that. He'd have Maddie live with him and he wouldn't need to worry about unlocked windows in the future.

He patted Scout on the head. "Looks like you're staying here. Even you can't climb a tree."

Jason crossed his arms over his chest, a dubious expression on his face. "I believe you can take out the guards around the house, and it sounds like you won't have any trouble getting inside the house. Just what do you plan to do when you get in there?"

Chapter Twenty-Five

Madison was in deep, deep shit. Fenton Jacks had a gun pointed at her and Tanner was miles away. She had a genius IQ, but it sure wasn't helping her at the moment. She had no idea what she should do or say. Instead she concentrated on her patient, blocking out any thoughts of what Fenton Jacks might do to her. She didn't hurry through the procedure, taking her time, and hoping against hope Sherry had realized something was wrong and called Deputy Sam.

The fact that Sherry hadn't waltzed back into the house after walking Scout gave Madison hope that help was indeed on the way.

"Aren't you done yet?" Fenton's henchman growled. He was pacing back and forth in the small room and making her even more nervous. She had to steel herself so her hands wouldn't shake as she worked. She had to hold herself together until help arrived. She wouldn't allow herself to believe she was going to die here tonight. She had too much living left to do to go out like this.

She glanced briefly at Fenton. His expression was one of disgust. He didn't seem to like the other man too much, but then Fenton didn't really have any friends in town.

"Shut up and get out of this room. Fuck, you're driving me crazy. Go in the kitchen and get us something to drink." Fenton pointed to the door of the exam room.

Madison bent over the wound and breathed a sigh of relief the victim was unconscious. She'd injected a local anesthetic in his thigh, and at the sight of the needle he'd passed out.

"So why did you break him out of prison? Is he a friend of yours?" Madison probed the wound.

Fenton chuckled. "Curious, huh? No, he's not a friend. In fact, he works for an enemy. That's why I want him alive. He has something I want."

254

"Tanner told me about the war over the drug route." Madison didn't know why she couldn't keep her mouth shut, but she was compelled by something inside of her to speak.

"That's old news. I won. They lost. Simple as that." Fenton leaned back in the plastic chair. "Where is good old Tanner anyway? I need to see him before I leave town. I was hoping he'd be here with you."

"He should be here any minute." The lie slipped out easily. She wanted Fenton to think Tanner was on his way even though he wasn't anywhere near here and wouldn't be anytime soon.

"Good. He and I need to have a...chat. Sort of a come to Jesus moment."

Fenton didn't look perturbed that the sheriff of Springwood was on his way. If anything he looked damn happy. That wasn't good.

Madison began to stitch the wound. She'd pulled one bullet from his thigh and dropped it in a metal cup to give to the police. She learned from her time in Chicago to save it for evidence.

"He's lost a lot of blood. You shouldn't move him for a bit. Actually we should really get him to a hospital. That much blood loss is dangerous."

Fenton shook his head. "You know I can't do that. He can stay here in your capable hands while I wait for your boyfriend." He scowled. "Shit, where is Hadley? I told him to get us something to drink."

Madison indicated the set of double doors on the far end of the small waiting room. "He couldn't have gotten lost. But the doors are very thick. My mother insisted on having privacy in the house from the medical practice."

Madison tied up the last stitch and placed a bandage over the thigh. "There. That should do for now, although I still think he needs to go to a hospital."

"Shut up." Fenton moved restlessly around the confining space. "Where the fuck is Hadley?"

"Maybe he was hungry. I think there was some popcorn on the counter."
It sounded stupid, but she was wondering herself what the man was up to.
He'd been gone awhile.

Fenton's eyes narrowed and he grabbed her arm, dragging her into the
waiting room and to the back door. He pulled it open, looked left and right
briefly, he cursed, and then slammed the door shut, locking it.

"Fuck. Fuck. My men aren't in position. Looks like we have company,
Doc." He placed the gun at her temple. Her heart raced and sweat broke out
all over. She was screwed. It wasn't supposed to end like this, but here it was.
She was at the wrong end of a gun of all things. All the crap that had happened
to her in Chicago hadn't put her in this kind of danger, but coming home had.
Now that she had stitched up the man, she was expendable.

Hopefully, whoever was here was on her side.

"It's too late, Fenton. If they're here, you're probably surrounded."

Her voice sounded more hopeful than sure.

Fenton's eyes were cold and hard, his grip on her upper arm merciless,
making her wince in pain. "They must be in the house. You're my ticket
through the cops."

Madison tried to take deep breaths. She needed to stay calm and think.
Think hard. She'd been given self-defense training in Chicago. Now her mind
was whirling through everything she'd ever been taught, read, or even seen on
television.

Conflicting advice made her head hurt.

Should she go limp and become dead weight? Should she try to knee him
in the groin? Maybe she should try and become friends and talk him out of
this?

He didn't give her time to make a decision. He dragged her through the
double doors and down the hall to the kitchen, the barrel of the gun pressed to
the side of her head the entire time. He came to abrupt halt in the doorway.

Madison's eyes widened. Fenton's henchman was sitting on one of her kitchen chairs, duct tape wrapped around his hands and feet and a strip over his mouth. He was jerking in his bonds, but clearly whoever had done this had done it well. The silver strips of tape wrapped around his chest and the back of the chair held him firmly. He wasn't going anywhere until someone set him loose. His eyes were bulging and he was trying to say something but his words were muffled.

Fenton's complexion went white, his eyes darting everywhere. Beads of sweat had popped out on his forehead and for the first time he looked like he wasn't completely in control.

A sound came from the living room area and Fenton fired at it, the blast leaving ringing in her ears and her heart almost stopping in her chest. He placed the gun back at her temple and tugged her into the center of the living room. He still kept looking around and his grip had tightened painfully on her arm. If she lived through this, she was going to have one hell of a bruise.

Another sound, this time from the left side of the living room near the foyer. This time Fenton didn't fire, but he jumped and yanked her arm hard enough to make her grit her teeth. His head was jerking from side to side and his breathing was ragged. He was genuinely shook up as he looked for the source of the noise.

Suddenly a cascade of marbles bounced down the stairs. Fenton pointed the gun toward the racket and shot off two quick rounds, a frustrated roar coming from deep in his chest. The loud bang deafened her and she didn't hear the sound of footsteps behind her. She gasped when she felt the presence of another person and fearfully turned to look over her shoulder. She gaped as a gun was placed on the back of Fenton Jacks's head.

Her heart in her throat, she tentatively looked over her shoulder and almost fainted with relief.

Tanner!

She sagged, her knees almost giving way, but she locked them in place as Fenton still had a hold of her arm with his left hand. His right arm was extended and had a grip on his gun. He hadn't moved at all, but he didn't appear to be giving up.

"Let her go, Jacks. This is between you and me."

Her gaze darted back and forth between the two men. Tanner looked totally calm and in control, but she could see a muscle working in his jaw. Fenton Jacks, on the other hand, had sweat pouring down his face and his complexion was a pasty shade of gray.

The door to the foyer closet swung open and Logan Wright stepped out with a long rifle pointed straight at Jacks.

"Should I call in the rest of the guys?" Logan asked.

The rest of the guys?

If Tanner actually answered, Madison didn't hear him. But the front door opened and two men entered the house, while at the same time two more men, one of them Seth Reilly, came down the stairs. She wanted to faint with relief, but this wasn't over yet.

All the men were wearing what looked like bulletproof vests and brandishing guns. If she were Fenton she would have given up by now, but he didn't look inclined to do so.

"Let her go," Tanner repeated. "The house is completely surrounded with federal agents. Even if you managed to get out of the house, which you won't, you won't get out of Springwood."

Fenton licked his lips nervously. "I have her."

"You have nothing," Tanner countered. "If you so much as move a muscle in your right arm, I'll pull the trigger. You'll be dead in a split second. Throw the gun down and let her go."

Tanner's voice was deep and commanding and for a moment Madison thought Fenton might do exactly as asked. Instead his jaw firmed.

"Fuck you, Marks. You won't shoot me in front of your girlfriend."

Her heart was beating so loudly the entire town could probably hear it. She tried to slow her breathing but the tenseness of the moment didn't allow it. They were all frozen, no one giving any quarter. A proverbial stand off. It seemed like forever before Tanner spoke again.

"Scout, fass."

Before Fenton could respond, Scout tore through the front door, snarling and growling. He jumped high in the air, his muzzle clamping down on Fenton's outstretched arm. Fenton screamed, his hand opening and dropping the gun. He fell to his knees as the weight of Scout brought him down to the floor. He was yowling in pain and at some point he'd let go of her.

She backed up a few steps and an arm wound around her middle. Her breath caught and she twisted to see who had grabbed her. She relaxed when she realized it was Logan. He was pushing her behind him and toward the door.

Tanner now had a gun pointed directly at Fenton who was writhing on the floor in apparent agony. She heard Tanner say something that sounded like "ows" and Scout let go of the man and sat down, looking up at his master expectantly.

"Shoot me," Fenton snarled. "Just fucking shoot me. I'd rather die than go to prison."

"That's exactly why I won't." Tanner shook his head. "It will be much more satisfying to know you're rotting in a supermax every day for the rest of your life. You're still a young man, Jacks. You've got many years to look forward to being behind bars."

A handsome man with dark hair wearing a DEA jacket walked into the room and smiled. "I see things are wrapped up here. Looks like I won't have to explain things to the brass after all." He motioned two more agents in. "Cuff and shackle this man." He frowned. "Where's Kerr?"

No one said anything. "Um, is that the guy who broke out of prison?" Madison asked. "He's passed out in the exam room. At least he was a few minutes ago."

A few more agents stomped through the house and down the hall. Fenton was led outside and she ran into Tanner's outstretched arms. He kissed her long and hard, and she lost track of everything and everyone. It was only when he lifted his head did she remember they had a roomful of amused onlookers. She pushed at his shoulder.

"Everyone's watching," she whispered.

"Everyone's jealous," he whispered back. "If anything had happened to you, I wouldn't have been responsible for my actions. Jesus, Mary, and Joseph, I love you, Maddie."

He kissed her until the room spun and her heart was racing again, although for a completely different reason.

"I love you, too." She pulled back, giving him a frown. "How did you get here? You had some assignment with the Marshals. You were supposed to be heading for Colorado. That's all you would tell me."

A grin broke out on his face. "My assignment was to escort Howard Kerr, aka the man in your exam room, to a prison in Colorado. Fenton ambushed our motorcade and broke him out. I figured he'd head here to get Kerr medical treatment. Sherry confirmed my theory when she found Sam."

"Sherry! Oh my gosh, is she okay? I completely forgot about her." Madison slapped her forehead.

"She's fine. Dan is with her and she's waiting at the station. They will have called her by now to tell her everything is over and you're okay."

Madison slumped against him, the reality of everything she'd been through starting to sink in. "How did you get in here? The doors were locked."

Tanner kissed her nose. "Sherry told us about how you used to sneak out as a teenager through your bedroom window and down the tree."

"You climbed the tree?" Madison couldn't believe her ears.

Behind her Logan chuckled. "We did. Then we snuck down the stairs and hid in the pantry. We got lucky when that guy," Logan pointed to the man in duct tape being cuffed and led away, "came out for a soda. We took him down and then waited for Jacks to realize his buddy wasn't coming back. Then all we had to do was distract and disorient him."

All they had to do?

"Meanwhile, the rest of us were outside taking care of the men guarding the house," Seth added. "We had the easy job, really."

Madison didn't think any of it sounded very easy but she was at the point where her head was spinning trying to wrap her mind around the events. She put a hand to her forehead, starting to feel faint.

"I think I may need to sit down."

Tanner reached under her knees and lifted her into his arms. He carried her over to the couch and set her down gently.

"You're okay but you scared the bejesus out of me."

He kept his arms around her and she took strength from his strength and warmth. She leaned her head against his shoulder and let her respiration return to normal. It wasn't easy as it appeared her home was a crime scene and there were federal agents making themselves at home, milling about, taking pictures, and generally making a mess of things.

"You're going to have to tell Dad why the house was shot up," she finally said.

"I don't think he'll care as long as his little girl isn't hurt." She could feel Tanner's chuckle deep in his chest.

She looked up, too overcome by how close they'd both come to death. "I love you."

He smoothed the hair back from her face. "I know. You told me earlier. I said it, too."

"No, it wasn't just the moment." She shook her head. "I really love you. Like the forever kind of stuff."

He tilted her chin up so their lips were a hairsbreadth apart. "I know, Maddie. I love you that way, too. The forever way. I should have told you sooner."

"Oh. Good, then."

She didn't know what to say. She'd never exchanged "I love you"s before. But Tanner was looking at her with the most wonderful expression. It was a mix of love, tenderness, and yes, passion.

"How long are these people going to be here in my house?" she asked.

Tanner smiled. "Does it matter, sweetheart? We have our whole lives ahead of us."

The DEA agent came to get her statement and Tanner helped her pack a bag. Until the house was released she'd be staying with him. As they walked out of the front door, she gave each of Tanner's friends a big hug.

"Thank you for saving me. I've never had anyone risk their life for me until today."

The men all looked uncomfortable, their faces turning a dull red in the early morning light. It had been a damn long night and she was dreaming of a hot bath and warm bed. Preferably with Tanner curled up next to her.

"Come on, Maddie. Let's get you home." Tanner threw his arm around her shoulders and led her to his SUV parked on the curb.

"Home. That's sounds good, Sheriff."

Chapter Twenty-Six

"Will you pass the fried chicken?" a smiling Stacey asked.

Madison handed Stacey the plate and looked down the long table in awe. Tanner's entire family, Madison's father, Sherry and Dan were having a picnic to celebrate the start of summer at the horse farm owned by Tanner's parents. They were back from Arizona and would spend the warm months in Montana. Chris, Stacey, and their little girl, Annie had come back with them. Chris was happy and smiling, and Stacey seemed relaxed and content. Annie was sitting on her dad's lap wearing a cute pink dress and making a mess of a buttered dinner roll.

Tanner sat down next to Madison and set a can of root beer at the top of her plate. "You look a little bewildered, sweetheart. Is anything wrong?"

He had the most wonderful smile on his face and Madison's heart squeezed painfully in her chest. She loved this man with everything she was. She wanted to spend every waking moment with him until the day she drew her last breath.

"There's just so many of us. I guess I'm just used to it being me and Dad."

"My parents adore you. Mom says she wants to invite you to the house so she can teach you to cook."

Madison snorted. "Fat lot that will do. I'm a lost cause. She mentioned that to me when I told her I could burn water. She seems determined that I should carry on the Marks tradition of making the best chocolate cake in the county." Madison licked her spoon with a grin. "It is heavenly."

"Mom doesn't get around like she used to, but she can still bake with the best of them. Did you even eat lunch or just go straight for dessert?"

Madison had learned to relax a little about her diet, and Tanner had learned to eat vegetables. He said it was because he wanted to live a long life so he could spend more time with her. She couldn't imagine anything better.

The last three months since Fenton Jacks had been arrested had been the best in her life.

His sojourn behind bars had been brief, however. While awaiting trial, he'd been knifed in prison by another inmate and had died. Madison didn't wish death on anyone, but Fenton had lived his life on the wrong side of the law. It was bound to catch up with him eventually.

Chris stood up and cleared his throat. "Excuse me." He clanged his spoon on the side of his soda can. "Excuse me. I have an announcement to make." He looked around the table and then his gaze rested on Tanner. "As most of you know, I've had a rough time of things lately. I want to thank everyone for standing by me. Especially my dad. He never gave up on me. And because of his persistence and belief in me, I'm here today to tell you that I'm the newest deputy-in-training for the town of Fielding."

Chris grinned and everyone clapped and cheered. Stacey stood and kissed him, a big smile on her face. He sat down looking proud but a trifle overwhelmed. Madison sought Tanner's hand under the table. She leaned toward him so only he could hear.

"Did you know about this?" she whispered close to his ear.

"Jared mentioned it. He's happy to have Chris and I think things might be finally working out for my son."

"Does Abby know yet?"

"You'll have to ask Chris about that. He visited her in Billings earlier this week so he had the opportunity. If he didn't, it's his choice."

Madison tilted her head. "How do you feel about Abby living in Billings?"

"It's none of my business," Tanner said in an exaggerated whisper. "I'm too busy keeping my young girlfriend happy to have an opinion about where my ex-wife should live."

"It's just you're so protective of your family." Madison didn't know how to explain it.

264

"That's true." Tanner nodded. "But Abby wanted to make a big change in her life. It's not my place to weigh in on that decision. I'm happy for her."

Madison smiled up at the man she loved. "I'm just happy. All the time."

"Let's sneak away." Tanner's voice was close to her ear and she shivered at the promise in his tone. With everyone in town, they'd barely had a moment alone in the last few days.

She nodded eagerly, as anxious to be alone with him as he was with her. They didn't say anything as they got up from the long table and walked arm in arm toward the old barn in the distance. Madison thought they'd managed a clean getaway when her father waved and called to them from the far end of the table.

"Madison. Tanner. Can I talk to you for a minute?" Greg Shay walked over to them and pulled a folded piece of paper from his pocket. "I've been wanting to give this to you."

He held it out for Madison and she unfolded it, scanning the document. She looked up at her father, not certain she understood. "I don't understand, Dad. This looks like the deed to the house."

"It is." Greg nodded. "I'm giving it to you."

"Giving it to me? But why?" Madison shook her head in confusion. Was her father planning to never come back to Montana?

"Gwen and I don't need it. You and Tanner do. If you move into the house, you'll be right there for work and Tanner will be closer as well. You both mentioned his cabin was too small for the two of you."

She and Tanner were tripping over each other in his one bedroom home. The man had closets the size of postage stamps, and she didn't even have that many clothes or shoes.

"Where will you stay when you come visit?"

"Maybe you'll let us stay with you? Besides, now that I'm volunteering at that free clinic, I doubt we'll make it back except at holidays. Hopefully you'll come to Seattle and visit us there, too." Her father had a grin on his face and she threw her arms around his neck.

"Thank you, Dad."

It would be wonderful to live in her childhood home with the man she loved. Her mind was already going a mile a minute as to what changes and updates she'd like to make. Tanner shook her dad's hand and thanked him, slapping him on the back. She was lucky these two men got along so well. They liked and respected each other.

They talked to her father for a few minutes before once again making their escape. Tanner led her into the barn and she giggled as he pulled her deeper inside.

"We're going to make out in the hay loft? What would my father say?"

"Your dad is a pretty calm person. A hell of a lot calmer than I've been about Emily and Matt."

Emily had brought her current boyfriend today. A shy young man with shaggy dark hair and liquid brown eyes which shined with love for Tanner's only daughter.

"Maybe Dad can give you some pointers," Madison teased. "I like Matt. He seems like a nice young man."

"I like him, too. I'd like him even better if I didn't suspect he was sleeping with my daughter."

"She could have brought home much worse." Madison was openly laughing now. Watching Tanner deal with his daughter's budding sex life was hilarious. This same man could strip her out of her clothes in less than ten seconds and have her screaming his name, but the mere thought that his daughter might be doing the same had his face red and his words tangled up.

"We really aren't going to have sex in the hay loft are we?"

Just the thought of all that itchy hay had her scratching her arm.

"Nope. Follow me."

Tanner opened the door to another room in the barn and stepped back. She went through the door and was surprised to find a huge RV parked there.

"Whose is this?" She walked up and down the outside, marveling at the size and what good condition it was in. It looked practically brand new for sitting in an ancient, run down wooden structure.

"My parents'. When Dad retired from raising horses, he and Mom took off for the open road. Six months later, her health wasn't so great so they came home. Now they spend the winter in Arizona and the summer here. The RV doesn't get used much. I loaned it to Seth when he needed to protect Presley."

"It's huge. When I was a kid, we had a tent."

Tanner pulled out a set of keys and unlocked the door. "That's what we had when I was a kid. Come on in."

Madison walked up the steps and gasped at the luxury. There was a large living room and kitchen area complete with a flat screen television. Everything looked new and comfortable.

"This is nicer than the apartment I had in Chicago when I was in medical school."

"This isn't the part I wanted to show you."

Tanner captured her fingers and led her through a door into the large bedroom with a king-sized bed.

"It's a bedroom. I guess I know what you have on your mind."

It was what she'd been thinking about all day.

He sat down on the edge of the bed and patted the spot next to him. "Sit down, sweetheart. I want to talk to you about something first."

She frowned but did as he asked. Normally Tanner was all action so it was strange to see him hesitate to get down to business. Especially as they had a dozen or so family and friends about a quarter of a mile away.

"Okay. What did you want to talk about?"

Tanner was studying his cowboy boots and not saying anything. She shifted uncomfortably, not sure she was going to like what he had to say.

Finally he looked up and grabbed both her hands in his. They felt rough and warm and her insides melted a little bit at the sensation.

"I love you, Maddie."

"I love you, too." Her heart picked up speed in anticipation.

"I've never felt this way about someone."

"Me either." Butterflies fluttered in her stomach.

"We just seem to mesh. To go together." His blue eyes were soft with love. "I was thinking we should get married."

She could barely breathe. Tanner was everything she had ever dreamed of and so much more.

"I didn't know you were thinking about marriage."

They'd been living together since the whole Fenton Jacks thing, but neither one of them had mentioned a wedding. Of course Sherry had been mentioning it on a weekly basis.

He gave her a lopsided grin. "Honestly, I was afraid to mention it. I wasn't sure I was what you had in mind for a husband."

"I think you would be a great husband." She squeezed his fingers with her own.

Tanner sat up straight, his jaw a determined line. "We could have children if you wanted to. I wouldn't mind giving fatherhood another try."

That was news. "You want a baby?" She sucked in a breath. She'd always assumed if she was with Tanner there wouldn't be any children.

"Only if you do. I guess what I'm saying is I'm happy to have more kids. If you want to. I'm fine if you don't."

"I sort of assumed you wouldn't want any more children," Madison said slowly, still trying to filter his words through her brain. "Until I fell in love with you, I really didn't give having children much thought. I was too busy with my career."

"I don't want to get in the way of that, Maddie. I just want you to be happy."

268

"I am happy." She really and truly was. She looked up at him and smiled. "I think I'd like to be your wife. I'll be Dr. Marks."

Tanner grinned, relief in every line of his face. "That's as close as my parents are ever going to get to having a child become a doctor." He leaned down, his lips hovering over hers. "Are you sure, Maddie? I love you so much."

"I love you." Madison cupped his jaw with her hand. "As for children, well, let's just take this one step at a time. We can get married and see how we feel afterward. I'm not one of those women who absolutely must have a child."

Although now that she knew he was open to the idea, the thought of having his baby was more than tantalizing. She was already picturing a little boy with her red hair and Tanner's blue eyes and stubborn nature.

He pushed her back on the bed, his body covering hers. "Sweetheart, whatever it takes to make you happy." He dug into his jeans pocket and pulled out a ring, holding it up. "Chris said I needed to be prepared. If you don't like it, we can get you something else."

It was a beautiful old-fashioned, white-gold setting with an emerald cut diamond surrounded by smaller diamonds. She wouldn't trade it for the world.

"I love it." She held out her left hand. "Will you put it on me?"

He slid it on her ring finger and smiled. "It was my grandmother's engagement ring."

Madison looked up, not as sure about the ring as she was a few seconds ago. "Did Abby wear this ring?"

"No," Tanner said firmly. "This ring didn't come to me until about five years ago when my grandmother died at the ripe old age of ninety. I thought it was silly when she willed it to me, but she had always insisted the ring was going to be mine."

"She must have known love wasn't done with you yet. You have longevity in your DNA. I'm glad. I'm going to want a really long life with you." Madison started to work at the buttons on Tanner's shirt. He grinned wickedly and began to tug off her clothes. In just a few minutes, they were both naked and rolling around on the bed, kissing and touching.

Tanner's fingers left a trail of fire wherever he went. Breathing raggedly, she captured his face between her palms and kissed him with everything she had. She wanted to put every emotion into it. She wanted to brand his soul with her love. By the time he lifted his head, they were both breathless.

His mouth trailed down her body, stopping here and there to explore more thoroughly. He nipped and licked until she was writhing on the bed, her fingers digging into his shoulders.

"Tanner, I need you."

"Not yet." His voice was deep with need. It never failed to fan the flames of her desire. His breath was hot on her clit and he blew on the button, sending arrows of pleasure through her body. He pressed two fingers inside of her as his tongue swiped at the swelling pearl. She half-screamed at the rocking sensation and tried to right her world. He never allowed her to regain control.

Tanner's lips, tongue, and fingers tortured her until her toes curled and her hands crumpled the bedclothes. Desperate pleas fell from her lips but he never ceased in his delicious campaign to make her explode with passion.

When the implosion came, the heat seared her from inside out. Her body was consumed with flames licking against her skin and she lost herself in its depths. She floated in the ecstasy until Tanner was lying on top of her once again, his condom covered cock nudging her thigh.

He pushed her legs further apart and pressed inside of her. Slick with juices, he slid in easily, groaning as he filled her completely. She wrapped her arms around him and whispered in his ear.

"Fuck me, Tanner."

Tanner shook his head. "No. We make love, Maddie."

Every stroke, every caress was a celebration of their love and commitment to one another. Their gazes were locked together as he moved in and out of her, rubbing her sweet spot and sending her closer and closer to the edge. She wanted to jump off that precipice with him, hand in hand.

"Tanner!" she gasped, the arousal so tight in her belly. "Please."

His thrusts sped up, each one rubbing his groin against her already sensitive clit. His lips took hers in a long drugging kiss, his teeth nipping at her bottom lip. Reaching between them, he barely had to touch her and she shattered. Wave after wave took over her body and she watched in fascination as he thrust home one more time before his own orgasm took him. His face contorted and his body shuddered before going very still.

As they lay close in the aftermath, she could feel him still inside of her, so hard and thick. She wanted to stay like this forever, but of course they couldn't. Reality would rear its head soon enough, but she would savor the present. Pressing kisses to his face, she ran her hands down his muscled back.

"I can't wait to marry you, cowboy."

He chuckled and kissed her hard. "I'll be right back." He disappeared for a few minutes then came back to cuddle with her, pulling the blankets over them. "I'd marry you tomorrow, Maddie."

"Sherry is going to want to organize the wedding."

He combed the hair back from her face. "You can have any kind of wedding you want. I just want to be your husband."

"You wouldn't mind a big wedding?" She turned so she could rest her head on his chest.

"Whatever you want. I'm easy on this."

Madison could hear the steady thump of his heart under her cheek. That was Tanner. Strong, steady, unflustered. He'd been through hell and come out the other side. He would take whatever life threw at him in stride.

And she would be at his side when it did. Just as he would be there for her. Hadn't he proved it already?

She would walk through life with Sheriff Tanner Marks.

It was a long way from the girlish crush she'd had on him at thirteen. He was a complex man. An imperfect man, thank goodness. But he would always be her hero.

Epilogue

Another Sunday meeting at the roadhouse.

Tanner pounded his fist on the table to quiet down the other men. "I call this meeting to order."

Logan laughed. "Anxious to get home? You probably have a tux fitting or cake tasting to go to."

The other men laughed but Tanner took the ribbing in stride. He and Madison were having a big church wedding with all the trimmings. Greg Shay had insisted he wanted to send his daughter off in style and Sherry had looked like her dream had come true when he'd said it. Tanner and Madison knew they were already married in their hearts so giving in wasn't an issue. In fact, the entire town seemed to have an opinion about the impending nuptials. Tanner figured it was only fair they got to have some say. This whole thing might not have happened if the town hadn't banded together and pushed them towards each other.

"I don't have anything wedding related today, but I do have a beautiful fiancée to go home to." He gave Logan a pointed look. "I highly recommend it."

His friend made a face. "No way. I'm happy the way I am. I come and go as I please. I like it that way."

Tanner smirked. "Whatever you say." He looked around the table. "Any updates on the drug war? Drug violence has gone to almost zero in my town since we busted both cartels in a big way."

Reed nodded in agreement. "I've made a few possession charges, but that's it."

"Much calmer," Griffin said. "It's almost back to the old days when I could spend the day fishing."

Everyone laughed. They all were aware of how much Griffin liked small town life. He was the sheriff of the town with the lowest population of all of them. He liked it when things were boring and slow so he could head off and catch some fish.

"What about the vigilante? Anyone had a run in lately?" Jared asked.

The table was silent.

"We haven't heard from him in a couple of months," Seth observed. "Maybe he's moved on."

"Or in jail for another crime," Tanner added. "I hope we've seen the last of him."

The meeting went on and they discussed the warmer weather and the rise in cattle rustling in the area. When the meeting broke, Tanner and Logan headed for their trucks, parked under the blue Montana sky. The weather was finally warming up, although summer was short in this part of the country. They had to enjoy it while it lasted.

"Listen, about that thing you asked me about," Logan began, his voice hesitant. "Are you sure?"

"Very sure." Tanner nodded. "I want you and Chris to stand up for me. Madison is going to have Sherry and Emily."

Logan looked down at the ground. Tanner let him ruminate on the request. Logan had some strange ideas about family and traditions, and Tanner would never ask his friend to do something he was uncomfortable doing.

Logan finally looked him in the eye. "If you really want me to, then I will."

Tanner loved Logan like a brother. A secretive, ornery, skirt chasing, hard partying, stubborn as a mule, enigma of a brother.

"Are you ever going to tell me about whatever happened to you?" The question popped out of Tanner's mouth before he could stop it. He'd always prided himself on respecting boundaries but Madison's upfront way of speaking was starting to rub off.

274

Logan shook his head, apparently not taking offense. "It's ancient history. I'm not the type of person to whine about how terrible my childhood was or what a victim I am. That's a bunch of shit, in my opinion. Men don't make excuses. They make things happen in their lives."

Tanner had heard Logan say that on several occasions.

"That's true. What are you planning to make happen in the near future, Logan?"

Logan shook his head and opened the door to his truck. "That's your problem, Tanner. You plan too much. You overthink things. Me? I think I'll call up the cute redhead I met the other night and let her rub my neck and shoulders. That's my plan."

Tanner just laughed and watched Logan swing up into the truck cab, start the engine, and pull out of the parking lot. Tanner climbed into his own vehicle and headed for home.

Home.

He really had one with Madison. He'd spent so many years with the crippling fear of not being enough. Now he had a woman who let him know every day that he was more than sufficient for her.

She was certainly more than he'd ever thought he'd find. She was everything. Madison had taught him so much, and given him more than he deserved.

She healed his heart and soul, and for that he would be forever grateful. Forever Maddie's.

The End

Continue reading for special bonus content…

Captured Innocence
CSA Case Files
Book One

By Kennedy Layne

"Why shy away from a lifestyle that you obviously desire?"

Lauren's hands stilled mid-reach for the sugar. He knew he'd taken her unaware, but that wasn't such a bad thing. People tended to answer honestly when taken by surprise.

"Why would you think I *want* to be involved with BDSM? Because I enhance the implements and toys that go along with the lifestyle?"

Well, that shot his theory down. She'd made a quick recovery and placed the conversation back into his hands. He could work with that.

"I guess you could say that," Connor responded. She still had her back to him, waiting for the coffee to stop brewing. "You have to admit, the field that you're in is vast. Why choose the items you do?"

"My sister got her degree in art," Lauren said, turning around and leaning against the opposite counter. She brought her elbows up behind her, resting her palms on the granite. "We're both creative and one weekend... I think I was twenty-one... she took me to an art gallery. The artist had the most sensuous pictures I'd ever seen, and with each of his models had these simplistic yet elegant jewels incorporated within the implements."

"And just like that, you decided you wanted to make them?" Connor asked, not understanding her thought process. "I mean, I assume a twenty-one year old girl would be wary of such a lifestyle, even on the outskirts."

"Let's just say my business mind went into a tailspin." Lauren shrugged and then smiled. "Sex sells. Jewelry sells. They always will. Blend them together, and chances are a person will be successful."

"And there is the calculating mind I knew to be in there," Connor said, smiling back at her. "So now I understand the business aspect of it. But you can't stand there and tell me that the nature of the lifestyle doesn't draw you in. You've never been curious?"

Connor knew he'd lost her the minute he'd asked the question. *Fuck.* She turned, and since the coffee pot had beeped while she was relaying her story, Lauren poured each of them a mug. She doctored hers while leaving his black. Turning, she surprised the hell out of him when she handed him his coffee and answered.

"Yes, but it didn't work out."

Although she'd actually replied, she didn't look him in the eye. Connor couldn't stand to see her brows furrowed so deep, knowing that he was the one to obviously bring up something painful, so he stopped her by taking her cup from her and placing both on the counter.

"Look at me," Connor murmured, moving in close to her. She lifted her head, giving him access to her beautiful green eyes so clouded over with torment. "I'm sorry. I seem to be saying that a lot tonight. It's obviously too much of a personal issue to share with someone you just met."

"We've had sex," Lauren said, tentatively resting her hands on his chest. "I think that's as personal as it gets."

"Sex is superficial," Connor said, in total disagreement. He slowly shook his head. "It's the underlying emotions that we keep hidden when we are at our most vulnerable. Sharing them just makes it more so."

"Do you share?"

Connor slowly shook his head again, realizing that he'd just gotten caught in his own trap. He leaned down and captured her lips, still tinted from the wine and tasting just as sweet as before. Wanting to learn more about her, he'd inadvertently opened himself up. He needed to tip the scales again, but Lauren pulled away before he could do so. When she bit her lip, he would have brought her back against his body so that he could take over, but she leaned around him for her coffee and headed into the living room.

"I suffer from claustrophobia. It stems after an event that happened when I was younger," Lauren stated matter-of-factly. "Being bound in any way isn't good for my mental health."

Connor grabbed his coffee, needing to see her face and wanting to know more. He was just about to join her on the couch when his cell phone rang. The sound did get her to look up at him, giving him full view of her beautiful face. He studied her for a few seconds, before giving in and placing his mug on the coffee table. She gave him little clue as to what she was truly feeling and that in itself said a lot. Lauren was expressive in every subject, except this one. There was something more to it, but unfortunately he couldn't ignore his call.

"I have to take this," Connor said regretfully, digging his cell out of his front pocket.

"Please, go right ahead," Lauren said, her words coming out a little too formal for his liking.

"Yeah, speak to me," Connor said, seeing that it was Kevin.

"Need your help down on Park near the Metrodome." Sounds from the passing traffic and honking horns could be heard over the phone. "How far away are you?"

"Close." Connor rubbed the back of his neck, knowing he had no choice. If Kevin called, it was for a damn good reason. "I'll be there in ten."

It fucking killed him to see the obvious relief cross Lauren's face. They'd both learned a little about each other this evening, and though he would have given anything to know more about her, maybe leaving this as is for a while was a good idea.

"Thanks for staying in for dinner this evening," Lauren said, leaning forward to place her coffee next to his. She stood and faced him, crossing her arms as if she didn't know what to do with them. "If I remember anything else, I'll give you a call."

Connor closed the distance, but instead of claiming her lips like he wanted to, he tilted her chin and gently kissed her forehead. Looking down at her, he wanted nothing more than to stay and hear those inner emotions he spoke of earlier, but knew that now wasn't the time. He hoped like hell that it was in the foreseeable future. She was becoming an enigma that he'd like to solve before things ended.

"Thank you for a wonderful dinner, Red." Connor released her and stepped back. "I'll be in touch, but if something *coincidental* happens that makes you feel uneasy, I want to know about it ASAP."

Lauren's lips curved into the smile she'd obviously been fighting at his attempt at humor and it alleviated his frustration at having to leave. However, he was dead serious about his request. Connor didn't believe in coincidences, which was why he was going to have Taryn check the traffic cameras in the area first thing in the morning once again. The angle into the alleyway hadn't been good for what they'd needed, but if the SUV was on the main street, they should hit paydirt. If someone was watching and keeping tabs on Lauren, he wanted to know who.

ABOUT THE AUTHOR

Olivia Jaymes is a wife, mother, lover of sexy romance, and caffeine addict. She lives with her husband and son in central Florida and spends her days with handsome alpha males and spunky heroines.

She is currently working on a series of full length novels called The Cowboy Justice Association. It's a contemporary erotic romance series about six lawmen in southern Montana who work to keep the peace but can't seem to find it in their own lives.

Visit Olivia Jaymes at

www.OliviaJaymes.com

6480191R00167

Printed in Great Britain
by Amazon.co.uk, Ltd.,
Marston Gate.